Fire and Apparition

A Novel

Inspired by True Events

by Alicia Connolly-Lohr

This is a work of fiction. Similarities to real people, places, or events are entirely coincidental.

FIRE AND APPARITION

First edition. April 18, 2024.

ISBN: 979-8224082322

Written by Alicia Connolly-Lohr.

For history lovers, believers and the curious.

"And you, Ring-bearer,' she said, turning to Frodo. 'I come to you last who are not last in my thoughts. For you I have prepared this.' She held up a small crystal phial: it glittered as she moved it, and rays of white light sprang from her hand. 'In this phial,' she said, 'is caught the light of Eärendil's star[1], set amid the waters of my fountain. It will shine still brighter when night is about you. May it be a light to you in dark places, when all other lights go out."

J.R.R. Tolkein

Author, The Fellowship of the Ring[2]

From the Lord of the Rings trilogy

---

1. https://tolkiengateway.net/wiki/E%C3%A4rendil%27s_star

2. https://tolkiengateway.net/wiki/The_Fellowship_of_the_Ring

SOURCE: National Weather Service, National Atmospheric and Oceanic Administration; https://www.weather.gov/grb/peshtigofire. NOTE: Champion WI is in the general map area identified as Tobinsville and New Franklin. Champion was named Robinsonville at the time of the Peshtigo Fire. The name may have been incorrectly copied down and transferred. The Sugar Bush location in the novel is where Middle Sugar Bush is indicated on this map.

1

For several decades, Peshtigo, Wisconsin flourished with the triad of the lumber industry, railroads and shipping. The city of some two thousand was nestled in the upper northeastern rural woodlands. From there, the Peshtigo River feeds into the Bay of Green Bay with the city of Green Bay at its southernmost point. The bay, in turn, opens into Lake Michigan, one of the five fresh water Great Lakes, commercially navigable all the way to the Atlantic Ocean.

On the evening of October 8, 1871, wildfire began sweeping through the Northwoods near Peshtigo. That Sunday, it intensified and burned through the night, destroying enormous swaths of land. After more than one hundred and fifty years, this genuine historical event, is still regarded as deadliest fire in American history. Inspired by true events, this is the imagined story of one family's experience.

SEPTEMBER, 1871
   Sugar Bush, Wisconsin

MEN GOT KILLED SOMETIMES working as lumberjacks in the Northwoods above Peshtigo. When he didn't luck into a sailing run, Anders Eriksson occasionally worked up there. During those working stints, he would stay at the lumber camp.

His wife, Illyanne, heard the rattle and jangle of an approaching horse and wagon from inside at their Sugar Bush homestead, five

1

miles north of Peshtigo. She didn't expect Anders back for another few days. People simply did not stop by out their way. Visitors might be just that. But it might also be the law, an outlaw, a land speculator, or some kind of bad news being delivered in person. She left her baking table where she had been cutting up apples for a pie. Stepping outside onto the porch she squinted, making out two men sitting atop a buckboard wagon. She leaned back inside the door and picked up the Remington rifle. She held the barrel down secluding it in the folds of her skirt but kept it at the ready. Anders had taught her the stillness required for hunting when spotting a deer. She practiced it now, forcing her breath to slow. If she had to shoot, she must be steady and they must not see it coming.

As the mysterious wagon pulled up near the house, her heart pumped faster. Her hand sweated as she flattened her finger alongside the trigger guard. She could see the men's faces now. It was even more worrisome that she did not recognize them. One wore bib overalls, the other had suspenders over a bulky long-sleeved shirt. What loggers wore.

What manner of business or problem might they be bringing? Bad news that she'd become a widow? Some kind of other trouble, from men who knew the man of the homestead was off working in the logging camp? Or, something else? The wagon stopped a good dozen paces from the house. She eyed them with caution.

At first and they said nothing, raising her suspicions all the more.

"Afternoon, gentlemen. My husband is out in the fields. What's your business?"

They sat still.

She felt a weird prickly sensation all over. A memory of a bank robbery story down in Missouri flashed through her head. A robber had posed as a customer asking to make change, just before he and his partners suddenly pulled out pistols. They took a big cash haul and killed somebody in the getaway. The locals around here just had a big payday. Maybe these two had got to drinking and talking and wandering to Peshtigo's outskirts to do something similar.

An awkward moment passed in which the two men didn't answer Illyanne. She didn't say anything else and they just looked back at her. Then, from the back of the flatbed, up popped fifteen-year-old Matthew, waving at his mother.

Illyanne let out a burst of anxious breath, set the firearm back inside leaned up against the wall and ran down to the cabin steps to the wagon. She saw Anders, sitting, one-armed, crab walking to the edge of the flatbed, his other arm in a sling. "What happened?"

The two logging men, still seated on the driver's bench, removed their hats and nodded to her. One said, "Missus. He's all right. Just got himself behind a ton wagon load of chopped branches piled too high."

The other one added, "Something spooked the horses and it all slid backward almost on top of him."

Illyanne tried to embrace Anders as Matthew helped him get down.

"Don't fret, Illie," her husband said. "It's like they're telling you. Ain't nobody's fault."

Anders was not speaking clearly which concerned her. She knew that could happen with head injuries.

"Medic said it's probably a small break."

"A broken bone!" Illyanne gasped. Anders was drunk and unsteady. She cast a scowl at her son and then toward the men, as she led Anders by his good arm up to the house.

"The doc had us give him some whiskey for the pain, Ma'am."

Shuffling and trying to look back at the lumbermen, Anders tried to turn his torso back toward them. He raised his good arm and said, "Thanks, fellas fer bring'n me home."

Before the driver snapped the reins, he called out, "Doc said to keep that sling on for a few days. Two months with the splint."

Once they got Anders settled, Matthew tried to explain how lucky Anders had been. "Mother, if he didn't have such sharp reflexes to jump out of the way so fast, he would've been buried in the branches. All the loggers said, that woulda killed him, for sure."

Illyanne had felt a disturbance in her spirit earlier in the day, about the time Anders and Matthew said the injury happened. Indeed, they were blood-bonded and spirit-bonded to each other. Well, she had her boys back home now and safe. She stuffed them with a big dinner. At times like this, she drew upon her native Menominee know-how. The ample supply of willow bark chew came in handy. To help him sleep, Illyanne prepared some Chamomile tea and put Anders to bed covered in wolf fur pelts. She set out ginseng root and honey, expecting she would have to prepare a morning curative to help with the after-effects of the whiskey.

It was the middle of September, 1871 and there were at least six good weeks of sailing left before winter. Weeks in which Anders wouldn't be sailing. Weeks in which he wouldn't be earning any money. Weeks in which the crops were at risk of rotting in the fields without Anders' use of both arms for the harvest.

She barely picked at her supper. Illyanne did not usually talk about household finances with Matthew. But he was fifteen and fit for handling most of the farm chores. This incident might just well have thrust him into adulthood. Later, in front of the fireplace that evening, while Anders slept, she took up her sewing in her lap. "This homestead is our life blood. Matthew, I don't know how are we going to get along. Who's going to help us with the harvest?"

"I guess it's on me, Mother."

"You can only do so much but you can't do the work of two men. We can't wait until late November and December to bring in the yield." She let up for a moment from her stitching and held out a pleading hand. "All the other homesteaders are going to be busy with their own fields. I don't know what we'll do." She paused a moment but could not calm her worries. She shook her head from side to side. "A whole year's earnings."

"We'll make do somehow. Like you always say mother, have faith."

"Yes, I suppose you're right." Despite using a thimble, she accidentally pricked herself. She nibbled the finger and then pressed on the spot. "At least I have my two weekends a month cooking at the Peshtigo Boarding House."

In less than a week, Anders was out of the sling but still wore the splint. He soon took to milking the cow, pitching hay and feeding the animals with his good right hand. The family attended Mass in town on Sunday and asked around for other young men who might be able to reap the fields with Matthew. Although everyone engaged in conversation and fussed over Anders' arm, nobody could commit to help them for the reaping. The prospect of a large financial loss silently hounded them all.

Quick to subdue her worries, on the ride back home, Illyanne offered, "Don't worry. There's time. Father Pernin will make inquiries. We will see to it again next week."

Lumber schooners departed from Peshtigo almost daily. Anders was acquainted with most of the ship captains. Against Illyanne's objections, on the first day of October, Anders announced he was riding into town. "I'm going to see what sailing captains are around and when I can go out on a sailing run."

Illyanne insisted it was too soon. "The doctor said you needed four more weeks of rest."

"He wasn't a real doc, Illie. No need up there. A lumberjack gets injured – he usually dies on the spot – or soon after." He put on his wide flat-brimmed Stetson. "Only going to find out what ships are coming and going. Promise, I won't take a job without talking to you first." He headed out toward the barn to tack up his horse.

In the late afternoon, he returned and sent Matthew outside to chop some more wood so he could talk to his mother alone.

Illyanne eyed him, searching for whatever might be the reason for his peculiar behavior. She walked around the high kitchen work table and scooped another handful of flour to spread to knead her dough for supper's bread.

"Illyanne, I'm not going to build up to it. I'm gonna tell you, right off." He placed his hands on her forearms as if he were about to deliver important news. "You can be hired on as the as ship's cook on the next lumber run to Cleveland."

There was a long silence between them face to face. She shook her head. "Oh, no Anders. I couldn't do that. Staying on the ship with all those men?" Illyanne spun away from his grasp. "You've told me how crusty they are. Go on now, I'm making bread."

He reached for her waist again.

"Watch out. You're going to get all full of flour." She twirled away from him playfully again, her skirt flaring above her ankles.

Anders stepped away but one-handedly pulled out a chair from the plank board dining table. He straddled it backwards and rested his splinted arm on the chair back. He set to working on persuading her while she rolled out the dough. "It's a one-week lumber run, Illie. Peshtigo to Cleveland and back. They *need* a cook." He informed her that there'd been women cooks on steamers for sure. And, he'd heard of one or two women cooking on schooners.

Illyanne shot him a dubious look. "More'n likely, just the one."

He ran over his points. It would be an adventure for her. It'd sure would help out with the family finances, him being without work, and all, until his arm healed. With the money, they might be able to take on a hired hand for the harvest. And, it was time for her to branch out from the homestead a little. Matthew was older, almost full-grown.

"Oh, I do I enjoy your sailing stories, Anders. Sometimes, I wish I could be there to see some of the places and things you tell me about but I don't know." She huffed. "And I have branched out. I'm cooking at the Peshtigo Boarding House now."

Anders let his good hand slap down to his thigh and sighed. "I mean, if you don't go, he'll have to find somebody else. I'll bet the first place he looks is the Boarding House." He paused for another ten seconds. "He might even hire that cook friend down there who you've been talking so much about."

"Beulah?" Just the other day Beulah had shown her how to make a roux from roasted meat drippings adding flour, milk, salt and pepper and simmering it until bubbly. Illyanne placed her wrist backs on her hips, palms back and upward, to keep the flour off her dress. "I'm sure I can do the cooking. I know I could do just fine in making all the meals for the crew of five." She cocked her head. "It isn't that." She came over and sat next to him at the table, wiping her hands on a dish towel. She looked distressed. "You know my reserved ways, Anders. Anyhow, I can't swim very well and have never been on sailing ship. I just don't see myself getting along on a schooner."

Anders took a deep. "I know you're a quiet one. But you got a lot more fortitude than you even realize."

She shot him a disapproving glance and felt the ever-present pull of those lake blue eyes and sandy colored hair. "What do you mean, fortitude?"

"Inner strength. Spirit. You aren't loud like a drunk, singing sailor and you don't say much but my lady, you got a will of steel sometimes." He exhaled deeply and paused. "Look. How about this? You make the captain a nice supper, if only for good relations." He held up both open palms in a conciliatory gesture. "If he wants to hire you, you don't have to go."

Twenty minutes later, he looked up from his chair by the hearth. "I just don't want you to end up feeling jealous if your cook friend ends up getting the job."

After a silent stretch of time, she stepped into the sitting area of their cabin. She tossed the dish towel over her shoulder, crossed her arms and cut her eyes toward him and sighed. "Does this captain like venison?" She smiled.

"That's my darling girl." He leaped up and twirled. "Oh, Illie, this is going to be a fantastic adventure for you. You're going out to sea. Uh, I mean, you might be." He got up and kissed her hard and noisily on her cheek. "The captain is coming tomorrow night for dinner. I already invited him."

Illyanne pulled the kitchen towel off her shoulder, bunched it up and threw at her husband.

She couldn't resist the challenge to cook the captain a great meal. As expected, he loved her venison stew. She created a sauce from mashed tomatoes, onions, and beef stock from portable soup tablets. And she whipped up something sure to win him over, her cornbread with cranberries, maple syrup on the side.

During supper, the captain offered Illyanne the job as substitute cook and she accepted. The rest of the night, she felt jumpy and worried she might spill the coffee or brandy or break a dish and ruin the mood. Thankfully, Anders talked a lot and reminisced with the captain about prior sailing runs, steering through violent storms and much-enjoyed port visits.

Once the captain finally said goodnight and was out the door, Anders tried to lift Illyanne up and twirl her around. His injured arm couldn't bear the weight and he groaned but the two of them giggled together at their triumph. "Oh, Illie, it's going to be such a thrill. You're going to ride the Great Lakes on a schooner." He raised his good arm, announcing, "The finest, fastest, most maneuverable cargo sailing ship in the world. I'm so happy, you'll be joining me in the working commercial waterways of America — well, at least Wisconsin, Michigan and Ohio for this run."

"It's mostly for the family's finances, Anders. And, it's just the one-week run."

"Then the adventure, my sweet, will all be extra." Anders threw his head back laughing. "I wish I was going with you."

2

October 7, 1871
Saturday

ANDERS LOCKED THE BRAKE on the wagon in front of Peshtigo's General Store.

Matthew jumped down from the back of the wagon, stretching out his back. "I'll stay here if you don't mind." He made an annoyed expression looking west. He squinted and raised an arm to bury his nose in his sleeve. "The air is pretty smokey today." A familiar yellow gray haze filled the sky. "Must be a lot of fellas out there burning leaves and stumps. Bigger chance of flash fires."

"The fire watch will handle it," Anders answered. "We'll only be a few minutes."

Illyanne looked back and saw Matthew raise himself up on the tips of his toes trying to peer into the saloon across the street. He then tipped his hat to a young lady walking by with her mother, making Illyanne smile to herself.

Anders held out his good arm to her and they stepped up onto the boardwalk and into the store. Inside, she dug in her little handbag and brought out a list, smiling eagerly. Her own collection of spices would accompany her on the trip. Anders would carry the onions, lemons and vegetables. The store would send a schoolboy to deliver the cooking oil, rice and potatoes to the ship. Matthew would shoulder carry aboard the salted beef and the hind quarter of a deer.

Illyanne browsed, stopping at a wooden rack set atop of some grain barrels. "Oh, look Anders, it's Worcestershire sauce. I'll take a bottle of that. It's a wonderful season for meat. Beulah showed it to me."

"Is that the one who was a slave somewhere down South?"

"Yes, a house cook on a Georgia plantation." Illyanne looked away from Anders, perusing items on the store shelves and glancing back to her list. "The older cooks taught her. The master held a lot of dinner parties. She knows how to cook just about anything. She's taught me a lot."

Anders only nodded and went to chat with the clerk in the long apron, while waiting to settle up.

They stood on the Peshtigo dock in front of the ship's gangplank. She'd been here before to see Anders off on voyages and greet him on return. The ship's masts and rigging appeared taller and more formidable than she recalled, almost ominous.

Anders boarded and from the ship's deck he talked Illyanne across. "All right now, here's where you're going to be glad that I had you wear sailor pantaloons beneath your skirts. Lift your dress up over your ankles and pull back so you can see your own feet. A good ten inches or so. That's fine. Now, careful of your footing on the steps. Do not look down to the water. Walk fast but don't run. If you feel yourself losing balance, you grab hold of the side ropes lean back, squat down and pull hard like you're trying to stop a team of horses from running wild."

Illyanne focused on Anders' eyes, then broke off and took a deep breath. She stepped forward, then walked briskly. When she stepped onto the deck, she let out a little laugh. "Oh, that wasn't bad. I've got it now." Matthew followed and came aboard.

Anders led her down the ladder well to the galley, showed her the cook stove, storage containers and mess table. In a few minutes, he had covered everything she needed to know.

"I'm all set here. I want to start my preparations to feed the crew supper tonight. You two young men be on your way now." She made whisking motions toward them with the backs of her hands.

"You sure?"

"Yes." She kissed Anders.

"God keep you, Illie-Nee. We'll see you right back here on October fourteenth. You have a great sail."

She warmed and smiled at the affectionate nickname he sometimes used, shortened forms of her first and Menominee middle name. Neenah was a proud moniker of tribal hope for future prosperity. The Menominee pronounced it as NeeNAH. It was a lakeside town which had grown up from humble beginnings in the 1830's. It had started as a Menominee industrial and agricultural mission. Illyanne hugged Matthew and they were off.

Standing now on the ship's deck at pier-side alone, Illyanne looked out over the river. The little hairs on her arms bristled with the uneasy sense that something would go wrong. She told herself that was silly. Anders would have said she needed to buck up. She watched two other cargo schooners as they majestically glided along the river. One sat high in the water, returning to port empty. The other rode low, laden with its lumber freight. The loaded one was heading down river to the Bay of Green Bay, then on into Lake Michigan, and out somewhere into the great beyond.

Watching the ships rang true to what Anders had said. It captivated, like seeing a bird high overhead, arc and turn and land on the water's surface in a gentle splash. No matter how many times, she'd seen it before, ships moving in the water were as wondrous and beautiful as the first time she set eyes on them. And when the ship docked in Cleveland, she would be able to go ashore briefly and glimpse the streets and shops in those faraway places of Anders' endless travel sea stories.

3

C*ity dock*
Peshtigo, Wisconsin

A THUMP FOLLOWED BY a commotion of men's voices down on the dock, drew her attention. She walked across the deck to the opposite side gunwale. A package of goods must have shifted while being lowered onto the dock with the big pulley crane. Four longshoremen were tending to a damaged crate. Angry men's voices wafted up, arguing how to transfer it onto a wagon. Packing straw bulged out from splintered wood in its side.

Off to the right among a group of men, a flash of orange caught her eye. She gasped. A dock worker's arm started on fire. A flying ember must have floated down from the sporadic brush fires often occurring around Peshtigo and landed right on the worker's shirt sleeve.

It had not rained in more than a hundred days. Occasionally, when it was dry like this in the Northwoods and when the winds kicked up, bits of twig and leaf, still lit, would blow easterly then fall like snowflakes. They would flicker for a moment, looking like graceful daytime fireflies before they snuffed themselves out. Sometimes, the small burning wisps would land on something flammable and ignite.

The flash engulfed the man's whole arm. "Ahhh. Heeelp," he screamed, He swung his arm back and forth then threw himself to the ground. He rolled and kicked and thrashed about. Perhaps this man had some grease on his sleeve making the fire worse.

"Man down," someone yelled.

Other dock workers dropped lumber they were carrying. Plunks and clatter rang out all over the dock. It echoed up to the ship's deck where Illyanne stood. A pack of workers ran, heavy-footed toward the man. More lit pieces floated up and burned out. The men swatted down the fire and clapped after burning flying bits in flailing motions as if swatting mosquitoes. Something sparked up near stacked boards, looking like fat spatter sparks from a frying pan. Saw dust. It was everywhere in Peshtigo. People even sprinkled it on puddles in the dirt roads to soak up the muddy streets. When the weather was dry, smoke, ash and saw dust blew about constantly. The air frequently resembled grain dust clouds which formed up when threshing and winnowing wheat.

"Fire!" Someone shouted.

She saw several men hollering and rushing to fill buckets with water at a trough. They stomped across the dock. All over Peshtigo, she had seen men do this from time to time.

Illyanne raced below deck to her galley provisions. Just before she descended, she glanced back to see the men throwing buckets of water on the stacked lumber. Cheers accompanied loud splashes from dumping whole buckets of water. They had hold of the fire now but oh, that poor man.

She grabbed her worn drawstring carry bag. There, she kept her precious spices and herbs. What might help? Something for pain and for a skin burn. Raw potato? Yes, but she would try the wild apricot leaf first, which Beulah, had shown her. A poultice with Spikenard Root would actually be the best thing to apply. But she did not have any. Nor did she have a mortar and pestle. And anyhow, there was no time to grind that up and prepare a cloth wrapping. She tossed a few medicinal things onto one of the ship's galley flour sack cloths, rolled it up and hurried back up on deck.

She hiked up the gathers of her skirt dress to mid-calf. She did not care that her sailor bloomer pants showed. She ran down the gangplank to the dock. It wobbled considerably, giving her a start. For a moment, she thought she might fall, drop her bundle, end up in the water and make a fool of herself. The boards bended and bobbed up and down as she ran. The thumps of the wood planks echoed her footfalls creating a confusing rhythm to her steps. She had to grab hold of the rope rails to keep her balance. She stepped off the ship and ran toward the burned man.

He was hidden among others clustered around him. She pushed gently into the huddle of men's backs. "Please, may I see the burn?"

They gave way, looking at her with curiosity. The man sat on a short stack of lumber cradling his burned arm at the elbow.

Illyanne pinched her skirts up and knelt down beside him to examine his arm. She twisted her head and looked up at the men, who looked on, baffled. "Does anyone have a knife?" Someone produced a folding knife. She cut off the remaining parts of his shirt sleeve. Most of it had burned away but she peeled back the remnants of fabric with the skill of a mother tending to cuts and abrasions on the farm.

The man winced and groaned as she pulled it off the blackened areas of blue plaid fabric.

"That's a good sign. That you feel pain, I mean." She looked up at him and feigned a smile. "Really, it would be much worse I assure you, if it didn't hurt." She lifted it off him and dropped the sleeve, sopped with blood and watery fluid.

The surrounding men had gone silent, keenly watching her actions. After a minute, one from among the group looking on said, "Hey Ben, you sure you want some Injun medicine woman meddling with you?"

Startled, the victim and all the others stopped moving and stared at Illyanne. Now, she could tell by their expressions, their apprehensive postures. They perceived the heritage in her facial features, narrow hooded eyes. They hadn't noticed before, the pastel caramel color of her skin. People supposed she was typically American with some kind of mixed ancestry, like everyone else. She wore her hair up and dressed like a homesteader's wife and spoke perfect English. Her medium brown hair and lighter skin made people overlook her subdued native features.

Ignoring their gaze, she unrolled her wrap of things. She stood up and turned toward them. She swallowed hard, "Yes, I am *Métis*. Half Menominee." She wiped her hands on the gathers of her prairie dress, her favorite, the maroon one with the tiny yellow and white flowers. She wore it today for her first-ever sailing excursion. "I'm a sailor's wife and mother, Mrs. Illyanne Eriksson." She made a demure curtesy and nod, then cupped her hands in front of her waist.

"My husband is Anders Eriksson. We're homesteaders, like all of you, I expect." She pointed in the direction of their farm. "We're just outside of town in Sugar Bush. Of course, I'm not a nurse or doctor." She looked down for a moment. "But I do happen to know some natural treatments for ailments and injuries. Things passed down to me from my Menominee mother. Surely, you've seen healing from natural Indian remedies." She waited a moment for a response. None came. She let her hands fall idle to her sides. She looked down. "I will be glad to step aside or wait until you can and get a doctor."

The muscled men murmured amongst themselves. The smell of their sweat collected in a cloud of pungent air that lingered about them. They had glanced at the raw burn and saw how red and shiny it was. Fur traders and explorers around here had married Indian women and mixed-bloods for more than a century. In recent decades, some people acquired a disdain for Indians with the advent of white assimilation programs. Illyanne overheard part of their conversation.

"I figure she's pretty much the same as us. Bill Handley's married to a woman who's got some Oneida and Ojibwe in her, and ain't nobody's ever made no mind about that." The other men shook their heads in agreement.

The burned man, Ben, grimaced and rocked himself, whistling in air through his teeth. "Listen, Miss. Never mind them." He jutted out his jaw toward her, pointing. "You go ahead now and do what you can."

Illyanne returned to her task. "All right, Mr. Ben, chew this please." She handed him a small cut piece of inner tree bark. "It tastes bitter but it'll help the pain." Next, from her spread dish towel she selected and opened a small container. "This is wild apricot leaf. It's from down South."

The fruit leaves had arrived by mail, dried in a small jar. Illyanne added golden droplets of olive oil to plump them up. She hoped that her effort would not now decrease their medicinal potency. Anyhow, wasn't oil an ancient healing aid? The Good Samaritan poured olive oil into an injured man's open wounds. She trusted that the oil would work with the curative ingredient still active in the apricot leaves. With graceful, cautious movements, she opened the bunched-up petals and flattened them.

Ben winced a little but allowed her to lay the leaves on his arm. She saw his pain ease right away and felt her own confidence surge. She spoke to the men behind her without turning toward them. "May I have a few neckerchiefs or bandanas, torn into strips for a bandage, please?" She knew they all had neckerchiefs to pull over their noses and mouths for times when the wind changed and blew the smoke of the Peshtigo's small fires at them. Sometimes it got down right noxious, like campfire smoke blowing in one's face when the wind abruptly changed direction.

Several of the dock workers hurried into action. It struck Illyanne as pleasantly odd that, the same men who moments earlier considered refusing her help because of her heritage, now jumped to respond to her request. The sound of ripping fabric surrounded them on the shipping dock.

"Here you go, Miss." One of them handed Illyanne strips from their scarves.

She fashioned an outer bandage with the scarf strips, loosely tying several together of them.

"Here's some more."

A burly man came pushing his way into the gathering. "Hey. What's holding things up over here?" He pushed his way in front of the men. "Break it up. What's going on? Somebody drop dead here or what?"

She tucked in the ends of the bandage she had made. "No, sir." Illyanne stood up and spun around to face him and made a little curtsey. "I was on the deck of that lumber schooner over there." Her arms dropped to her sides. "I saw this man catch fire from a floating ash. I came to help his burn with some natural treatments until a doctor arrives."

"Go on. Git." The man swung his arm in a lateral sweep. "Everybody, get back to work." The men cleared away and returned to their tasks of loading lumber and goods.

"My thanks to you, Ma'am." He nodded at her. "I got it from here." He nodded toward her. "Much obliged." The man helped Ben up by his good arm and started leading him away toward the dock warehouse.

"Wait, sir, there's one more thing."

They both stopped and looked back at her. Illyanne approached them digging something out of her rolled up towel. "Here's a potato." She held out the lumpy brown thing toward them in earnest.

Ben and the burly man glanced at each other then looked back at her with perplexed facial expressions. "A potato?"

"Yes. Take it, please."

The foreman squinted. "Uhhh."

She spurted a laugh at their quizzical looks, touching her fingertips to her coiled pinned braid at the nape of her neck. "If the apricot leaves don't help in an hour's time, and you haven't found a doctor, cut thin slices of the potato and lay them on the burn and wrap it the same way I just did."

The larger man, the boss, reached out and accepted the potato. He didn't speak but only nodded and held a curious lingering gaze at Illyanne.

As if to apologize, she added, "That was such a freak accident." She made a casual smile, and scanned the Peshtigo sky. Blue was not visible through a heavy smokey mist. "It seems the fire dousers may need to double up their efforts tonight."

"It happens a lot more often than you would care to know," the burly man said. "We stamp out little flare-ups like that all the time. He cast a blaming glance at Ben. "The men are supposed to be on the lookout for that sort of thing. Nothing really to worry about. Thanks for your help." The two of them turned and walked away.

Back on board in the galley of the Henry B. Jones – her galley now – Illyanne made herself some tea. She sighed and sat down, nervously stretching out and retracting her fingers over and over, trying to stop the slight tremble in her hands. Dear Lord, give me strength to endure for all that is coming. I fear I may have taken on too much.

For heaven's sake, running to bring pulverized goldenrod flower for scrapes and bee stings to her husband and son was something she ought to go running to – not to a worker on the dock who had caught fire. Her breath quickened, recalling her boldness at the way she had butted in – a lady and common cook, on the docks. What was she thinking? She reminded herself of Anders' words, "Yes, it'll be a tough adjustment being out there in the shipping world, but it will be all right, Illie. I can promise you it will be an adventure. And don't you worry. It's not dangerous or anything."

In the short time since her family dropped her off at the ship, Illyanne felt that everything had already changed.

4

Aboard the ship by herself, Illyanne was ready to sail but she still fretted. Sailing on the open water out of sight of land was going to be strange. She could swim – a little, in rivers and lakes, where she could always see shore. She knew that that in Lake Michigan, at times she would be completely surrounded by water. The incident with the dock worker magnified her alien feeling. How different her nature was compared to Anders. This was his world, not hers. She would rather be at the homestead, feeding the chickens and milking the cow, walking the woods and cooking. Oh, how baking bread or cooking a stew which her family liked gave her a pleasurable glow inside. It was only a few days ago, wasn't it? A week at most, when her life turned such a momentous page. She felt homesick already. It quieted her restless spirit to think of home. . .

On a typical day, Illyanne carried a pail of cow's milk up the front three steps to the cabin. She poured it into a glass bottle and set the rest of it back in the sawdust-lined box. Sometimes, humming she'd break half a dozen eggs, pour in some milk and scrambled them on her prized iron cook stove. She toasted bread at the same time in her oven and swirled the striker inside the hanging iron triangle outside to call Anders and Matthew in from their chores for a hearty breakfast.

She had Mason jars of all her jams. Last week, it was apple-plum. Some days she'd have sausage from trading in town, and always coffee. Fika, from Anders' Swedish tradition. One of them would usually mumble the prayer before meals and dig in. It always made her feel proud and satisfied.

Illyanne remembered the years they had getting their homestead settled. Living in a tent for over a year, chopping down trees, brush and her cooking squirrel and fish a hundred different ways. It seemed like she had cooked on a campfire for ages before she got her stove. Then came the hard work of planting. She had mentioned to Anders before his injury how well they were finally doing.

He had teased her, asking what was making her get all philosophical on him and wondering whether she was expecting again.

With her new twice a month cooking job, working every other weekend, she'd come home with some new recipes. Honey-Bourbon glaze for ham. Anders feigned shock over that. Liquor? Mother! And one night she fed them buttermilk fried chicken. She laughed at the crazed look Anders gave her for it. Yet, he and Matthew gobbled it up.

They didn't often stand back and take stock but God had been good to them. Despite a few hardships, it was a pleasant daydream to remember scenes from home – all the more so, that she wasn't there now.

Illyanne smiled to herself at the nostalgic memories but it faded quickly. She could hardly believe how she ended up on a ship. The preparations, purchases and menu planning had gone by so fast. And then, she was here.

It made her recall a time as a child when she visited her grandparents at the Menominee reservation with her mother. One evening, she sat under the stars with other Indian children who were telling entertaining stories and legends around a big campfire. Some Oneida children were there. One of them told a shapeshifting tale about their Iroquois ancestors. Soldiers had chased some Iroquois tribesmen over many miles of woodlands. The Iroquois got far ahead, ran into a clearing and changed themselves into stones. The children laughed, clapped and whooped over the story of how clever the Iroquois had acted. The soldiers caught up to them in the open field. They walked amongst the changed Iroquois and complained to one another about having lost their trail.

Illyanne found it disconcerting that today, she felt a kindred spirit to the soldiers in the story, not the Iroquois. She knew how they felt when they couldn't find the Indians in the field of stones. Although she understood it was temporary, her own home and family had disappeared from her sight and surroundings. Before now, she had always felt the closeness of their spirits. It put her in a brief temperament, well-known to sailors as being 'in the doldrums.'

The schooner's crew arrived during the day on October 7th, a Saturday. It was scheduled to set sail early the next morning. It perturbed the crewmen that Illyanne Eriksson was the wife of a sailor who sometimes worked with them. The mariner brotherhood held its own customs and traditions. Women and families only came aboard and visited when the ship was docked in port. The captain's hiring-on Illyanne as the ship's cook was an unappreciated invasion of the sailors' inner sanctum.

Illyanne heard their grumblings when they boarded. People around these parts generally gave little thought to a sailor marrying into Indian stock. This part of Northeastern Wisconsin had still been mostly pioneer land not much more than a couple of decades ago, when all the industrial expansion started. White-Indian intermarriage was relatively common.

If being part Indian was a source of the crew's coldness toward her, it was secondary. She knew what the main problem was. Anders told her that the men might see her as a wife poking her nose into her husband's business. And then of course, there was the ordinary teasing or playing of some prank on any newcomer. 'Every sailor's rite of passage,' Anders had called it.

She laddered up and down the deck bringing in supplies and setting up in the galley and getting the evening's meal started. The gentle lapping sound of the water against the docked ship's sides became a pleasant background as she began her preparations. Below deck in her galley, the space was cramped but the sounds of walking on wood and clanging her pots and pans all muffled in the cozy area.

By late afternoon, the men began reporting aboard for the voyage to set sail the next morning. Two of them kept their backs to her, when she came up looking for a dry goods delivery. She overheard a pair of them.

"Did you see we got Anders' half-breed woman as cook for this run?" One sailor muttered to another. Both of them jiggled with wheezy laughter.

The second man snickered, "Yeah, it'll probably be pig corn and 'tatoes for the duration."

Anders had tried to explain that men would sometimes latch onto jibes and digs that they didn't even believe in for the sake of going along with the group. She didn't understand. Finally, he dismissed the subject saying, "It's like how kids act, teasing each other. It's just a maritime tradition."

Illyanne saw the men slap and box with each other playfully. When walking the decks, she observed them spar jokingly with one another as they checked rigging and equipment.

She frowned, waited until the crewmen walked out of hearing range. She mumbled to herself, "pig corn and potatoes might make an interesting dish." She might very well dress them up with roasted squash, nutmeg and cinnamon, butter, salt as a side dish. Wouldn't *that* be a surprise to serve? Quickly, she realized Anders would probably disapprove. Too contrary. The men's eyes might pop right out of their heads and make her their enemy from the start.

"Always remember sailing is team work, Illie," Anders told her. "There's not much worse than being an outsider on a lumber run.

The men ain't necessarily friends. Still, when you're on a sail, they all form a friendly working connection." Sailing was a man's world but she hoped they would get used to her.

The men came below to store their gear in the bow where they bunked. They brushed by her briskly in the small space making their way through the galley to their sleeping quarters. Two averted their eyes from her. The other two stopped by the galley, one with scraggly long hair and wool cap, the other, muscular, and missing a tooth. He asked, "Shouldn't you oughta be at home making soup for Anders to nurse 'im back to health so he can get back to work?"

She swallowed the slight and answered in a singsong manner as if she had been interrupted in a daydream. "Oh, soup wouldn't help a broken arm." She flashed a smile and swung her head back to look at the stew she was stirring. "But I left instructions with our son about how to make a poultice if there's any swelling. And if he has any pain, I prepared willow leaves and inner bark chew." She could feel the man and his friend standing behind her, thwarted in their jabs and not understanding what she had just said. Their silence was like honey. She carried on humming to herself. She started slicing up vegetables and tossing them into the pot. She smiled to herself, thinking in that moment, this was her mother's kill-them-with-kindness approach coming out through her.

Sailors! Anders had warned her about the seagoing culture of insulting kinship. Illyanne heard them calling each other Gollumpus and Chowder Head and they laughed together. Sailors insisted on carrying out their senseless, beleaguering initiation practices even with her. She could not imagine what they gained from it. 'Just grown men being small,' she imagined her mother would have said.

Anders had tried to explain to her how to deal with them. "Be firm but make light of things, too. Don't take their guff, Illie-Nee. Throw it back at 'em – but in a way so's they don't know it." It was difficult to find that middle way but Illyanne felt that she had managed it well on this first encounter.

One of the men stepped closer to her as she was bent over her stove and leaned in to speak in a low voice. "Don't you pay them no mind, Miss Illyanne. They don't mean nothin' by it. They're just taunting you about any old thing 'cause you're new. Same as they would for any sailor." He sighed. "Truth is, it'd be more worrisome if they didn't act like that."

She remained standing in front of her stove and didn't turn toward him to speak. "Oh, I know. I still don't care for it but I understand. My husband has told me many things about sailing." She nodded in gratitude for his comment. Soon enough, she would see the crew choke on their own insults. She aimed to put into her food something like what those Siren women put into their singing in that story by Homer. Anders collected epic sea tales of all sorts and was forever regaling her with them. The Sirens particularly enchanted her with their ability to subdue the sailors – though she'd only lure them to dinner – not to their deaths. The Sirens had lodged snugly in her memory. Illyanne was the crewmen's cook now aboard the Henry B. Jones, three-masted lumber schooner. The men might not think she was important now but she took great pride in having taken charge over their most primal need to eat. She would woo them with her cooking like the Sirens wooed those sailors with their singing. Tonight, it would be a basic stew, but tomorrow, when they sailed, she'd make them something special to win them over.

In her peripheral vision, she saw the man still standing at the opening of the galley, watching her. "You can let the other gentlemen know that supper will be ready soon," she said sweetly.

"I think you're gonna hold your own, Miss Illyanne," he said to her as he touched his cap toward her and walked away.

She smirked to herself. His comment reminded her of the new arrivals, who often came in groups to eat at the Peshtigo Boarding

House. It fed up to two hundred men a day. A logger or a factory worker at the woodenworks, acting as a mentor usually helped them get settled as boarders and showed them where to take meals when they first arrived. They came by boat in droves to make good money, purchase land, find a wife and settle into family life.

Time and again, she'd seen it, cooking for the men at the Boarding House for the last several months on her every other weekend shifts. They acted tough, haughty and demanding because of their work when they came in for a meal. They didn't expect much more than campfire slop or a lumberjack's stew. She thought of the times she greeted new arrivals, those brash loggers, and factory men – and now these sailors.

The crewmen stirred a similar annoyance in her. Aboard ship, she felt even more under the thumb of working men. None of them knew what she could conjure up in the kitchen. And it was her people, the Menominee, who had lived here in northeast Wisconsin for centuries, farming, fishing, hunting, logging, gathering rice and trading. The workers, like these sailors, were from out East, or immigrants from Europe, Britain and Scandinavia. She wished she had a good reason to explain it all to them. Why, the very town where they now lived, derived its name from Indians. The Ojibwe called the Menominee the people of the rice, in their language, *Peshtigo*. It only took a few days for the boarding house men to appreciate a supper that was filling and tasty. The crew of the Henry B. Jones was about to learn the same lesson.

5

O*ctober 8, 1871*
Sunday

WHEN THE CAPTAIN BOARDED Illyanne's ship early Sunday morning, he grumbled about the dock longshoremen running so late. All day, the noise of the dock workers' loading filled the ship, piling up stacks of lumber in the hold and shoving them different directions.

Crew members had come through the galley randomly during the day for bread, apples, sandwiches as they helped the dock workers. It was near sunset when the captain finally came down to the galley for a cup of tea, still grousing about recording the late departure. "Confound it all! I had to put down our departure time as 7:00 p.m., October 8, 1871 in the ship's log. We were supposed to leave at sunup this morning. Hope we can make up the time. I'll be hearing about it if there's dock workers in Cleveland sitting around waiting half a day for us to arrive."

At last, at dusk the ship cast off and started down the Peshtigo River for the bay of Green Bay. Then on to Lake Michigan, into what Anders called the fantastic mystery of the vast, inland seas. A new universe loomed before her, where the divine kissed the waters under the sky, the province of men, mariners and sea creatures.

As Anders had kept saying, maybe it would be an adventure and she should enjoy it. Illyanne stood on the deck, trying to stay out of everyone's way. The first days of October had remained warm. Tonight, the sky to the west glowed like a low, orange cloud, sunset in the haze of the Peshtigo area's unremitting little fires. "It's mighty pretty," Illyanne offered as men noticed her on deck after she had come up for a break, seeking some fresh air.

The buoyancy of the ship moving in the water made her shift her weight and feel a momentary queasiness. Yet, it felt delightful. It reminded her of a time when she sat in a bark canoe with her mother. When she was eight years old, she was finally old enough to go out with her to harvest wild rice.

Back then, a Menominee Indian elder long-poled them along the edges of the lake in a dugout canoe. Once they came close to the water's edges, they could tap-tap-tap with their sticks against the rice stalks and collect the kernels in into big woven baskets. Illyanne and her mother laughed and put their faces up to the sun and lolled in the canoe when the poler moved them along to the next spot. The water glistened and birds swooped and sang. Illyanne reveled in the idyllic memory of perfect ease. Later, the men would process the yield of the day, loosening the husks by 'dancing the rice' in holes in the ground lined with animal skins and wearing special moccasins. It was fun to join the women to do the final winnowing, tossing the trays of rice in the air and catching it again to separate out the lighter chaff that blows away.

The Peshtigo wind kicked up, snapping Illyanne out of her memories. The ship's captain began calling out orders to the crew, to open up some more of the sails to carry them down river faster and into the bay of Green Bay on into the celebrated Lake Michigan. It was roughly ten nautical miles to the bay but the fully loaded ship moved at the pace of a slow walker.

Minutes later, the captain barked, "visibility is bad. Slack off the headsail sheets. Take 'em down to half-mast."

Illyanne knew to stand clear of the captain, who now turned red-faced and fast-walked toward her, yelling past her. "She's going too fast in this thick smoke." He hurried to the port side and then starboard in the walkway between lumber stacks all over the deck. He leaned out to look ahead. "Bloody heck, this is worse than any pea soup fog I've ever seen." The smoke had not dissipated since the day before. "Ascend the mast," he ordered. "Lookout to the bowsprit." One of the crewmen scrambled up the webbed rope ladder of the center mast. Another crawled out onto the pole that was the protruding spar at the ship's bow.

The captain waited on deck, looking upward with a handkerchief to his face. The buttons of his old Navy service coat glinted faintly. "Lookouts, report."

"Can't see a thing, sir," the man overhead called down. "Nothing but a few lights along the river's edge." The bowsprit lookout yelled back the same thing. The men all sounded strained and worried. The captain ordered the crewmen back to the deck and to lower away all but the main sail down to slow their speed. The current carried them along.

Illyanne felt an urge to do something, to somehow help light the way for the ship to makes its way through the smoke. Maybe this was the time that her dream vision had portended, back when she was ten. Girls didn't spend nights and days in the wigwam with their mothers like the boys did for a guardian spirit vision. But, Illyanne once felt ill at her parents' cabin and went to bed without supper. Feverish, she experienced her own dream vision and took it to be comparable to a boy's dream vision. She became a bird soaring high over a dark landscape without trees, carrying a light on her head. Accompanying this sight was the strong feeling of euphoria.

Illyanne's mother didn't know the dream vision's meaning. She only told her, "When the time comes, you will know." This might be her moment. If she went to the ship's bow, she might provide a guiding light from overhead. Up on deck, she planned to help somehow but the yelling and worry in the men's voices squelched the sentiment and she went back down below deck.

Anders' words pounded in her head. "By God, Illie, if there's anything ever going on, the ship taking on water, getting too close to another ship or a bad storm, you get yourself below." He shook his splinted arm in the air. "Let the sailors do the sailing. Nothing's worse in this world than somebody in the way during some kind of crisis at sea. Keep your mouth shut and do your work. Aye?" He kissed her hard on the head and added, "Illie-Nee, I'm darned proud of ya."

The galley stretched about four by six feet. This was her refuge now, the wood counter, cupboards and little iron stove set on top of bricks inside a sand-filled box. She stirred the stew and peeked in to check on her bread. Nothing to do but curl up and sit in her hot little space across from the iron oven stove and wait, rocking with the ship's sway.

She must have dozed for some time. Something incredibly loud blasted outside waking her. Its echo reverberated through the ship and she felt a sudden jerk of the vessel in the water. She tensed all over and coiled herself up, her heart racing. What in heaven's name was that? She shivered. Did a steamship's engine blow? Was there an explosion back at the saw mill? It sounded like the echoing crack of thunder that comes after a great bolt of lightning but there was no storm outside. It sounded more like the veterans' Civil War stories at the Boarding House. She had never heard cannon fire but this sounded like what those men described. Earth shattering, ear splitting.

Illyanne scaled the ship's ladder quickly and stepped out of the hatch door onto the deck to find out what she could. The stacked lumber around the ship's deck left small passageways for the crew to walk through. Night had fallen but the sky toward Peshtigo had lit up with fire. The wind blew strong but felt strangely hot. Then, the breeze reversed. Air seemed to be getting sucked upstream toward town. Then, while gazing back at Peshtigo, the fire jumped up. It climbed above the tallest forest trees. It was freakish sight. Even through the smoke, she could see how it swept upward very rapidly in a spiral. The sky itself seemed to be burning. The roar sounded like being close to a heavy waterfall.

She stared at it, mesmerized. She whispered, "It's a pillar of fire." She felt tears roll down her cheeks. The image came to her, God's presence as the pillar of fire in the book of Exodus. It lit the way for night travel in the desert. That fire served as a powerful sign of constant protection and a promise the He would not forsake his Chosen People. It was supposed to be as comforting as a campfire burning through the night, to keep predator animals away.

Her mother had told the story before, lifting a lit twig from the fireplace to demonstrate what it might have looked like in miniature. With her arms out wide, her mother said, "the real fire was hundreds of times bigger and reached up to the sky." Illyanne recalled feeling scared but her mother cooed, "The people had no fear of it. They loved that God lit a big candle for them to see. He was there all night to watch over them."

But this pillar of fire screamed with a continuous hellish rumble. Nothing about it was lovely or reassuring. It was other-worldly. It appeared to betray the original purpose. It was as if the Devil himself leapt into the fire and was wreaking havoc with it, destroying everything, for what reason, she could not fathom. The colossal fire horrified and transfixed. She stepped closer to one of the ship's masts, and wrapped her arm around it. Inside, her spirit kicked and screamed but no sound came out. Yet, she could not look away from the fire. It held a dreadful magnetic power over her. Was God abandoning her town? Illyanne almost forgot to breathe and she felt strangely chilled, even in the warm air.

The crewmen stood nearby on deck, their arms limp at their sides. The inferno commanded their stares and the men's mouths gaped as the ship slipped slowly away, bobbing along on the gentle river current. They only let out groans at the sight. Several miles downriver from the Peshtigo dock now and still, they could see the flames spread and reach and twist like a giant kerosene lamp broken and spilling onto a miles-wide haystack landscape. One crewman staring back at it, wiped his brow and hung his head for a moment. "Must be over a hundred feet high for us to be able to see that from all the way here down river."

The conflagration rendered them all still. There were no words for this catastrophe, as they witnessed it, helpless from afar. All the crew's brawn and animated horseplay stopped at the devastating sight of Peshtigo burning. After a minute, some of them glanced back at Illyanne. The eyes of those gruff, strong men of the sea had all turned glassy.

"What was that loud blast?" She asked them.

One of the men answered, "Fire that size – it was probably roots and tree trunks exploding. Underground peat burns and smolders. Like a campfire that isn't fully doused. If there's something to feed it, it grows back and goes up into tree roots and up the trunks."

The thumps of the captain's footfalls running to where they all stood broke the trance. "Looks like the jaws of Hell have opened up on Peshtigo," he said.

His words sent a shudder through her. Yes, this was hellfire, not something heaven sent. She murmured, "How can it be?" Against the black sky, the shafts of flame glowed a brilliant angry orange. It wounded her spirit. What had she or the people of Peshtigo done? She even wondered, as she would discover others did too, whether this might even be the start of the end of the world.

The captain choked up as they all stood still, side by side. "Say a prayer, boys for your homes and your loved ones." He bowed his head. The ship moved along in the gentle, black silvery waves of the river. No one spoke for several long breaths. Then, the captain pressed the crew. "We've got to navigate out of here. Not a thing we can do." He raised his voice. "Let's get to it, men."

Only then, Illyanne gasped. Why had she not thought about Anders and Matthew? She almost slid back down the ladder well. At the bottom, she collapsed into a ball. She held her hand over her mouth to stifle her cries as a shiver penetrated her whole being. Those trees all lit up must have been the forest behind Peshtigo. The fire must have been close to their Sugar Bush homestead. Did they get away in time?

Illyanne had once seen a widow crumple up and sob when she went to meet her husband's ship at the dock. Somehow, the man had died at sea and the crewmen brought her to the Peshtigo Boarding House to sit and have tea and break the news to her. For a few seconds, Illyanne felt like she was living in that woman's skin. Illyanne whimpered for a moment, doubling over in silence as her gut wrenched.

She suppressed the thought that Anders and Matthew might have been burned or killed in the terrible fire. What of their home and farm? The animals? Was Sugar Bush far enough away to have been spared? Dwelling on it now in this other world of the sea was useless. There was no possibility for her to get off the ship and try to go to them. She wiped her eyes and the slobber from her mouth and cheeks. Pushing it all down, down deep, she tended to supper. The men would be needing to eat soon.

Overhead, she heard men reciting a familiar sea shanty, one of those ancient mariner chants to set their deck work to a rhythm. Anders sometimes sang one when chopping wood or baling hay. Some of the sailing songs thrived as an outgrowth of the Catholic faith, successfully transplanted in these parts over a hundred years ago by the French Jesuit missionaries. That evening, the men's voices carried a plaintive quality. As Illyanne stirred her stew, she heard the other men's voices join in to chant the ode again.

Oh Mary, Star of the sea,

Light of all waters,

Guide us through all dark and stormy seas.

Protect us from being lost at sea.

Lead us to that haven of peace and light

Back to our home port,

Found only in Him who calmed the sea.

The lyrics only compounded Illyanne's perplexed state. The incident rattled her understanding of calm and home. The Great Spirit and God-man sent his beloved human mother as a constant guide. But incomprehensibly, like a slap in the face, he had also sent the violent fire.

6

S*unday night*
October 8, 1871

ILLYANNE FINISHED PREPARING the meal and found herself idle and fidgeting for a long time, in front of the iron stove. Her mind failed to track on the simplest prayer, even after having seen the disturbing horror of the rotating shaft of fire. She tried to shake off the lingering fogginess she felt. This was not at all the adventure Anders had described.

Time dragged on and the sound receded above as they wended their way further down the river. At last, news came when one of the men hollered down the hatch, "We're in the Bay of Green Bay now. First crew is coming down to eat, then we'll swap out with them."

Illyanne let out a sigh of relief to become busy. With tasks to complete, she managed to set aside the repetitive intrusive thoughts of whether or not she still had a family. She dished up two bowls of her beef, carrots, corn and potatoes in a sauce with bread on the side. And two big glasses of cold water.

Wet and smelly from sweat and smoke, the men passed by and sat down. The mess table was in a dining cubby adjacent to the galley, lined with light grainy Douglas fir planks. There, four crewmen could eat, six, if tightly packed together. She set their meals before them.

They ate in silence, sopping up every bit of sauce with the bread. One got up, "Thank you Ma'am. That was awfully good."

Illyanne nodded to him. She smiled to herself. Yes, her choice of sauce creation had the intended effect, beef stock with cranberries mashed into a paste, and the secret, an enchanting pinch of cinnamon and dollop of maple syrup. In the Northwoods, syrup was the golden nectar product adopted from Indians who made it, Oneida, Ojibwe, Menominee and their closest neighbors, the Stockbridge-Munsee, migrants from out east who were Mohican and Munsee Delawares. The other crewman took his last spoonful of the stew and met Illyanne's eyes with a thank-you nod. She felt glad she had chosen this for her first meal, just right for a working sailor's supper.

The second pair of men who came down for dinner also ate well. The captain came down last. He ate with relish as the others had. He glanced toward her as he ate.

Something prompted Illyanne to offer a friendly word. "At least sir, we've made it into the bay safely."

"Yes, but we can't afford to rest too soon. The smoke persists. There's flying sparks and debris all about. I've got to have a man posted aloft, so the sails or masts don't start on fire." He took a long drink from his cup. "It's hard to see but it looks like there may be fire on both sides of the bay now."

Illyanne inhaled deeply and began kneading her hands. "Oh, dear."

"We have to be on watch. Burning ash is blowing all around." He gulped his water and clanged the metal cup on the table. "And, Missus, we still got quite a night ahead of us. We have to pass through Death's Door at the far end of Wisconsin's craggy arm peninsula to get into the main body of Lake Michigan."

"What's that, sir?"

"Ah, Anders has spared you hearing about that, did he?" He let out a little dastardly laugh which rattled her. "Sorry, but we're not home free yet. Death's Door is the main navigational passageway into our great Lake Michigan." He pointed to a map nailed against the mess table bulkhead. "See this finger tip of the peninsula here?"

Illyanne leaned forward over the table and peered at the map.

"What looks like a torn off fingernail there? That's actually Washington Island. We don't go around the tip of that like you would think. We go through the strait right here. That's Death's Door. *Porte des Mort* is what the Frenchmen around here called it. She's got rocky shoals that extend far out from the shore and the lake winds can be fierce and unpredictable. It's a famous spot for shipwrecks. And because of our late start, we'll be transiting at night."

"Oh my. I hope –." She didn't want to say anything about God or the Great Spirit, Mecawetak, but rather, something nautical. "I hope the Star of the Sea keeps us safe." She knew he would understand from the shanty the men had recited earlier. It was an old-world title of the Virgin Mary, who lit the night sky with a guiding star. She served men's spirits too, as the navigating patroness of seafarers and faith.

"Indeed," he said as he finished his last bite, swallowed, got up and handed his dishes to Illyanne. He saw her distress and touched her forearm. "Try not to worry yourself. We've transited the Door many a time before. You just do the best job you can, as I see you have. That was a fine meal, Miss Illyanne, hearty and delicious. "We'll be there in the next few hours. You'll want to set out some bread or apples for the men's night watches."

She cleaned up the dishes and put them away. She decided to set out bread and jam for the night shift. Over the bread, she laid a slightly damp towel to keep it from drying out. The breakfast plan was bacon, eggs and she'd bake her buttermilk bread biscuits. If the dough was made tonight, it would rise well in the heat already captured below deck. Half of the dough would be for making ordinary biscuits. The rest, would include mixed dried berries, currants, elderberries, and gooseberries, as a tryout of the men's tastes.

In preparation for a night's sleep, she rolled out the bedroll. Illyanne managed to say a few Hail Mary's on her knotted twine rosary before she climbed over the half-foot bracing rod to sleep in her little galley perch. This space was probably meant as a staging area for larger food containers but she claimed it as her bunk area. All the shelving in the galley had similar bracing bars, wooden dowels which kept supplies from sliding or falling over when the ship pitched or rolled.

Being on water continued to unsettle her. Right now, she could have been getting ready for bed in the dim lantern light of home. She imagined combing out her hair and rewrapping Ander's splint. She wanted to be there, having her usual quiet evening. After she fed her family, washed the dishes, she and Anders and Matthew sat around a glowing hearth chatting while she mended clothes, sewed some quilt patches together or occasionally worked on weaving a basket.

Anders and Matthew might have been telling her tonight who they saw in town today. There might be news on the Miss Jennifer, the young lady who sometimes clerked at the General Store. Matthew seemed to fancy her. She wondered if they made it to Sunday Mass this morning without her prodding. Illyanne hoped Mrs. Harriet Barstow had given birth by now. She was dying to know whether it was a boy or girl. She thought of Beulah and felt a twinge of guilt. Cooking alone, Beulah must have been frantically dishing up dozens of supper plates at the Boarding House.

The ship's easy rocking and the gentle creaking wood with its sweet, clean, fresh-cut scent should have calmed her. Instead, she managed only brief cat naps through her first night at sea. Worries about Peshtigo and her family tormented her. She had trouble ridding herself of images of dead sailors floating in the lake near a large iron gated door beneath the water – the Death's Door of her dreams. The treacherous sight and sound of the fire replayed in her head. She had to chide herself of fearful thoughts of Anders and Matthew dead or burned by the fire. She must have faith, but her thoughts conspired against her, causing tossing and turning and stealing much of her sleep.

The winds from Peshtigo continued to propel the ship forward on its already unusual journey.

7

Sometime during the night, a screeching grinding sound jolted Illyanne awake.

With it, a loud scraping noise resonated through the ship's ribs and cargo of timber. She felt the abrasive movement in her bones and teeth. It was like riding in a fast-moving wagon when the wheels were running over ruts of dried mud. A sudden stop in the vessel's motion threw her forward. She heard a thud as she banged her head against the bulkhead. She groaned. Her hands went up to grab her head. Hanging pots and pans clanged together. Her head throbbed but she managed to sit up.

Overhead, men's feet stomped across the deck. Men's voices shouted unintelligible things. Somewhere below her, came the unmistakable sound of rushing water. The cargo hold was filling up. She grabbed a dish towel, ready to throw up into it but she was able to hold off the urge. "We hit something." Might she end up drowning in Death's Door?

Jittery, Illyanne stood in the dimly lit galley. She could not stand up straight but in a moment, she realized it was not her dizziness. The ship had come to rest at a tilt. It was difficult to steady herself and overcome the tremble in her hands when she reached for the oil lamp. She turned up the wick on the brass lantern. The little ship's kitchen brightened but her eyes were bleary. Holding the light over her kitchen work space, she slid the bread and apples back to the center of the counter, back from the bracing rack.

She started to climb the ladder to find out what was happening on deck. The hatch door would not open. She pressed harder and harder, trying to ram it. Soon, she figured out that hundreds of pounds of wood planks stacked all over the ship had shifted, slid and now pressed against the door. It trapped her below deck, alone.

Her insides cringed and her heart rate increased. Sweat beaded up all over her. Illyanne tried to holler through the hatch door. "Help. Captain. Anybody. I can't get out. Help. Pull the boards off the hatch. Please. Help."

No reply came.

Over the hiss of the water rushing in, her voice simply did not carry. The lumber overhead insulated the sound too well. She heard a muffled exchange between the captain and a crewman directly above through open walkway in the deck boards.

"Helmsman Amidships!" The captain called for the man steering the ship to come to the center of the deck. "What happened?"

"That bloody smoke's marooned us, sir," the sailor said. "I couldn't see a thing. Had a spotter up at the bow after the tough time we had earlier."

Quickly, she stepped down and grabbed a wooden spoon to hit against the door and ship's frame to signal for help. Illyanne banged away frantically and yelled again for help. The muffled voices overhead moved further away. The fire flashed in her mind again. The pillar of fire. So incomprehensibly destructive and frightening.

Thoughts of the Menominee underworld monster flooded her mind. The Horned Hairy Serpent was a giant eel-like serpent in tribal lore. It capsized boats. It pulled people down into the abyss. The French priests taught about a Devil with horns who did the same thing to souls. Illyanne wasn't sure whether the Menominee or the Catholics had the right understanding or if they both taught the same thing in different words. Right now, the fatigue and fear were turning into defeat. She could not get out. No one heard her pleas.

Water continued rushing in and she was alone. She knew God was always with her but it didn't seem so just then.

The drumming thoughts intensified in her head. Some horrible creature might be coming for her very soon. She fumbled around and grabbed a long knife in the galley. It was doubtful she could fight off the mythical beast. Her breathing became like panting. Would it bite, bleed her out or pull her into the water to drown? How long would it take? A minute? Two minutes of horror and then peace and rest? Like Anders's stories of men tossed into the ocean and surrounded by sharks?

The air below deck turned warm and stagnant.

Overhead, she could make out the captain's call. "Ladder over the bow. Damage report."

A crewman replied, "I'm going over, Cap, starboard side."

She heard more poundings of rapid footsteps. The pounding in her head decreased to a dull throb. Illyanne rallied all her energy and screamed for help again. She beat the wood spoon against the hatch door once more. Then there was only quiet. Very tired now, she sat back down in the galley in a slump, out of breath, unable to cry.

"Got a good look at her from here, sir," the sailor yelled from somewhere. "She's sitting pretty straight in the water, sir, listing a little to starboard."

"We've run aground, sir. She mighta broke her back, on the shoals." the sailor added. "Can't tell for sure 'til mornin'. We'll have to swim underneath her in the daylight to get a good look at the keel."

"Blast!" The captain started making rounds about the ship. First, he ordered, "Drop anchor to the starboard side." A voice called to "abandon ship" over and over and moved around as Illyanne heard it through the galley ceiling, the passageways in the deck above that were free from the blockage of stacked lumber.

Minutes and minutes of time rolled by. Then, more muted voices now came to her ears. Three or four men? Further away. She could not tell what they were saying at all but the voices came from different directions. They signaled some hope. Still, no one came when she resumed hitting the spoon on an overhead beam inside the galley.

The waiting made everything worse. Had fifteen minutes passed? A half hour? However long it was, it crept into longer. More than an hour. At least the swish of rushing water had stopped and none had seeped into the galley. So, perhaps no beast of the sea was going to pull her to the underworld. And, she wasn't going to drown. Now, it appeared she would be left alone, forgotten inside the ship. Could there be anything more sad and lonely than being abandoned with no way out of a shipwreck? Fatigue set in again after the desperate and excited spell. Illyanne lay back down to rest and sleep.

After some time, footsteps sounded again from overhead. Then, above her came the glorious sounds, wood planks being slid back. Soon, she heard voices calling her name through the hatch door.

"Miss Illyanne. Hold on. Miss Illyanne. Are you alright?"

Grabbing her spices and carpet bag, she went back up the ladder and waited there for the hatch to be opened. A great lump formed in her throat so that she could only faintly answer the men hovering over her. "Yes, I'm here." Through tears, she managed, "I'm alright."

She heard the last board get pulled off and the hatch opened. To crewmen lifted her out of the galley shipwreck tomb. Looking out, she saw the faces of two crewmen and the moon and starlit sky behind them. Seeing the stars, especially the brightest North Star almost seemed to smile at her. It brought tearful relief. It was a joy to be alive.

Illyanne stood near the hatch opening on deck. Overwhelmed, she was only able to nod and smile responses to her rescuers. A crewman led her toward the bow. She could see now that the ship was not sinking. It stopped in the water. A sweeping lighthouse beam on land somewhere rolled past them.

Down on the land, two silhouetted figures stood in front of partial light talking to each other. The sailor who had her arm said, "You have to climb down this ladder off the bow and walk ashore."

A shadow of herself in her own body, she looked back at the crewman. She blinked at him as if he had told her to go into the water. "What?"

"It's fine. The water isn't deep. There're men on the shore to receive you."

The captain arrived now and stood next to the sailor. "We all have to go down like this. It's safe. Two men have already gone and they're waiting for you."

She readied herself to step onto the first rung of the rope ladder with wood slats. She paused. "But, sir, what about the p-p-provisions?" She realized her mouth had gone dry and her lips quivered. "Shouldn't I save something to cook later?"

"No, not now."

"I could fill a basket." The thought made her feel useful and less afraid for a moment. "Lower it down on a rope?"

"Never mind that." His voice had a firm tone. "Lives come first. At daybreak, we'll see about rescuing food and cargo. Go ahead now and get down the ladder."

His irritation ripped through her. She was being troublesome to the captain.

"Yes, sir."

When she hit water, she felt a deathly cold slap. She gasped and the shivering began instantly. Her teeth chattered. The lake water smell of fish and minerals drenched her. She was waist-high in the water. Her skirts got sopped. Her footing was bad. She slipped on the shoals, soaking her from head to toe. Illyanne felt nearly paralyzed in the freezing water and black night. She stood, wobbly and coughing and horribly alone. The fire and shipwreck bled her energy.

"This way. Walk toward my voice," someone shouted from the shore in the eerie dark void with the nearly blinding sweep of the great lighthouse lamp. "Come on. Keep coming. Come toward me."

Behind her, from the ship, some crew members called to her, perhaps a hundred and fifty feet away. "Keep going. Do not stop or you will drown."

The killing coldness of the water sapped her. Moving in the water felt even colder. Standing still, arms wrapped around herself shivering felt a little warmer. Or the illusion of warmer. She thought she would rest for just a minute. Then, she understood surrendering to the sea now, like one of the people in Anders' sailing tales. It was so cold and so far to go to reach land.

Those voices could not know how frail, how deathly tired her entire body felt. They weren't coming out to help her. So easily, she could yield herself to the water, become part of the inky cold, go numb to it. It would be like falling asleep. If she went under, she hoped they would retrieve her and lay her in a ghost house or mourning house grave marker like her parents. She would sleep in a dugout with a traditional two-foot house built over her and an opening to the world where she would receive food. Her spirit would link up with her parents. Yes. She lifted her feet off the lake bottom and floated. The voices faded away. Her eyes focused on the beautiful stars in the sky, that almost seemed to be watching and waiting for her.

Hold on. What of Anders? And Matthew? She had to shake off this urge. She scrambled back up and stood again. She had to concentrate hard on dragging each leg and foot, heavy as rocks in the deadening frigid water. The pull to rest was also very powerful.

In the shallower water, she stumbled again and took in an unwanted shocking gulp of lake water. Hazy, she lifted herself and rung out her skirts and tucked a gathered handful into her waistband. The water was at her knees now but the shore was still fifty feet on. She stood there in the cold, stilled.

Oh, God, what a day and night. Her worst fears had all come to pass. First, fire and sickening, gut-wrenching worry, now before the night is through, shipwreck and near drowning. The freezing sensation returned. She felt so feeble and small. Raising her heavy arms part way, she looked up for a moment and whimpered, "Jesus." She fell into a near delirium, adding the name of the Menominee Great Spirit, "Mecawetok." Her eyes rolled back in her head for a moment.

Death hovered right there, reaching for her. The alluring peace of death was so close. Her soul ached for Anders. Maybe the fire took him and Matthew. Maybe it was a blessing that she would drown and join them now. Somehow, she moved forward. It was as if someone else was moving her limbs for her.

A woozy sound blew past her. Oh, it's a voice. A woman's? A man's?

"Don't stop. Don't quit. You're almost there."

"Keep moving. This way. Right here. Take my hand." The boy reached out from the velvety black night and grabbed hold of her arm. "What's that you were saying, Ma'am?" Over them, the blazing rotating light streamed directly out to sea. The bottom portion of the beam swept past her. She could only see the slightest outlines of the world, like walking in the forest behind her homestead on a moonless night.

"Come on Miss. My mother's making hot tea for you all right now. The person, a boy threw a double blanket around her. "Come sit by the fire, get you out of those clothes. My mother will loan you something to wear. You're tired and confused and all out of sorts but you are safe now." He leaned down and scooped up her up. "The good Lord has landed you on a lighthouse island."

Illyanne took two more steps and collapsed. The boy caught her and picked her up and carried her into the house while water streamed off of her.

8

T*he day before*
          Saturday, October 7, 1871

"ALL RIGHT, MATTHEW, now that we have your mother all settled aboard, let's go."

"Can I take the reins this time, Papa?"

"Sure, you're practically the backup man of the homestead these days, anyhow. Why not? Anders moved over on the bench and handed the reins to Matthew.

They headed out of town, not north toward home but east. "Papa, I was just dying to know when we'd finally be able to get started on our secret journey. I was about to bust from fear that mother would see something was up." He snapped the reins. "Hah." Following a pensive moment, he added, "I think we should have told her. She should know where we are."

Anders took out his pocket watch to check the time. "I suppose we could have told her. But she would have fussed and pecked at every little thing. Who's going to feed the animals, turn out the horse for the day, milk the cow? And worried on and on." He paused for a moment. "And, besides it's just plain fun. She won't fret now," he beamed, "I tell you, there's no harm in it."

"So, we've spared her. Any chance we'll miss the ferry?"

"No, we will be there in plenty of time to drop off the horse and carriage at the livery stable and get on board."

"Sturgeon Bay, here we come," Matthew said as they headed toward Marinette. They'd ride through it and cross the bridge over the Menominee river there and into the Michigan town of Menominee. There, they would board the steamship ferry to cross the Bay of Green Bay.

They both smiled that their planned trip on the sly was now underway. They would tell Illyanne all about it when they met her back at the dock on the fourteenth. In the meantime, a neighbor would watch the homestead. Nothing could be done about the harvest that week anyhow. They would deal with it when they returned. It would take an hour or so to steam across to Wisconsin's Door peninsula. They planned to camp, fish and make their way southwest to the farm of Anders' old sailing friend, Karl. After a few days' visit, they planned to reverse their tracks, pick up Illyanne at the Peshtigo when the Henry B. Jones arrived back in port and head home.

As soon as they boarded the ferry, Anders and Matthew ran up to the open deck. They leaned against the railing and raised their faces to the sun feeling joyful and free. Matthew said, "I can see why you love the big open blue water and sky so much, Papa." He closed his eyes, set his face up and let the cool breeze ruffle his hair. "It's so different from the river."

"Yeah, that's sea air." Anders breathed in deeply and puffed out his chest. He stood on his sea legs, his feet wide apart and his knees slightly bent. "And this is a much better view, higher up than sailing on a schooner. See the ships out there?" He pointed at small white patchy figures in the distance. "It's a different world out here." He threw his head back for a moment. "I've been watching ships sail since I was a boy. As fascinating today as it was then. A man becomes part fish out here." He stood peering out over the water. "I sure hope your mother will enjoy it."

"She'll be below deck most of the time, won't she?"

Anders grabbed the railing again. "Yes, but she'll feel the ship's movement, come up and see the waves and night sky and feel the cool air change."

The ship rolled over a larger swell. "Whoa. Oh, my stomach."

"Queasy? You'll get used to it. Most do anyhow." Anders laughed and leaned down. "Feel that cool sea spray?"

"What happens if you don't get used to it?"

"Well, you sure won't be any kind of a sailing man." He patted his son on the back. "Take slow, deep breaths and fix your eyes on the horizon."

Matthew fell quiet.

Anders looked over at him, amazed. His son was so close to fully grown. At fifteen, he had fleshed out. He could do all the jobs the homestead required. Now, they were off on a young man's adventure.

"What would you think if I wanted to be a sailor like you?"

"It would be good to learn but farming and having a little business sideline is better. Sailing takes you away from home a lot."

"That's what I would love about it."

"Ah, son, it's a love all right, and an adventure for sure. But it's a curse, too. When you're on land, you can't wait to get back to the sea. When you're at sea, you pain to be home again and all the while that you're loving it. It's a fish hook into the soul. It grants great freedom and exciting voyages, but oh, son, it also makes you its slave. You know, they say every sailor's mistress is the sea." He looked at Matthew, who shrugged in response. "And it can be dangerous too, let me tell you. There's plenty of ships decorating the bottom of the Great Lakes that never made it back to port. Weather mostly. Storms on the Great Lakes would chill the blood in the veins of any saltwater sailor."

Anders started gesturing with his sea story narrative. "Out here, steep waves and high winds will capsize a boat lickety-split." He snapped his fingers. "Oh, and you better hope you don't have to sail in November. The weather is witchy. It can change in a minute to snow and hail and you're out there bobbing around like a cork in a giant bowl of soup. The gusts can roll a ship and snap a mast like a match stick. Freezing rain or a heavy snow can glue you to the deck and sink you straight down, like a stone in a bucket."

"None of that scares me, Papa. And skilled sailors can find their way out of trouble, right?"

"True but there's plenty a sailor who's never been seen again and we don't know the conditions they faced. I've heard everything from sea monsters and mermaids to the ancient Greek god, Poseidon helping or tossing sailors and ships. There's beauty out there like nowhere else." Anders went silent a moment with his thoughts. "Great companionship among shipmates, though. And, after dark, on a clear night, the stars punch through the sky and grab hold of your very breath." He nudged his shoulder against Matthew's as they stood side by side along the ferry's topside railing. "Aye, the stars light the right path in more ways than one." He inhaled deeply and scanned the panoramic view. "The Great Lakes are endlessly fascinating."

Anders paused, looking dreamily out over the waters and slapped his hand over Matthew's shoulders. "Well, you are still young. You finish up your schooling and learn the basics of farming and running a homestead. Then, we'll see about you sailing. You still have to learn the business side of it all. Now, let's get on with adventuring."

As the ferry boat entered the mouth of Sturgeon Bay, the stretch of land on the southern part of the bay gripped their attention. Anders peered through the binoculars his ferry pal had loaned him. "You gotta take a look at this." He handed them to Matthew. Steep sandstone bluffs and craggy cliffs came into view. "Look at that," Anders said. Patches of green plants sprouted out from the white and tan crevices between layers of rock. Thick pine and deciduous forest topped the heights, at least seventy-five feet up.

Matthew looked through the glasses. "Never seen anything so incredible." He paused and let out a little laugh. "Those layers of stone with the brown and green tufts of grassy things growing out of them actually remind me of Mother's flaky biscuits." It looked powerful and mean, lovely and kind, all at the same time.

Anders hugged his son around the shoulder. "There's so much for you to see and do. And today we start with a ferry, camping and a trip to an old sailing buddy's house."

In this Door County peninsula area, the leaves of the trees had turned yellow and red and the water was the same deep blue as the bay. The sunny sky seemed infinite. "Papa? Do you think we might see a bald eagle out here?"

"We might. Keep a sharp eye out." The trees and rock adorned the edges of the landscape scenery in a way Matthew had ever seen anywhere else.

Both of them remained in quiet awe and the ferry steamer glided past the nature show toward the city dock of Sturgeon Bay. This land was much different than the thick forest back home where the rustle of the wind on tree leaves and the sound of birds dominated. Back at the homestead, cool shade stretched everywhere and the sun only pricked through a canopy of heavy foliage with freckled spots of light or cleared acreage. And almost always, smoke dimmed the colors and thickened the air from someone burning brush or tree roots.

"I am still a little confused about the lay of the land. Where we are again, Papa."

Anders pulled out the stub pencil and paper any good farmer kept in his pocket for writing down a list of supplies. "Remember mittens when you were little?" He drew a crude line drawing of a left-handed mitten. He explained the gap between the thumb and fingers was the bay. At the hinge of the thumb was the city of Green Bay. Peshtigo was about half way up the first knuckle of the index finger, and Sturgeon Bay was straight across the bay in a downward slant line.

Coming ashore, they walked down to the water. They set down their gear, a single-sided saddlebag and a shoulder-strap travel valise. Trees at the top of the slope gave way to scruffy bush, then a worn path to the water. It was a wonderful summery day for October. The wind sent a rain of colored leaves floating down every few minutes.

"Let's find some thin branches to use as fishing poles," Anders said. Amongst the people at the shore was a group of Indian families. They wore a mix of traditional animal pelt clothes and American pants and shirts. They were cooking fish over a campfire.

Matthew noticed a pretty Indian girl near his age among them. She had long dark hair. He picked up several small branches and tossed them aside as he wandered toward her. He asked her, "Where do you find the good branches to fish with?"

The girl only looked at him with a puzzled look. An Indian elder looked over toward Matthew. "Why are you talking to her?" Another said gruffly, "What do you want with us?"

Matthew walked over and spoke to him, explaining that he was part Menominee.

The elder Indian stood face to face with Matthew and in a prolonged look. "You Menominee?"

"Yes, my mother is half Menominee, so I'm a fourth."

"Good. You come. Eat fish."

Matthew sat with them. "That's my father over there. He's looking for sticks to make fishing poles."

The girl sat across from Matthew and he watched her. He smiled and she beamed and giggled. Matthew felt his heart flutter. The elder called her Chepi Redleaf. "That girl is daughter of my brother. Not for you."

Anders came over and introduced himself and sat down on the grass. He explained he had married Illyanne more than sixteen years ago. "Your Chief Oshkosh even came to our wedding." He told them Illyanne's parents had later died from fever. Anders felt embarrassed that he knew so little of Illyanne's or her mother's heritage. "I am not sure but I believe she was of the Menominee Moose clan, the protectors of the wild rice beds."

No one in this group of Menominee remembered Illyanne's mother. But the elder assured, "back on our land, maybe someone who knew her. Where is your woman, our daughter, Illyanne?"

"Uh, she works sometimes as a cook. She has a job to cook for one week. I usually sail on ships but – ." He raised his splinted arm. "I have a little break in the bone. Can't pull sails, for a few weeks. Matthew and I are visiting my old sailing friend near Champion."

"Champion?" The elder's eyebrows went up. "This is near the chapel," the elder said. "We know this place. Sister Adele lives there. Teaches our children." He made the sign of the cross over himself. "She is good sister. Knows the Great Spirit. Does good work. She has a bad eye but is a good woman."

After eating, Matthew and Chepi Redleaf wandered off together in the distance, appearing as darkened silhouettes along the shore. Matthew bumped shoulders with her teasingly. The elder still kept a vigilant eye on them as they skipped stones into the water. He was too far away to see the smiles and gazes between them.

Matthew asked her, "Why are your people around here in Sturgeon Bay?" He tried to avoid saying reservation. He knew there had been bitter land disagreements. "I only mean, uh, that the Menominee land that I know is way across the bay and west of Peshtigo."

"Some of us still travel here for many generations. Pottawatomi and Ho-Chunk and a few others. Government agents came to move us but some come back. Some stayed." She smiled. "We return to see them." Chepi Redleaf told him, "We like this place but, we are woodlands people."

"We are too," Matthew said. Their smiles at each other lingered.

"We visit other Menominee here," she said. "We camp and fish. I come with my uncle."

"Do you fish for sturgeon?"

"For that we mostly go to the big lake."

"Why not here? This is Sturgeon Bay."

She laughed. "Not because of sturgeon fish here. There are some but it is called Sturgeon Bay because the shape of the bay is like a big sturgeon." She picked up a stick and drew the shaped in the sandy dirt. She made a long body about three and a half feet, with a shark tail, spikey back and long snout.

"Oh," Matthew slapped himself on the head and laughed at his ignorance.

Chepi Redleaf laughed along with him. "When there is a late summer like now, we come to get more fish to have in winter. We smoke or salt them. We take sturgeon too if we see them here. Usually, they are in lakes near where a river flows in to the big lake."

Matthew only nodded. "Did you catch any sturgeon today? I've never had it."

"We don't catch them. We spear them when they come into shallow water. It is past their run but sometimes there are a few. We could see some but most are gone now until spring. Sturgeon is a big fish. We eat a lot of it in the winter. Don't you know Menominee have great respect for sturgeon?" She tilted her head and asked. "Do you know sturgeon? It's a big, dark-colored fish." She stretched out her arms wide. "With wild rice, this is a main food for us. We honor the sturgeon's spirit. We have the Fish Dance."

"The Fish Dance?" Matthew laughed.

"Listen, this is Menominee. You should not laugh," she chided. "You should learn as one who is part Menominee."

Matthew nodded, accepting the scolding coming from the attractive young girl. "You're right. I don't really know that much about my own ancestors. Show me. How does the Fish Dance go?"

In a hunched posture, she started marching in a circle and tapping her feet. "First, the dancers flap their hands like the sturgeon's fins." She imitated it and Matthew watched, holding himself back from giggling. "There's a part where dancers jump back." She demonstrated with some backward hops. "This is how the fish moves when it comes into shallow water."

Matthew stood by clapping and smiling.

"The last part that I know, you lay down on your stomach, like this. Then, you stand on your hands and your toes or knees. You lift up one leg and wiggle it, then other and do it again. This is like the sturgeon's tail." Chepi Redleaf stood back up. "There's singing and drum beating with it. I watch the men dance."

"Well, I think that was a wonderful. You dance well."

She smiled and he admired the glistening of her dark eyes.

"Hey, how come they call you Chepi Redleaf? I mean it's two names."

"It's Algonquin and Menominee. My real mother died when I was born."

"I'm so sorry."

"It's all right. I don't remember anything of her or my father. He was a trader, always traveling so he left me with the Menominee. I grew up with them. It was the best thing but my father wanted me to keep the name Chepi. Redleaf is from my Menominee mother. I am usually called Chepi." They rejoined the group with the elder and Anders.

They were all eating fish and talking. Anders was talking. "Oh, yes, my Illie, makes the best wild rice dishes with cranberries and mushrooms for meat, deer, duck, fish, anything. I wish I had some to give you now."

This made the Indian elder laugh. "You should come to our land and bring this food."

"All right, we will visit." Anders replied. "We live in Sugar Bush, just a few miles north of Peshtigo."

The elder gave Anders and Matthew tree branches for use as fishing poles. They fished with strings of yarn from Illyanne's sewing box. They gave their yield to the Indians when the day's light began to shift.

"We have to get going now. We need to see if we can get some horses."

The elder told Anders what road to take. "You have a good chance to ride with someone passing by."

They began walking away from the Indians.

Matthew whispered to Chepi, "Walk with us." He motioned for her to come along.

She rushed out in front of her uncle, "I'll be right back."

Anders grabbed him by the arm to hurry him along and climb back up the slope. Chepi followed Matthew. Her uncle stood watching them go. When Anders looked back, the uncle seemed to be frowning but turned away and muttered to the other Indians.

Matthew tripped several times among the brush and slid backward. He fell forward on his hands but found his footing again. He tripped again on purpose and pulled Chepi down with him. For a precious moment, he had his arms around her and pulled her close. He kissed her while they were low and hidden behind a bush. "I think you're beautiful Chepi Redleaf and I want to see you again." He stroked her dark hair.

"We have to go. If my uncle sees – ." She scrambled back up and started brushing dirt off her buckskin tunic. She looked up the slope and saw Anders standing, looking down at the two of them.

Anders called down, "Come on, Matthew."

When Anders turned to climb again, Chepi patted his back. "Come to the reservation at harvest time with your family. Bring something your mother cooks." She stepped back where she knew her uncle could see her and waved at Matthew and Anders.

Matthew blew her a kiss, hoping she would understand the gesture.

Chepi giggled, kept waving and then turned back to walk down the incline toward her uncle and the others.

At the top of the embankment, Matthew said, "Papa, that Chepi has bowled me over." He arched his back and raised his arms overhead and clapped.

"Oh, nonsense. It's calf love."

"No, it ain't. She invited us to the Menominee lands at the harvest. I already can't wait."

"Well then," Anders said, with a slow smile and a slap around Matthew's shoulder. "Sounds serious."

They retrieved their bags and began walking west. Matthew chattered on about how nice it would be to visit the reservation, see Chepi again. He hoped Mother could cook something special to take out there. "Gee, Pa, I really think that would do the trick. They might accept me as a suitor."

"Let's see how it goes. You're going to meet other pretty girls."

"Oh, no, Papa. This is going to be the one."

"All right son, let's step it up."

9

O*ctober 7-8 1871*
        Sturgeon Bay and
Brussels, Wisconsin

ANDERS AND MATTHEW began walking west toward Champion. Their footsteps crunched and slid on the pebbly dirt road in the warm afternoon sun. Two men on horses ambled by and raised their hats in a passing greeting. Soon, a farmer driving a wagon piled high with hay came along and asked, "Where are you heading?"

Anders looked up, squinting, "Near Champion, to visit an old friend."

The man had slowed his horse but the wagon kept rolling along. "It is too far to get there today, Mister. I go to Champion tomorrow. I trade goods with them." He spoke with a European accent and seemed very good natured. "Today, I come from city market in Sturgeon Bay. Come to my home tonight. Meet my family. Have a good meal and a rest. You ride with me tomorrow."

The man, named Jakoh, said he drove to the chapel there, used as a trading post for his wife's pies and cheese. Anders and Matthew hopped into the back of the wagon. They chatted with Jakoh as the wagon paraded along beautiful pastoral fields, quaint little farm houses, trees and livestock.

"Orchards," Jakoh said, pointing from his driver's seat. "Ya, apple and cherry trees." In a few hours, he pulled the wagon up to a barn and jumped down. At the back of the wagon, he pounded the sides of the flatbed. "Welcome to Brussels." He threw out his arms wide and chuckled watched them rousing from their slumber.

"Isn't that a city somewhere in France or something?" Matthew asked.

"Quite right. Ha, your boy is smart. Belgium. We are from Belgium." Jakoh pointed his thumb to his chest. "Most families live here, from Belgium. Wallonia. Dat's southern part. The better part." He flashed a big smile. "In the north, dey are Dutch, Flemish." He frowned and shook his head from side to side. "Come in. Come in. Willkomen. Bienvenue. Meet my wife and boys."

They could see Jakoh's whole frame now. He was of medium height and muscular but a little stocky.

His wife, Lina, came scurrying out in a pinafore to greet them. She was a petite, energetic, light brown-haired woman, with two boys, seven and nine in tow.

They stepped into a cozy living room of log and mortar walls. A large blackened hearth took up one side of the room. A bench and two wooden sitting chairs rimmed the fireplace. The family had placed an assortment of animal pelts and woolen blankets over them.

Jakoh steered everyone toward the dining room. The family and guests sat around a large circular dark wood table. A good fire was going in the smaller hearth there.

When Stefan, the older boy of nine, returned, he said grace for the family. Serving dishes of bread and cheese were in the center of the table.

Jakoh informed his visitors, "Stefan is to start learning how to work da farm." He patted his son on the shoulder. "He has chores but he's going traveling with me, planting, buying supplies. Learning the business." He pointed across the table to his younger son. "Todor just had birthday. He's seven." Jakoh surveyed the table and called to his wife. "Lina, where's our beer?"

"Coming." Soon, she set down large glasses of beer in front of each of them. "Oh, Mr. Anders, is it all right? For your boy?"

"Papa, please."

"How about half a glass." Anders looked up at Lina, smiling. "He's fifteen and ought to try it but I think half would be fine for tonight."

Matthew did not complain too much about getting only a half glass for his first beer. Lina returned with an empty glass and poured off half of a beer into it.

"Jakoh, you must have more beer for them tonight," Lina said.

"You see what good fortune I have, my friends?" He raised his hands in cheerful celebration. "Can you imagine a better life, loving wife, who has your sons, cooks delicious meals and tells me I must drink more beer for supper? Hah!"

Anders and Jakoh laughed together.

Lina spouted something to him in French in a disagreeable tone. She went out to the kitchen area and brought a tray of bowls. She set a bowl in front of each person. Bowls of thick brown mush with meat bits and corn, peas and carrots. It smelled good but to Anders and Matthew it looked repulsive, something like pig slop.

Anders and Matthew reached for the bread and cheeses. Everyone began eating in earnest. Slurping sounds abounded. When Matthew tasted the first spoonful, surprised, he asked, "What is this called? It's very good. My mother is a good cook and I'm sure she would like to have the recipe."

"This is Booyah," Lina replied. "Belgian food, a common stew. It's chicken, sometimes beef and pork. Many vegetables. Onion, carrots, potatoes. I can write it for you. Oh, and lemon, too, in the pot. Cooks all the day."

That led into questions about where Matthew's mother was.

"She's sailing on a ship?" Jakoh grunted, making his shock and disapproval clear. "I wouldn't go. After what we went through, I wouldn't go. My wife not go sailing either."

"What happened?" Anders asked.

"We sailed to America on Atlantic Ocean. Eleven years past. Terrible. Very rough seas. Crowded." He waved his hands around as if to slap down the bad memory. "Dey were sick much of the time. Da food was bad, quarters too small. Cold, storms."

Anders cut in, "She's sailing the Great Lakes. It's what I usually do but – ." He lifted up his wrapped splinted arm. "It's not as bad as the ocean, though they can have bad storms."

"Ya, you see what I say?" Jakoh said in a raspy irritated voice.

"Schooners are different. They're small and fast," explained Anders. "They're cargo ships but a passenger could be on the deck most of the time. Only a five or six-man crew. A much nicer kind of sailing."

"I wouldn't go out on a ship. Never again." Jakoh grumbled. "I had enough. For whole life."

Lina broke in. "I think I like this wife of yours," Lina said. She looked at Jakoh. "It might be a good idea for me to go cook for sailors and travel. One time, eh? I think this would be good, Jakoh."

"No, Lina, no."

"Well, I wish I had the chance to take you out, Jakoh to sail on the bay on a summer's day," Anders said. "I think you would be surprised what a joy it is to floating along out there."

Jakoh only returned an adamant cold stare. "I don't think so."

Anders guided further discussion away from sailing. Laughter and goodwill abounded with the good food, talk of family, farming and cooking. After the meal, Lina sent the boys off to bed. Jakoh and Anders finished their beers and retired to the front sitting room. Matthew tagged along. The sun had set and the fireplace now glowed with orangey warmth.

"Well son, we certainly are having a pleasant adventure, aren't we? Tonight, we've made a new friend and tried Belgian beer and Booyah for the first time."

"You must have more." Jakoh turned his head to shout, "Lina, please bring da chocolates."

"I'm stuffed, please, nothing more tonight," Anders said holding up an open palm.

"You must. Dis brings Belgium to America. Like you are flying in da clouds and over da ocean to our old home with one bite. You must try one. Just one."

Anders and Matthew ate the chocolate. Jakoh made pleasurable humming sounds and they all laughed and ate.

"So, what is the yellow flag with the red rooster?" Matthew asked. "I saw three of them as we were riding through town."

"This is Walloon flag. We are from Wallonia. Yah."

Jakoh stoked the fire and added some smaller wood chunks. He slouched in his chair and stared into the flame. Anders and Jakoh drank their beer. Jakoh turned to Matthew. "So, what are you going to do when you are all grown?"

"I was interested in sailing like Papa."

"Oof. Again, this nonsense."

Anders quickly added, "I'm with you on that, Jakoh. I want him to learn the farming business. He can practically run the homestead now, do all the chores, plant. I've told him we can discuss it in a few years."

Matthew went on. "I was interested in sailing . . . but now I am thinking my future is Chepi."

"Chepi?" Jakoh looked confused. He tossed his head back and yelled, "Lina, what is Chepi?"

Lina had gone upstairs and was helping the boys get ready for bed. She did not answer and did not come down.

Matthew had trouble stopping his chuckling. "Chepi isn't a thing. It's a girl, an Indian girl. Chepi Redleaf."

Jakoh sat up in earnest and leaned in toward Anders. "Ohhh, Anders I must talk to you about dis." He lowered his voice to speak to him in confidence. "It is very bad to mix people like this. We Belgians have problems with our own, Walloon and Flemish fighting and angry, different languages. All the time. If anyone marries the other kind. Big problems. Many years." He threw up his hands and shook his head with his eyes closed. "Even in America. We got train to Milwaukee and they said no more. You walk. We walked and camped. At Sheboygan, dey were Belgians but give us no work. Flemish. Dey said, Green Bay is for you and we walked here."

"You walked here?" Anders and Matthew spoke in unison.

"Men, women and children. Over months. We walk and camp. It's like your war between states. Understand?"

"Not exactly but a little." Anders said. "But we get along fine with the Indians around here. Illyanne is half Menominee and Matthew is one fourth. There's good relations."

"Yes, I know dese things. The Indians here saved us. Helped us ice fish, hunt, preserve meat, tan hides, how to tap trees for sap and make syrup. We are good friends with dem." Jakoh wagged a finger. "Friends but no marry."

"Don't worry, Matthew is fifteen and I've told him, there will be other young ladies to meet."

"No, Papa."

They all laughed at their disagreements and Jakoh signaled, "Time for bed. We get up early before the sun. "Tomorrow you will have Belgian coffee." Anders and Matthew held their sides and groaned and laughed.

October 8, 1871
Sunday morning

Jakoh was up early, rousting Anders and Matthew. He jostled Anders' arm. "You come now. Lina made breakfast. You take Belgian coffee with me. We have some bread and cheese and we go then."

The first hint of morning light had broken as they dressed and came to the kitchen table, shuffling and squinting. The ear-splitting rooster's crowing came in from outside near the barn. It was cold but Jakoh started the kindling and soon the growing fire spread warmth. The coffee was rich and stimulating, the slices of Belgian pie pastry, substantial.

While they were still inside finishing their coffee, Lina and Jakoh loaded up Belgian pies, large flat pastries with fruit and topped with baked sweet cream cheese. Lina and the several other Belgian wives spent all day, one day a week baking dozens of pies in a communal oven built on to the back of a home. They set pies on shelved crates. Small blocks of cheese filled two baskets. Lina came back to the dining area, sat down next to Anders and wrote down the Booyah recipe for Illyanne before leaving.

Anders and Matthew rode along without saying anything for a while. Then, Anders commented, "These people are really something. And, son I know, never in your life, are you ever going to forget that brown, muddy stew, Booyah, are you?"

Travel along the bay coastline included stretches of tree and brush, clumps and patches of long grasses that revealed a frequent view out into the bay of Green Bay. The intensity of the blue water and sky rendered them silent observers for a long while. This was its own little earthly Paradise. Anders imagined how pleasant and peaceful it would be to float up and into the sky. A few sailing ships slipped by in the distance.

In the first few hours, they wrapped themselves in blankets in the crisp Autumn air. By mid-morning they shed them, having turned inland. There, the landscape grew dense with trees and it became more shaded and cooler. Anders and Matthew again pulled on their blankets back on. By midday sun soon made it too warm again.

Jakoh turned his head sideways to speak to his passengers and keep his eyes on the road. "We'll be coming up to the chapel soon on the edge of Champion. That's where you get off."

Anders and Matthew sat up from their lounging positions in the back of the wagon. Inside the flatbed, they moved closer to the bench seat to converse with Jakoh.

"Hello there, sleepy heads," Jakoh said, talking with his head turned to the side.

"Thanks for everything, Jakoh. You have been a great host, feeding us, giving us lodging and a ride today, not mention introducing us to Booyah, Belgian beer, coffee and chocolates."

Jakoh only nodded with a hand up and smiled.

Anders and Matthew hopped down from the wagon and spoke to Jakoh. "If you ever get up near Peshtigo, come visit. Ask around. People know our homestead."

"Now, before you two set off, let me tell you about Champion and the chapel. You heard about Sister Adele who saw the Virgin Mary here some years ago." He counted on his fingers. "Ten, no it was twelve years ago."

"Our priest has told us a little." Anders stood with his carry bag over his shoulder and shifted his weight back and forth from one foot to the other, squinting up at Jakoh. Matthew held his valise in his arms and planted his feet wide apart in a firm stance.

Jakoh noticed and said, "Fine. I tell you shorter story." Still seated on the wagon bench, he twisted to face his guests, who set their bags on the ground and listened. He related that the young Belgian woman, got surprised seeing a beautiful lady standing between two trees years ago. "The lady said she was Queen of Heaven." Jakoh raised an index finger and raised his eyebrows. "She told Adele she didn't want her Son to punish people. If dey pray, do penance and convert hearts, they could stop it. The lady told her to teach the children. Ever since that day, Sister Adele got the chapel built and teaches da faith to children. It was a sign, what she saw. Champion is first place Belgians lived here. Everybody respects her, what she's done. If you see her, giver her our greetings."

"We're just going to visit my friend," Anders said. "Just two nights on his farm and then we head back home."

"Just in case, Mary chapel is that way. Your friend's farm, I think, is that way." Jakoh tipped his hat, shook the reins and started driving the wagon away.

10

O ctober 8, 1871
Near Champion, Wisconsin
Midday

ANDERS AND MATTHEW hiked the road, a worn, wagon-wheel path over tallgrass. Anders breathed deeply and let out a great sigh of pleasure. The vast fields of grain and blue-green distant clumps of trees here stood out as decidedly different that the shady woodlands back home around Sugar Bush. There was something invigorating about all, the wide-open space and bright sunshine. Yet, the sight of neighbors' homes and barns was comforting too. The pastures with farms held a countryside ease.

"Good thing, we traveled light," Matthew said, wiping his brow as they trudged along the trail toward Karl's place. They had walked past a wood post which held up a flat board with burned-in lettering: Karl Scholz Farm. Anders felt a rush of goodwill but also laughed inside himself at Karl's ego. He was soon to see a sailor friend and he would be able to show off Matthew. It was clear that Karl had established himself well and they would have that in common. He would tell Karl how the years of slugging work on the homestead had finally paid off and he, Illie and Matthew were living well.

"Sure is warm out here, a lot warmer than I would have expected for this time of year, that's for sure." Anders took off his hat, swatted it against his thigh and replaced it. "Can't be too much farther now."

He looked at the sky. "It's getting late enough in the day that Karl might well be back at the house after doing his chores."

They walked for a spell longer and heard something. Karl's old imitation seagull call. He looked ahead, squinting. He saw a blurry figure cupping his hands to holler down the roadway.

"Is that you, Anders, you old sea dog?"

Anders recognized the voice. Good. Karl was keeping an eye out for him. Anders had wrangled a favor from a shipping clerk at the dock and sent a short telegram to Karl's business office in Green Bay. He told Karl he expected to arrive yesterday but then Anders and Matthew had miscalculated their timing. Anders could barely see Karl in the distance but a figure was positioned outside a large log cabin just coming into view. He recognized his stance. Karl had thrown his arms open wide and was smiling broadly.

Anders yelled back, "Is there some kind of landlubber swabbie out there talking to me?" Picking up his pace, he could soon make out his friend's features. He started running toward his old shipmate.

Matthew hung back on the path observing the two of them.

Anders and Karl came together in a crash hug, laughing and spinning 'round and slapping each other on the back. By the time, they disengaged, Matthew had come up, dropped his shoulder bag and stood watching them.

"Hey, this is my boy, Matthew."

Karl shook Matthew's hand. "Mighty fine to meet you, son. Anders, you have done well. This one's almost grown." He grabbed around Matthew's upper arm, then slapped him on the back. "And fit for sailing, too."

"More than likely, farming, Karl, not sailing."

"Papa!" He turned toward Karl. "I want to be a sailor but it'll be after I learn everything about farming the homestead."

Anders ruffled Matthew's hair with affection.

"Well, c'mon in. I'm awfully glad to see you made it."

They stepped inside. Anders and Matthew stared up and down at the lavish interior. The house was a large but simple log home. On the inside there was knotty pine wood on the ceilings and the thick log walls he had painted white. Cow hide rugs covered the floors. A stone-faced fireplace must have measured ten feet high. A set of sitting furniture formed a half circle around the fireplace.

Karl's furniture awed Anders and Matthew. They both ran their hands over the arms and back of what Karl said was a "Chesterfield sofa," It had a tufted back with buttons. Its wine-red color shouted money and refinement. "I got lucky in a card game one night," Karl said. "Got it and these sitting chairs in payment of a debt of fifty dollars."

"Oh, Karl." Anders grimaced and shot his friend a secretive no-no head shake for talking about gambling in front of Matthew.

"Shipped it to Green Bay and brought it the last fifteen miles by wagon out here. Have a seat."

Anders eyed the surroundings, leather chairs, the small table against one wall with scrolled carved designs all over it. "Looks like you have done quite well for yourself."

"Yeah, I've done all right. Would you two like a drink?" Karl lifted his head and called out. "Jiao-Long!"

A Chinese man servant came in wearing black pants and vest with a high-buttoned white shirt.

"Would sarsaparilla suit you?" Karl asked.

"Yes, fine."

Karl nodded at Jiao-Long. "Sarsaparilla. And, bring me some whiskey, too."

"Aw, I don't drink much anymore, Karl."

"You didn't used to be such a snore. We'll just have one for old time's sake."

Jiao-Long waited for Karl's nod, then walked out to a kitchen in the back of the house, Anders guessed. He and Matthew looked at each other with raised eyebrows.

The sarsaparilla quenched their thirst and Anders and Karl started reminiscing. There was that raucous a time in a tavern in Buffalo and another in Cleveland. They reminisced about their sailing days together and traveling life. Together, they had encountered many an interesting character among fellow sailors and shore acquaintances. There was a sailor who used to sketch wonderful seaside scenes but neither of them could recall his name.

"And there's also the great mystery sea stories," Karl said. "I always liked the one about the sunken Confederate gold ship."

"Stolen Union gold, you mean," said Anders. He looked at Matthew.

"Yeah, they say it was intended as pay for pay Union soldiers," said Karl. "Well, there's different stories about where she came from but she sank somewhere on the eastern shoreline of Lake Michigan, with the gold. If anyone could get good information on where to look, it'd be you. A fella told me all about these special suits that a man could wear to dive deep and stay down for an hour. Haw, wouldn't that be something if we had those and discovered the gold?"

"That's just a story," Anders said.

"Today it may be a story but with money put into experimenting, there will be such things sometime."

"And one day, men will fly, too," Anders said. Karl bent both arms at the elbows, his thumbs at his arm pits and flapped like a chicken. They both laughed.

The old friends sang sea shanties. Matthew chimed in at a few places where he knew the words to *Blow the Man Down* and *Haul Away Joe*. Anders and Karl chuckled as they recalled more old times.

"Oh, we had good runs. Especially on shore."

"I don't think we need to go into too much detail on old times," Anders said, shifting a quick eye glance toward Matthew.

Anders and Karl each took a shot of whiskey. Anders had to admit it relaxed him after the day's traveling. After a second round, Anders slouched on Karl's sofa.

"Come on, Matt, why don't you have one with me and your Pa?"

Anders held up and open palm. "No, Karl. He's just fifteen."

Karl was on his way to being pickled from the whiskey and was already slurring his words. "Aw, come on. Aren't you gonna teach the boy 'bout the world, women, drink and song?" He swung one arm side to side in midair.

"Karl!" Anders stared him down and shook his head no.

"Before he settles into old manhood?"

"No, Karl. No. Let him alone."

For a moment, Anders and Karl eyes locked onto each other's.

"That's all right, Papa." Matthew started to get up from the Victorian arm chair where he'd been sitting. "I'd like to take a rest anyhow." He picked up his shoulder bag. Can you show me where we'll be sleeping?"

Karl motioned, "down that hallway, door on the left."

Anders called after Matthew. "We'll see you for dinner in a couple of hours."

When they heard Matthew close the door, Anders and Karl both burst out sniggering.

"You didn't used to be such a shameless rake, Karl."

Karl put his feet up on a footstool and said, "But I've always been a rogue at heart. Just not so obvious."

"So, I guess you are a rich rogue, now eh, Karl?"

"Well, I'm on my way, old shipmate." Karl laughed at himself. "I'm in business now. The biggest thing out there now is land. I heard that over and over from all the high rollers playing cards in Chicago and Milwaukee." He pulled his feet back down and straightened up in his sitting chair to pour another drink. "I just missed the getting into railroads. Steamships are going to be the gold mine but right now it's land." He threw back a shot and eyed Anders for another but he declined. "Only a few years ago, I took my sailor savings and started with twenty acres right here. Once you learn about balance sheets and investing and meeting the right people, Anders, I tell you, the sky is the limit."

"You have certainly done well. I see you even have a servant."

"Oh, Jiao-Long? He's on loan. He'll be going back to Chicago soon."

"Another card game?"

"Something like that. Business. I wanted to try him out. He's great but I think I like doing things for myself. I might consider getting a woman housekeeper though."

"You really are a bottom feeding scoundrel. Only now you have a big house and wear respectable clothes."

Karl let out a howl of laughter. "You see, Anders. It's just like back in our old days. It's awfully good to see you. And a fine-looking boy you've got there."

Settled into comfortable sitting chairs inside, Anders commented, "I wish you could meet Illyanne and see our homestead. If you ever get across the bay that way, you must stop in. We have a nice house, simple but nice, a barn, ten acres. We trade a little and I still sail. Mostly short lumber runs. Looks like you're settled in nicely, except for a wife and family, community and church."

"I've never been much of a church goer and I have even less time now, although there is a chapel near here, down the road a ways."

"But you have the voice for hymn singing," Anders said. "Remember? You were always the loudest singer of any sea shanty cantor. Star of the Sea, Our Sailor's Prayer and such."

"Mostly, going along with the crowd, I guess. Fellowship on my way to something better."

"Naw. You enjoyed it back then." Anders eyed him for a moment. "You've changed."

"Well, I aim to become a self-made man. And, I'm not finished climbing. I try to follow the example of Mr. William Ogden. He is in railroads and lumber. He owns the Woodenware factory up in Peshtigo, you know. I've actually been to his home in Chicago for a dinner party. Friend of a friend. Wow. It had tall pillars in the front. They call Greek Revival style. First mayor of Chicago, you know. Just for one year but he was prominent, a real business pioneer, a true builder.

Anders cast him a perplexed look. "What about the simpler things in life? Wife and family?"

Karl only responded with a negative facial expression and threw back another shot of whiskey. "Not for me. I got my sights set on bigger fish, at least for now. Oh, and I've got an iron in the fire about a paper mill up your way. Some investors are pooling together. Down the Fox River near Lake Winnebago. I'll send you more on that after a meeting next week."

Anders had to wake Matthew for supper. The three of them enjoyed a hearty dinner of roasted duck, corn, carrots, potato and cherry-apple pie for dessert. Karl wanted to take them outside and show them around the property before the sun set. Matthew begged off saying he had found a good book to read in the guest room about the Lewis & Clark expedition. "You two go talk about old times together but I'm enjoying this book."

"It's nice to meet your boy. But if it was just you and me, I'd take you to Green Bay and show you some fun places. Good food, women and song."

"I'm not much into that sort of thing any more, Karl. Haven't been for some time. I haven't seen you in more'n five years. I think Matthew was nine or ten when you had your sendoff. Illie and I and Matthew have been living a quiet life. It's busy running the farm and

I still sail." A wave of self-reproach moved through him about the old days spending in saloons drinking and carrying on in sailor mischief, but he had matured now. "This old sailor is plenty settled into family life. I'm gonna be thirty-six soon."

"I get it. I'll be coming up on thirty-two myself. Too much of the drink doesn't mix with business."

Before Karl and Anders turned in for the night, they took a stroll outside and Karl pointed out his land holdings, his prairie view. The sun had lowered and the evening buttery light washed over the gentle fields and woods. "Past that clump of trees over there is my neighbor's land."

"It's all very nice, Karl. You've done all right for yourself."

"Thanks mate." He slapped Anders on the back and flashed a big smile. "Come by in ten years' time. O' course by then, I might be living in a big house closer to Green Bay to be closer to my business interests." He laughed and suggested they head in to sleep off the big dinner and drinks.

11

October 7, 1871
        Sunday night
Karl's farm and
the Chapel in Champion, Wisconsin

BY THE TIME ANDERS tip-toed into the guest room, Matthew had already become one with the pillow. A small candle on a dresser dimly lit the room. Anders could see Karl had dressed the beds in coverlets of deep brown with a gold leafy pattern and matching pillows. He discovered that the corners of the pillows had little tassels attached to them. He snorted a laugh and muttered, "A far cry, Karl, old mate, from the hammocks and racks under the bow of a schooner."

Late in the night, the fast pounding of a horse's hooves interrupted their slumber. Outside the house, a man's voice yelled "Karl! Fire. Come quick!"

Anders went to the window. He saw Karl, who'd run outside in the dark, barefoot, confused and fumbling, his pants sagging, suspenders hanging down to his sides. Anders and Matthew heard a muffled exchange of excited words outside and the faint moonlit outlines of Karl standing next to a man on a horse. In the next moment, the sound of the galloping hooves faded off into the distance. Karl came back inside the house shouting and pounding and bursting through the guest room door. "Anders, Matthew. Get up, get up. Now."

"We're awake. What's going on?"

In a harried Karl told them, "Get dressed. There's a fire at my neighbor's farm. We have to go help. I'm bringing the wagon around to the front."

Karl yanked up all of his cowhide rugs off the floor and ran out to the barn.

The scent of burned material hit them as soon as they got outside. Sitting in the rattling wagon with the horse racing along fully woke up all three of them. When they got to Gustaf's farm, about a half mile down the road, the fire was roaring and crackling and moving quickly over the fields. It sent a wall of hot air toward them. The fire lit up the night. The wind blew the flames and smoke toward them and it made them hack and cough.

Karl hollered at his neighbor, "Gustaf, I'm here with two men. Where do you want us?"

Through the low roar of the fire, he hollered back with an arm pointing, "Beat back the line coming from the west field."

Anders, Karl and Matthew dragged the rugs off the back of Karl's wagon. "Use them to beat out the flames," Karl said. "Like this." He demonstrated how to grab the rugs with both hands and slap it down over the flames. All three of them ran to the line of the approaching fire as it fed on crops with a low growl. Anders splinted arm was too weak to be the main force in swatting flames with the rug. He had to force himself to power his left hand as dominant to fight the fire.

Gustaf went toward the barn. After a while, he did not respond to Karl's calls for him to return. The flames made the men sweat and it sucked up much of the breathable air. The fire spiked in spots to three and four feet high in the tall prairie grasses. Whacking the flames as they moved over some grassy crop, probably wheat, took a physical toll. In a few minutes, they stamped out a fifty-foot wide swath but the smoke kept blowing at them, stinging their eyes. Lateral parts of the fire kept burning and encroaching on them.

When Anders looked back for a moment, he realized the flames had jumped over the cleared spots and continued coming toward him. Soon, it was advancing in an arc around the three of them. Anders and Karl backtracked out of the fire perimeter. He tried to tell Matthew to get back but he could not be heard over the rumble of the fire.

The smoke rose and clouded everything. This was a landlubber kind of dread that neither Anders or Karl had ever known. Even in the worst gales at sea, men could always try to swim to save themselves. They had to squint. They were coughing and the hot fire was sucking the moisture from their bodies.

Anders had walked back to the place where he had just left Matthew but he was gone. Matthew kept working at beating back the fire and it had surrounded him.

Anders walked into another creeping wall of flames and walloped it. This time the fire burned the soles of his feet. Flying sparks singed his hair and he felt the searing heat jump at him. He backed away. "Matthew. Matthew, run to the sound of my voice. Matthew. . . Matthew. Run to me." He was out of breath for a minute, coughing. "Matthew." Anders turned to look at Karl and Gustaf with the expression of a desperate man.

Gustaf stood twenty feet further back. "We have to go. We can't stop it. I'll follow after I let the animals out of the barn."

Defeat and disbelief made Anders go limp and stand still in a stupor. He bent forward with his hands on his knees, breathing hard. Matthew was in there somewhere, lost to certain death. How could Anders leave when he knew his son was in there among the flames?

Karl hollered at Anders again. "C'mon. We have to go now. Maybe Gustaf will find him. They'll be right along behind us."

Anders tried again. "Matthew." He waited.

Karl had wrapped a shirt around the horse's eyes. It whinnied and stepped around nervously. "We have to go," he said again.

Anders felt like a man disintegrating. He took a step toward the fire, to go in and find Matthew but he knew it would kill him. His knees went wobbly and he almost crumbled down to sit on the ground in grief.

"Now Anders. Let's go."

Anders hung his head and looked into the flames in anguish.

In another few seconds, Matthew leaped through the flames and right into his father, knocking him down. With tired limbs they embraced each other, laughing and crying and trying to get full breaths of air.

Karl hollered over the bellowing of the fire. "No time for that. Let's go."

They climbed back up, silent, bracing against each other, still panting. Between gasps for full lungs of air, they smiled at each other and laughed at themselves, in relief and for the joy of it as they bounced around in the back of the wagon.

"That was a close one, Matthew."

"Yeah. But I knew if I didn't make it, Mother would've killed me."

That set them on another round of nearly painful laughing, lying flat with their arms stretched out to open up their lungs to as much air and they could get.

In a minute, Anders was able to sit up and ask, "Did you get burned?"

Matthew shook his head, no.

"What happened to you?"

"I don't know. I guess I got confused. It's like the fire it grew around me while I was beating it back with the rug. Then, in a second, I couldn't tell which way I had come in. I thought I heard you but I got spun around and I just leaped with hope it was the right way."

"An incredibly lucky guess, Matthew. The fire could have taken you."

"And you too, Papa. I swear my heart almost quit on me even after getting out safe." He placed a palm on his chest. "I'm glad we both made it." He reached for his father and they clutched each other's hands for a few seconds as the flush of the excitement receded into exhaustion.

Anders smiled with the orange red sky raging and the blackest of nights in the periphery.

They rode back to Karl's s farm. His cow, goats and chickens were loose and heading away from the fire. Anders, Matthew and Karl roped up the cow, tossed some of the goats the flatbed bleating like crazy. The other goats sidled up to the wagon moving alongside the cow. Anders and Matthew helped to calm the animals and keep them inside the perimeter of the wagon.

"Where are we going?" Anders yelled from the back.

"There's only one place," Karl said.

"Where's that?"

"The Chapel," Karl yelled over the thundering fire.

"That's in the path of the fire, isn't it?"

"Yes, but it's the only shelter there is."

"What about the bay, Karl? We can get in the lake and sit it out there?"

"That's five miles away. I'm not willing to gamble we can outrun this fire. Besides, we might well freeze to death in the water. So, the Chapel is the best chance for safe haven. And do your praying my friend. Pray."

The wagon rumbled and clattered along with Anders and Matthew trying to hang to the buckboard's sides. The horse ran like a racer but the cow could not keep up and the ride was jerky, moving forward fast and then slowing for the mooing cow to catch up.

Soon, Anders and Matthew and Karl saw other settlers running toward the Chapel. When they arrived at the gate, they encountered a family running in with two cows and carrying chickens. They let the animals loose inside the chapel fence. The fire rumbled in the distance.

They ran inside the sanctuary with the other family, nearly tripping as they bumped into them. They panted, out of breath. Inside it was surprisingly quiet yet packed with people. Everyone was exhausted, bleary-eyed, having been rousted from their beds by a fiery night terror and run to what they hoped was safety. A nun in black dress and wimple veil stood up from a chair in the back of the chapel and greeted the family first. They spoke briefly and then took seats in the chapel pews.

Anders, Karl and Matthew were all gasping, two of them holding their sides from the run.

Karl told the nun, "We just ran for our lives. We tried to stamp out the fire at my neighbor's farm. It turned into an ugly monster." He realized the people in front pews were reciting something together in soft tones so he lowered his voice. "Barely got my animals out. Rode like mad in the wagon to get here. Almost went off the road. And my friend is coming behind us." They people in pews up front looked like farmers with families. Several nuns also knelt there with farm families.

The nun remained serene in the face of the obvious disaster going on outside. "Yes, others have seen the same things. You are all welcome to stay and pray with us. We hope the Virgin Mary will intercede for us and keep us safe. Many healings have happened here. We believe she will protect us." She paused for a momentous, few seconds. "If not, when we are found later, we will be seen to have demonstrated our faith."

Anders gulped at her words. A curdling chill pulsed through him.

An eerie stillness had settled into that place. The air was warm and stagnant but the lit candles emitted a calming glow. People were coated in beads of perspiration. A desperate feeling radiated off of them. They all might soon die by fire. Yet, in a moment, Anders could feel the hopefulness of their hearts. It reminded him of walking into a low spot back at the homestead and into patch of fog, feeling the cool moisture envelope him.

Karl blurted out in response to the nun's words, "What if I don't believe as you do?"

"Then, you should pray, 'help my unbelief.' And if you cannot do that, we will pray for you."

Anders found it oddly funny in this solemn setting that Karl offered no retort.

Inside the chapel, people crammed together in the pews. Big lighted candles on crude wood-carved holders stood four feet tall on either side of the altar. One of the sisters came in and knelt in one of the front church pews. She was unhurried in her movements, a profile of bravery and faith. Anders felt amazed at sensing a joining of his spirit with the others. There was a steady muffled moan of the approaching fire outside but serenity prevailed inside.

Anders knelt and bowed his head, praying along with the group up front.

When they finished the rosary, several minutes of an unnatural quiet passed. A nun with a disfigured eye came into the chapel from a side door and whispered to another smaller nun. They had a book between them and flipped pages back and forth as they spoke. The smaller nun, calling herself Sister Angela announced the pages of hymns they would be singing. The group began singing, following along with books placed in the pews.

The voices of ordinary men, women and children with the nuns took on a transcendent quality, rising to the crude brown rafters. Anders never felt that core emotion in church before. Good voices were mixed with bad and mediocre ones, which on any other day would have challenged him to stifle his laughter. Here and now, it created a beautiful quilt of sound, a togetherness and ease.

Anders realized all those people with him might very well die in the fire, perhaps even within the hour. It was coming fast and there was nowhere to go to get ahead of it. The melodic singing helped him put that worry aside in a way he could not explain. He began to sing too and felt swept up in the prayer. It was a mystical, soulful prayer of a group in unison. Dear God, if you take me, please spare Matthew. Let my son live. If you cannot do that, please help Illyanne. She will be so crushed without either of us.

When the hymns ended the stark silence returned. The crackles with the low steady taunt of the fire outside now grew louder. The nun with the damaged eye that the Menominee elder and Jakoh had described, stepped in front of the altar facing the pews. Of course, that must be Sister Adele, the one who'd seen the apparition.

Sister Adele began speaking to the people in French. Sister Angela translated explaining that while Sister Adele knows some English but her pronunciation was not very good. "She says that the Virgin Mother told her this would keep her from talking too much."

The people managed a round of polite laughter.

Sister Angela continued the translation about every other sentence. "I am not supposed to preach but our situation is urgent. Many of you are not of our faith but we always welcome you." Sister Adele opened her arms and smiled. "Often times, our devotions to the Blessed Mother are misunderstood. I wish to explain now because – ." She swallowed and looked down for a moment. "It's important."

From inside, something hit Anders hard in the chest. She feels afraid too, yet she's here organizing people and pressing on in the face of the fire.

She continued, "We pray to our Lord *with and through* Mary. Like at the wedding in Cana, the Lord often grants for his mother the petitions she brings to him from the people who have petitioned her. She intercedes for us with her Son, like the mother of King Solomon. He refused nothing to his Judaic queen mother." She nodded calmly and began to step away.

Sister Angela, still translating, announced, "We will carry a statue of the Blessed Mother, which we do today as we do every year on the anniversary of her appearance here. Please keep in mind that we do not worship Mary or the statue. It only helps us picture her and focus our prayer. We will walk side by side in twos outside around the rim of the fence of the chapel grounds to sing and pray, remembering her apparition here and asking for her intercession with Jesus to spare us. I need four men to shoulder the poles of her platform."

Volunteers stood up and walked toward her. They spoke privately with Sister Adele.

Anders was sweating and now he gulped. Death was pacing and prowling like a hungry lion nearby. His insides cringed. His choices were now to die in the fire or march in prayer, and maybe still be burned to death.

12

C hampion, Wisconsin
The Chapel and grounds

FOUR MEN APPROACHED and took places around the platform like pallbearers. They lifted the poles of the rack onto their shoulders, the statue resting on top of it. Sister Adele stood in front and led the procession out through the center aisle of the chapel. It was a commanding site, the plaster Marian figurine, raised high. It was painted to match the described vision of the apparitions here, robed in white, with a crown of stars around her head of long golden hair, a yellow sash at the waist. The carriers moved gracefully down the aisle.

Anders watched Sister Adele close up as she processed by him. He flinched at her disfigured eye. It looked as if she'd been branded and scarred over her eye. He had heard of farm accidents like that. It must have been devastating. Slowly, others began to follow.

Anders muttered, "Why are they going out there, walking into hellfire?"

One of the carriers passing by overheard it and said, "Though we walk through the valley of the shadow of death we fear no evil."

Karl sputtered back, "That's just a poem."

The carrier called the others to stop for a moment. The man looked at Anders, Matthew and Karl and spoke in a kindly tone. "It's about trusting God. Remember the men who the Babylonian king threw into a fiery furnace for refusing to worship a statue. They sang praises to God and came walking out of it unharmed." The procession resumed.

Anders, Matthew and Karl watched in stifled amazement as the processors walked on. Something in their movements proved contagious. Anders found himself stepping out of the pew. He followed and stood outside watching them. The group walked right out onto the grounds. The orange lines of light crawled toward them, jumping up at points along the fire line. Visible from all sides, perhaps two thousand feet away, now. The fire had trapped them. Its snaking death march would eventually reach the chapel. In hours? Less?

Anders observed the group for a few minutes from chapel entrance. The procession drew him in. Even while feeling a partial aversion, he stepped down to join the group.

"Papa, don't go out there," Matthew said, rushing forward to grab his father's arm.

Anders yanked himself free. "If I am going to die, I'd rather it be quick. If you stay here, you'll watch us die out there first." He turned back face to face with Matthew and placed his hands on his son's shoulders. "You have the best chance by going back inside. Your mother and I love you. You're ready to run the farm." Both of their eyes glassed up. "If I don't make it, take care of your mother." Anders hugged Matthew and joined the procession.

Anders didn't know all the prayers and hymns but he followed along in his head and they walked. Around a five-acre perimeter, with the panting fire advancing, their fear dissipated. They were all together in a sweet trance as they recited all three mysteries of the rosary, focusing on the Annunciation through the Resurrection. He looked back and saw Matthew and his friend standing at the chapel door. The heat increased and Anders' sweat began rolling down his face and body, dampening his clothes. It dried up in the hot air almost as quickly as it came. It was like how Illyanne had described the Menominee sweat lodge and dream visions.

As the flames crept closer, the smell of burned brush wafted in, too. They sang louder to combat the sounds of the blaze. He willfully ignored the outside world beyond the procession. He supposed if the fire came close enough, they would all stop and try to beat it back with the clothes they were wearing. When it came, if it came, they would probably relent and resign themselves to dying. Many joined hands and looked at each other for strength, acknowledging the screaming and horrible pain that was coming, yet it quelled their fear.

Midnight came and went. The fire continued but its advance had slowed. Anders thought the fire would have arrived at the chapel by now. They kept marching, singing and reciting various prayers. Another hour or two passed. Its pace slowed; the walkers had become tired. Conversation fell off. A faint sound from the world broke in and penetrated his ears. The soft noise blended with the fire. It was like putting his ear up to one of those large conch shells that sailing port shops often stocked. 'You can hear the ocean in it' is what the shopkeepers always said. And Anders now heard that same gentle, shushing sound.

"Rain. Hey, it's raining," someone said. Several in the group stepped out from the procession and raised their arms and faces upward. People twirled around with their arms extended outward from their sides and laughed. In the light of the distant fire, Anders found their profiles striking. For a moment, they resembled twirling, dancing human crosses. Anders took it as a sign that heaven had sent the rain. He waved to Matthew and held up his palms and lifted his face in relief.

The procession kept going in the light steady rain. Cows, chickens and goats, grazing on the acreage, moved aside as the people marched by. Anders stopped and sat on the chapel steps twice for a few minutes. The second time, Matthew returned to the parade with him. When Anders rested a third time, and few people remained inside the chapel, Karl too, joined in the outdoor procession. The drizzle continued steadily through the remainder of night. Before dawn, a heavier rain fell but they did not stop the procession.

13

Monday, October 9, 1871
The day after the fire
Green Island, Wisconsin

ILLYANNE CAME TO AN hour later. Someone had wrapped her in double blankets in her wet clothes. A woman was tending to her on a big brass bed covered with a patchwork quilt.

"Hello, Miss. I'm Emma, the woman of the household here." She was bent over Illyanne dabbing at her forehead with a small wet towel. "I'm very glad to see you."

"What happened?" Illyanne's eyes darted around the room. "Where am I"?

"Green Island."

For a moment, she thought the woman said Greenland. A flash of horror and abandonment ripped through her. "Green?"

"Green Island."

"Where is that?"

"It's in the bay of Green Bay, Miss."

"What day is it?" Illyanne asked.

The woman answered, "It's Sunday night," but she glanced over at a wind-up wall clock ticking away. "No, actually, it's after midnight so, it's Monday. Now, if you please, we need to get those wet clothes off you so we can get you into something dry. Are you all right to undress yourself?"

Illyanne nodded yes, sitting up slowly.

"Put this on and come out when you're ready. There are more dry blankets in the closet. All your sailing shipmates are out in front of the fireplace. They are all safe. I've got tea and bread for you all."

"My bag." She wriggled trying to run out of the room. "Where's my bag?"

Emma held her back. "It's in the kitchen. It got soaked too. I've taken everything out and laid it on towels to dry and hung up the blanket and your extra clothes. After everyone goes to sleep, I'll dry your dress and undergarments by the fire. It'll be ready by morning."

When Illyanne had changed clothes, Emma took her arm and led her out into the sitting room. A fire roared in a cozy fireplace in a room with wood-planked walls. The four sailors and the captain all huddled around the fire, wrapped in blankets, drinking hot tea. Almost in unison, they turned to look at her as she came out of the bedroom. She could hardly take in her own surprise at their smiles and words.

"Ah-hah, there she is."

"Good to see you're all right Miss Illyanne."

"Thank God, you came through all right."

"C'mon over here and get warm."

Illyanne made a self-conscious smile and sat down in a spot they cleared for her in a grouping of wooden dining chairs. Emma handed her a cup of tea. She touched her hair, tucking back the loosed strings that had wrestled free from their pins. "I must look a fright."

"You're alive and seeing you is no fright," the captain said.

She could think of no response but to smile and sip her tea.

"I'll help you to comb-out your hair later," Emma whispered to her.

They all sat in quiet. Illyanne kept touching her head and rocked herself gently. "The provisions. Did anyone get them out?"

"Not tonight, Miss Illyanne," the captain said. "Water didn't seem to rise too far so there's a good chance the galley food is safe." He sipped his tea. "It's getting it out that might be the challenge." He sighed. "We didn't lose anyone so, all in all, I guess we're lucky. Can't say the same for the ship."

"Well, I'll be better by morning," Illyanne said. "I'll be able to go in and get the food supplies."

"Oh no, no." He laughed and several others chuckled too. "A quiet one but fastidious, she is," he observed out loud. Illyanne did not know what he meant. "It's much too dangerous. I'll send a crewman in on a rope. Not much of a current here but she could break up and shift position some and the waves might break her up further. It could be dangerous inside. All that lumber could fall on top of a man or crush him sideways if the ship moves too far one way."

Illyanne sipped her tea with the others, listening to their sailor talk. Soon, everyone bunked down for the night. The drama and tribulations of her first night at sea made Illyanne sleep well in the Green Island lighthouse home. She rose later than the children of the house. Their squeals and chatter romping outside woke her. Shuffling out of the bedroom, she first saw the crewmembers' blankets rolled up in the main sitting room by the fire.

She smelled coffee. Emma was ironing shirts when Illyanne lumbered into the kitchen. She set the iron back down on the stove top.

"I'm sure I look like a wreck." She twisted her long mane into a manageable cord of hair, which Emma had helped comb out the night before. Illyanne sat down at a dark-wood dining table across from the big black iron stove.

Emma smiled. "Good morning. You had a pretty good knock on the head last night." She motioned toward a dining chair. "Come, sit." She set a plate of bread and cherry jam in front of her. "How do you feel?"

Illyanne remained silent for a stretch, thinking. "The only word I can think of is one my husband uses when he sometimes scolds our son." She snorted a little laugh. "Unmoored," she sighed. "I feel unmoored. Adrift at sea."

"I rinsed your dress and wrung it out last night. I spread it over a chair by the fire to dry." She pointed with her chin at the garment folded up next to Illyanne. Emma reached for a dish towel, picked up the coffee pot on the stove top next to her iron. She poured coffee into a cup and handed it to Illyanne. "I can iron your dress for you, if you like."

"No, it's fine." Illyanne smoothed her hands over the bodice of the dress. "Thank you."

Silence came between them again. There was only the gentle sizzling sound which came with Emma flicking water on shirts and streaking the five-pound iron across them.

Illyanne sipped the coffee and sat looking out the window, pensive. "I'm so worried about my husband and son. The fire. Our homestead is a few miles from Peshtigo. Sugar Bush. I'm very afraid for them." She choked up and looked away from Emma. Her voice turned creaky. "And if they're alive, they don't know where I am. They think I'm on a schooner lumber run to Cleveland."

"You poor dear."

Illyanne wiped her eyes. "I've got to go looking for them as soon as possible."

"Uh, you may have to put that off for a bit."

Illyanne looked up. She wrapped her arms around herself and rubbed her upper arms as if she felt a sudden chill. "What do you mean?"

"First order of business has got to be that." Emma pointed sharply toward the outside. "Unloading that, of course."

The view from kitchen window showed a clothesline and vast green lawn. "The scenery is nice here," Illyanne said, spreading some jam on her bread. It looked like some of the smoke had cleared from her view of the sky and bay, since the ship had left port – was it only last night? On the far shore, a few lines of dark smoke meandered upward, blowing to the east. Patches of blue sky broke through from the smoky haze in spots. The lighthouse land curved down to the water and out of the kitchen window, she could see the upper half of the Henry B. Jones, standing still. The crewmen were down there moving around. "What they're doing down there?"

"The men are all out there with my husband, Hans. Taking measurements and trying to figure what can be done. Hans runs the lighthouse here. He should be asleep now after working the light all night." She threw up her hands and shook her head. "But instead, he's down there with them tying to help unload safely. The children went too, to watch. We've got five. You met Daniel, our oldest last night. He carried you in. I expect your ship isn't going to be repairable. They're taking off what stores and cargo they can from her." She turned the shirt laying on the ironing board, lifted and ironed another section.

"And wait for waves to break up the rest of her, I suppose?" Illyanne asked.

"Yes and no. They'll salvage everything they can and then probably burn her. Dry as it's been, they might wait until it snows if they can, as long as pieces don't start floating into the bay to be a danger to other ships."

Emma chuckled at the dazed expression on Illyanne's face. "Sorry, Miss. Eat up. You don't look so good. You need to regain your strength."

"Call me Illyanne." She spread the jam on a wedge of bread and bit. "Hmm. This is good. Never had cherry jam before."

Emma smiled.

Illyanne got up to change out of the nightgown Emma had loaned her and put her hair up. Returning to the kitchen, she told Emma, "Thank you for rescuing us."

"We see our fair share of sailors come ashore here, usually in storms. But this –. This fire's been a real disaster. We haven't seen anything like this – ever. And, we've been here seventeen years. It was on both sides of the bay last night."

Illyanne's eyes grew wide. "That was the most fearful thing I've ever seen. Did you see it from over here?"

"Oh, yeah. Fire surrounded us last night from across the water. I had to have two sons stand fire watch all night around the house. Flying ash. Didn't want the roof to catch fire. The lighthouse was safe because it's stone and mortar." Emma picked up the iron again off the stove and dragged it across one of her own dresses.

"You're looking at Marinette out there," She pointed. "And out back, you walk a spell and you can see Egg Harbor on the eastern Door peninsula." She ironed out another sleeve, the blouse upper, and then the length of the gathered skirt. She placed the dress on a hanger and laid it over a kitchen chair.

Emma appeared to be a woman who was always in motion, happily working. Over the course of an hour, she drew Illyanne into conversation. Illyanne raised Matthew and Emma was raising five. Both had run households. Both had participated in quilting bees, cleaned fish and game, made bread, syrup, grew vegetable and flower gardens on their land. Matthew was close in age to Emma's eldest, Daniel.

Illyanne explained her cooking, "I guess I learned mostly from my mother. She used to grow herbs. I used to help tap maple resin and make syrup with her. Hunted mushrooms, gathered rice. From knee-high, I suppose, I learned about cinnamon, onions, ginger, garlic, salt and pepper, watching her cook. She talked talk to me about spices and flavorings. It just got into me. Whenever Anders told me he liked something I made, I wanted to cook more." She told her of working at the Peshtigo Boarding House, of Anders' broken arm and the ship's loss of a cook and need for a quick replacement. "That was a big mistake. Never again. Anyway, that's my life's story 'til now." Illyanne flushed. "I don't usually talk about myself much. How about you? It's must be a different way of life being on an island."

"I expect so, but it's mostly what I've known. I was nineteen when we came here. It took some getting used to. We had to clear land and work. Children came on fast."

"Doesn't it get lonely being out here by yourselves?"

Emma shrugged. "We keep busy. We get mail once or twice a month from the mainland and from late spring to early fall, we take a boat over to shore, go to church, get supplies and dry goods."

They both sat in brief silence, ruminating on their similarities and differences.

"It is a different kind of pioneer life," Emma said. "We get shipwreck visitors from time to time like yourselves. Sailors are generally a colorful lot." She smiled and Illyanne nodded in agreement. "Great for story telling by the evening fire. Mind you, I've had to cover children's ears more than a few times."

They enjoyed a small laugh together.

"What's on the other side, what you called out back? Is that what the captain called it the craggy arm of Wisconsin?"

"It's quiet farm life over there. We've only gone south from there, not all the way out to the tip of the peninsula."

"So, not to Death's Door?"

"No. Those sailors been tellin' you horror stories 'bout that?" Emma laughed and gave Illyanne a long look. "I can see you tend toward the delicate, don't you? And it's true that there's been many a shipwreck there. It's shallow and rocky but I think it's more a case of the weather at the time. So, it's probably not as bad as whatever you've heard."

Illyanne backhanded the air and fiddled with her coffee cup.

"Let's see what else is over there. Oh, here's something for a cook. There's some cherry and apple trees out that way. There's lots of recipes. There's Sturgeon Bay, beautiful place to fish and camp. There's a lot of people in the spring and summer who go there. The Indians often come."

"That's me. I mean half. My mother was Menominee. My middle name is Neenah, after the town. We say NeeNAH. Used to be all Menominee living there. I didn't grow up with the tribe but we visited on occasion."

"Oh, yes, I see it in you now. It's almost hidden with your medium brown hair and dark brown eyes – and in the shape of your eyes." Must've been difficult growing up with a foot in each world."

"I guess so." She flinched her shoulders. "My mother tried to show me both ways of life as best she could. Don't have anyone to light the way anymore. My own family's everything now." Illyanne looked down and kneaded her hands for a moment. She thrust her head back up to shake off the fear. "Anyhow, you've found me out. I'm a mutt. That's what Anders says about the both of us. Jokingly of course. He's Swedish and German and English."

"You're a lovely mutt then. I've always admired the raw beauty of Indians. God has blessed you. I'm from rugged mutt stock, too, German, English and Scottish. We're the Schumachers." Emma tilted her head and flashed a big smile. "Anyway, going down the craggy arm, as you call it – that's the Door Peninsula – there's more farming towns, more people as you go south toward Green Bay. And, there's that Mary Chapel. Have you heard of it?"

Emma looked over at Illyanne who absentmindedly nodded yes. "They say there was an apparition there. A vision. Good ten years or better now. This young Belgian girl said the Virgin Mary appeared to her. After that, she helped build a shrine and started a group of nuns. They teach children the faith. They walk all over for miles and miles to spend a day here and there teaching farm kids. You ever hear about this? Father Pernin talked about it."

Illyanne snapped out of her blasé state. "Father Pernin? I know him. French-born. You go to his church? We attend in Peshtigo. Oh, I guess you probably go over, in Marinette. I know he covers both parishes."

"Yes, that's where we go – when we can."

"He's a good priest," Illyanne added. "He loves tell stories of the French restaurants in Chicago. He had a parish there before. He can really carry on."

They laughed together.

Emma said, "I never saw a priest crinkle up his face like he did when talking about food. You'd think he's practically committing a sin," Emma said. Both women giggled. "His Coq Au Vin, souffles. And oh, Crepes."

"Yes, Crepes." Illyanne held her stomach. What a relief it was to laugh. "I once asked him for some recipes. I made Beef Bordelaise. I thought it was great. Anders and Matthew thought it was good but it tasted strange."

Emma craned her neck looking outside. She put down her iron on the stove with a clunk and stared out the window. "What's got into that boy?" She went toward the window.

Daniel was yelling something. His voice grew louder as he came closer, running toward the house. Emma opened the door for him.

14

M onday, October 9, 1871
Champion, Wisconsin

AS THE LIGHT PEELED back the night, the people who had been walking the grounds saw that the fire stopped at the fence line perimeter. A burned scent permeated the air. People in the procession fell out of order. They wept and laughed and shouted about the wonder they could now view. Some fell to their knees in thanksgiving. They looked and sounded jubilant for every muddy-stained knee among them after the rain.

Anders' heart burst with the happiness of simply being alive, being with these people and most of all, truly and deeply uniting with the divine. This night changed him. He tingled with amazement. It reminded him of the stories of sailors who'd survived rounding Cape Horn at the bottom of South America. Tierra del Fuego, the land of fire. Those men lived to tell spellbinding tales of the treacherous Williwaw Winds. Those powerful airstreams swept down from the mountains to the sea, causing massive waves and wicked storms on the water. Many a ship and sailor perished there.

The people disbursed, meandered about the chapel grounds, with the animals, chatting with one another. They discovered that the fire had blackened the outside slats of the white picket fence which enclosed the chapel ground. Yet, the interior sides of the same fence slats remained free of any burn marks and white. The chapel suffered no burns. Everyone was saying it was a miracle.

A feeling of happy goodwill lingered in the air around the chapel and grounds the day after the fire. When the sun came out, it delivered an eerie beauty over the burned landscape. The chapel and school seemed to rise out the middle of the darkened ground, sporadic little swirls of smoke still rising in the distance. The sisters sent people out to milk the cows and goats and others to start preparing something to eat for those who had fled their homes for the chapel.

"Look, you have mud on your pant legs," someone said to Anders.

He brushed at his pants. "I don't mind. It's a sign of what happened here." He lifted his arms up high and twisting one way and then the other, among the backdrop of green grass and grazing animals. "If anyone asks, I'll tell them the story. Let's just hope there's someone out there to tell."

The man answered, "Yes, that's right."

A practical thought ran through Anders about what he should now do. "Would you help me? I think we ought to organize some men to go out and bury any dead outside the fence. I know that's grim but it's now God's work for us." Soon, Anders gathered a group of fine, including Karl.

They found Gustaf on the road. Karl stood over him, without moving or showing any emotion. The man lay on the ground, a crusted, blackened form overcome by the disaster.

Anders watched as a clammy shaken look came over Karl, who held back tears. "Karl, he must've gotten caught. When he went back to let the animals out of the barn, he lost time trying to outrun the fire." Anders touched him at the upper arm. "Nathan and I can take care of this one. Why don't you stand back?"

"No, he was my friend and neighbor." Karl choked up. "I have to help him. It's the last thing I can do for him."

The three of them dug. There was nothing to cover Karl's friend with. None of them even thought to bring anything to wrap bodies in for burial.

"He can have my shirt," one of the men said, unbuttoning his outer shirt. "I've got two. You never know when a sudden chill will come up in October. This time of year, my wife's always havin' me wear two."

That's just what Illie always told Anders this time of year. "The temperature can change in a minute." His mind saw a wistful image of Illyanne at the kitchen work table. He yearned for her and the homestead so much. He had to bend forward for a moment to ease the twinge.

The burial party wrapped the fragile burned body as best they could and rolled it into the grave. After the men shoveled down to dirt and piled it over the dead man. They fell still standing around the grave site. The area had been mostly trees, and fields and brush. The fire consumed the plants and must have moved past the man quickly. They found little remains of farm animals. Anders said, "I wonder what happened to your Chinese man servant."

"I don't know," Karl said. "I woke him and told him about the fire but I never saw him after that. Maybe he made a run for the lake. Maybe I'll find him back at my homestead. I may never know." When they were done burying Gustaf, Anders, Karl and the others stood around the grave with bowed heads.

Anders asked Karl, "Would you like to say a prayer? I don't know what ones you say in your faith."

He looked at Anders with glassy eyes. "We just pray from the heart. I don't know any of the hymns or anything so –." He gulped, crossed his hands in front of himself and lowered his head but said nothing. After a moment, he added, "And, I guess we can say the Lord's Prayer together."

Anders did not speak his thought out loud. *We call it the 'Our Father.'*

They all said the prayer aloud together. They all remained silent and standing still for a while longer praying silently over the small heap of dirt over the burned body that had been Karl's friend.

It seemed like it was all they could do or say for the man. Anders remembered Illie telling him that some of the workmen at the Peshtigo Boarding House used to get into arguments over religion. Protestants believed they automatically went straight to heaven if they were believers. Catholics had to see to it that they remained in a state of grace in order to die in grace and be saved.

Peshtigo men were lumberjacks, saw mill workers and woodenware factory laborers who, by and large, weren't at all that religious. However, they got awfully feisty and ready to fight over someone criticizing what their mothers had or had not taught them. Karl was a sailor and a businessman now but he was still more like the Boarding House men than not.

At a time like this, Anders didn't want Karl, who was some kind of Protestant, to bristle at a Catholic prayer. So, in a whisper, Anders added the part of the Catholic prayer for the dead that he knew. "Eternal rest grant unto him, Oh Lord, and let perpetual light shine upon him. May his soul and the souls of all the faithful departed, through the mercy of God, rest in peace. Amen."

The three young men, with shovels over their shoulders walked a good way further down the scorched roadway but they found no one else. After a while, Karl said, "We might as well go back to the chapel. I didn't think we'd find anyone else. There's nobody else who lives around here in this rural area. And it's charred as far as the eye can see. Looks like anyone who was able to run, made it to the shrine."

On the road back toward the chapel, the men chatted a bit amongst themselves. Mostly, there were only the crunching sounds of their footfalls on the gritty, burned ground as they shuffled along. "Karl, are you going to be all right?" Anders asked. "I know it was hard finding your friend like that."

Karl took several steps, not speaking but choking back tears again. "It's not that. I mean, yeah, that was terrible. But at least I know he's with God now. It's Inga I'm worried about."

They shuffled along the roadway without talking for a moment. "Who's Inga?"

"She's Gustaf's fiancé. She had written him from Sweden that she would be coming soon. I don't know how to contact her."

"Maybe the sisters at the chapel will have an idea. Someone to write to and inquire."

"In Sweden? Aren't those sisters from Belgium?" Karl said. "And anyhow, there's no Catholics in Sweden. Who would they write to?"

Anders scratched his head. "Well, you've got your Saint Bridget, haven't you? There must be some Catholic church over there somewhere."

"I think that was hundreds of years ago. There's only the one Church of Sweden now. And it's not Catholic."

"Sorry, I don't know much about Sweden or how and why Protestants broke away from the Church or any of that. I know there's other churches in Peshtigo but we never have any interaction with them. I guess I ought to know more about that. Maybe sometime I could ask you about all that."

Karl gave him a long look. "Sure. I guess so. Answering a couple of questions couldn't hurt much." The dramatic events of the night and day bonded the two of them together in an unbreakable way, like battlefield soldiers, in spite of their differences. Karl once again acquired the sassy, mischievous look that was his trademark as he stopped walking and leaned on his shovel. "Even if it is from what some other people call – not me, mind you – a papist idolater."

Anders stopped and his shoes ground into the burnt road, sounding like sand on a wood floor. He saw that that Karl was smirking. Anders assumed this was a type of gallows humor that had come over Karl. He felt free to return it in kind. They had been walking side by side and now Anders reached out and slapped the back of his companion's head. "All right, if you don't mind a few questions from me, I guess I don't mind talking to someone, who other people – not me – might say is a heretic turncoat." Anders laughed. "I guess we know the starting positions well enough, eh?"

Karl laughed too and started walking again at a leisurely pace. "I suppose you want to ask me about Mary. Well, you can save your breath, sailor. I don't believe in her the way you do. I ain't about to go changing my religion any time soon."

"That's fine but I say the Blessed Mother interceded with the good Lord for us all last night. You've seen the proof yourself. There's no way that fire up and stopped on its own just outside the fence all around the chapel grounds. Karl, you and me would've ended up like Gustaf, if she didn't plead to her Son to spare us." Anders stopped and stabbed his shovel into the ground, grinning. "You gotta admit, it's mighty hard to pass that one off as some kind of coincidence."

Karl kept on walking and Anders caught up with him. They both flung their garden tools over their shoulders. "Yeah, all right, I'll give you that." Karl said. "I can't explain it. And, it was strange." He paused for a few seconds. "But, so is a fish with two heads. I've seen that get pulled out of the sea in a net. Sometimes things happen that just can't be made sense of. All that Star of the Sea stuff. It's just a myth, nothing more than a working song, a sea shanty."

Anders puffed a laugh and swiped his hand dismissively toward Karl. He walked ahead, shaking his head to himself. There was just no knocking any sense into the heads of certain people. Some preacher put a version of everything in their head and that was it – forever. People could be mighty darned pigheaded.

It confounded him that even among the devout of Karl's faith, they didn't have the slightest idea about how Mary is an extra mother for everyone to help them out of jams and in times of trouble, can light the way forward. They didn't believe in her just because it was some kind of rule not to. It didn't matter that the first miracle at Cana was at Mary's request, or that she was at Pentecost, or that she went on trips with the apostles and Jesus. She was there for Jesus' carrying of the cross and crucifixion.

And she even appeared before people somewhere in Mexico back when Spain ruled down there. Hundreds of years ago. He remembered Father Pernin saying something about how lots of the Indians down there used to kill people as offerings to pagan gods. But after one of their own tribesmen saw the Virgin, they all quit doing human sacrifices and changed to Catholic.

Anders didn't say it out loud only because he figured it would have started a worthless round of talk on faith disagreements. But he voiced the thought in his head. You can lead a horse to water but you sure can't beat 'im purple with a stick to make him drink!

During the next several days a number of survivors left the chapel to try return home. The sisters and the remaining group of about thirty had put together a dinner of fresh bread and a stew. Sister Adele said the prayer, thanking the Lord and the Virgin Mary for interceding to keep the fire back and providing a good meal. They ate and talked about what chores they had all done that day.

After dinner, Anders asked Karl to join him for a walk around the grounds of the chapel shrine and get an idea of what needed to be done for the next day. They helped guide some of the animals back into the barn. Incredibly, there seemed to be enough hay in the barn for the animals for a good week.

Karl strolled out into the open pasture of the grounds and looked up at the stars. Anders came over to join him. "I really am so sorry for the loss of your friend today. I can't imagine."

"We were friends, neighbors but I wouldn't say we were close."

"Still."

"The thing I am most worried about now is Inga." Karl sighed. "Anders, what if she arrives by train and gets a ride out here to the chapel? I'm sure that's where they'd bring her now. Naturally, I'd take her in and help get her settled and find work in Green Bay." He kicked the ground. "I'll have to break it to her. She'll be in mourning. She won't have money to buy passage back to Sweden." He paused and looked searchingly at Anders. "I just wonder. Seeing how houses and barns all burned down and it's going to be a long struggle to rebuild." Karl paused again and looked down.

"What?"

"Well, I mean she'd have come all the way across the ocean and she'd be here. No money. No Gustaf." He did not look at Anders as he spoke. "I wonder, if she's nice, do you think it would be all right if I married her?"

"What? What is wrong with you?" Anders gave him a shove. "You must've cracked your head out there, old mate."

"It's not like I don't know her. Gustaf showed me her picture. Read parts of her letters to me. Told me all about her. I think he'd want me to take care of her. And you said yourself, I ought to settle down."

"But, she doesn't know you," Anders said. "And, weren't you just telling me yesterday that you had no time for having a wife and family? You have other things to do."

"Well, look around. Things have obviously changed." He stretched out his arms and looked up to the sky. "I mean, I'd give her some time and all."

"The fire must've made you crazy in the head." Anders turned away from him and stomped off toward the chapel building, wondering whether saying a prayer for him would even help.

15

M onday, October 9, 1871
Green Island, Wisconsin

DANIEL CHARGED INSIDE with his arms full of rolled maps and charting instruments. He dumped the items on the table. The sextant and the ship's log book landed with a thud. It knocked Illyanne's plate into the jar of jam. Emma cast Daniel a scolding glance.

"She's shifting and they're starting to pick her bones. Hurry. The captain sent me to bring back any rope we've got."

Both women stood up. "What does he want with rope?" Emma asked.

"The ship is moving from the waves. It's causing more damage. The captain says the situation was worse because the ship was fully loaded. He said the momentum of all the lumber weight ground the ship's hull into the shoals. Anyway, he wants to sort of try to lasso the ship and hold it steady so she doesn't drift in the waves while the crew get that lumber out of there."

Emma rushed to a closet and grabbed two fresh braids of rope and handed them to Daniel. He dashed back out and ran toward the ship. She returned to the kitchen where Illyanne had been watching. "For all the good that'll do," Emma muttered.

"Why's that?" Illyanne asked with a concerning look.

"I don't think they'll be able to hold back that ship if the water and waves have a mind to move it. If anything would work, you'd need a team of twenty mules – no, double that – to handle that job," Emma said. "We probably ought to go down there so see what provisions we can save."

As they hurried down the slope, Illyanne told Emma, "I've got a hind quarter of deer meat in there, salt pork, rice and beans – all the provisions for good meals for six for a week. Flour, sugar, coffee and four dozen eggs. We're shipwrecked on this island with you, your family and the crew and that's thirteen mouths to feed. We need those provisions."

Their skirts blew up to midcalf in the breeze. It provided them a few moments of panicked tittering while trying to hold their skirts down. They sat on the grass. It was still mild outside for October and they sunned their faces periodically. Illyanne closed her eyes for a moment and prayed that Anders and Matthew had somehow come out of the fire alive. They watched the men with curiosity and admiration, climbing up and down from the ship, walking and diving around her in the water, shouting things back and forth to one another and stacking lumber on the lawn in crisscross patterns.

Daniel ran back and forth delivering food items which had remained dry to his mother and Illyanne. They carried them up to the house going back and forth for an hour.

Emma sighed and sat down again in the kitchen. "I guess, we better start thinking about what kind of cooking to whip up for tonight. There's gonna be some mighty tired hungry ones about the place."

Illyanne smiled. "Have you got a roasting spit outside? We can roast that venison and prepare some vegetables and bread in here." After some of the men rescued the foodstuffs, the remainder of the day, Illyanne and Emma worked together cooking for thirteen people. The children helped turning the crank on the rotisserie spit to cook the meats. All day, from the kitchen and outside, they watched the men unloading lumber, laying braces and stacking it up crosswise all over the land. It was a best effort under the circumstances to dry out the wood.

Illyanne was glad to have work to take her mind off of Anders and Matthew. She was glad to cook for the large group. Emma had the idea to jam two picnic tables together and the men carried the dining room table outside from the house. They all dined outside in the open air with the view of the water and pink and purplish setting sun all around them. Moving the lumber had been hard work and the men ate like wild hungry beasts. The conversation was light but pleasant among the crew and the Schumacher family.

After dinner, during clean up, Illyanne's worries crept back into her mind. "Emma, can I go speak to your husband? I want permission to go ashore with one of your rowboats tomorrow morning."

"Illyanne, he's sound asleep. I told you; he stayed up most of the day to help with the work. I can't disturb him now. I will speak to him before he goes up to the lighthouse tonight. I'll ask him to send out a Morse Code message about your shipwreck and to send a salvage ship."

"I'm desperate, Emma." Illyanne twisted a flour sack towel in her hands. Her gaze hit Emma's heart, mother to mother. Her glassy eyes relayed her deepest concerns. "Wouldn't you do anything, absolutely anything if you didn't know whether Hans and your five children were out there dead or in desperate need of your help?"

"I know. I know." Emma laid her hands over Illyanne's. "I'll talk to him about sending a message tonight. There should still be shipping traffic in the bay. By morning we might have word that a salvage ship is on the way. Let's wait and see. I'll pray with you if you like."

"No, Emma. I mean, no thank you. I'm just so, so tired. I'm not much in a praying way if you know what I mean after everything that's happened. I'm so worried and afraid that I can't even pray."

Sleep came to Illyanne that night with difficulty. The thought confronted her over and over. She had to find a way off the island.

Tuesday, October 10, 1871

Two days after the fire

In spite of tossing much of the night, Illyanne awoke early and found Emma in the kitchen. "What did Hans say this morning? Did any ship answer the message?"

"Nothing yet, I'm afraid." Emma poured her a cup of coffee. "I wanted to get you sitting down, before I got into it."

"Is there some news?"

"Hans thinks we need to wait another night. To see if a reply comes through."

Illyanne's face fell.

Emma put her hand on Illyanne's shoulder for a moment." If a ship saw our message, it would be at least twenty-four hours, before they'd reload and are back sailing. The Green Bay dock knows there's only a night watchman at our lighthouse. No ship is going to try to message a Morse Code response during the day. I'm sorry. If you go ashore and head for Sugar Bush today, you might miss important information that comes in tonight."

Illyanne slumped in one of the kitchen chairs. "I was so hoping to make the crossing today."

"I don't think they'll let you go," Emma said. "The captain needs his men to keep offloading lumber. And, Hans won't let you take one of the rowboats alone. It's too dangerous to cross open water by yourself. The waves can get high enough to sink that little skiff. And ships might not see you. You might even roll over in their wakes."

Illyanne stomped a foot. "So, I'm as good as a prisoner here for the time being!" Her eyes glassed up.

"No, it's just we've never had anything like this." Emma cast an unusual look at Illyanne, annoyance mixed with empathy. "We aren't holding you against your will. It's just the abnormal situation. Please try to understand." Emma reached out in a soothing manner toward Illyanne but did not actually touch her.

Illyanne pulled away and walked outside and headed down toward the water's edge.

Emma called out to her back. "Don't go do anything stupid." She walked outside and cupped her hands. "The water's freezing now. You'd cramp up and drown. Think of your husband and son."

Illyanne didn't turn back but raised a hand acknowledging she had heard Emma. She kept on walking and paced when she reached the shoreline. The breeze, and cooler air and open space worked their mystical calming effect on her.

When she returned to the house, more than an hour later, she said she told Emma she was going to lie down. Illyanne curled up, wrapped herself in a blanket. She prayed that she'd find Anders and Matthew soon and cried quietly before falling asleep. After a few hours, Illyanne had cried out her frustrations and slept some more. Emma was outside hanging laundry on a clothesline. "Emma, I owe you an apology. I was just so worried and upset. What can I do to help?"

She spent the remainder of the day working with Emma and trying to think of ways to search for her family. They cooked, washed clothes and hung them outside to dry in the sun and fresh air on Green Island. It was indeed, a safe haven from the fire. Most of the haze had blown clear now. On both sides of the island, Illyanne could see a smudged black line on the horizon. Unlike the morning after a raging storm, when sunlight and recovering plant and animal life peeked out, the fire left long-lasting damage. The blackened shoreline must have once been lush with green trees.

With Emma at her side, Illyanne held wooden clothes pins between her teeth and fastened clothes to the line. "You know, workers at the Peshtigo Woodenware factory probably made these." It was a strange observation about a little household item. She and Emma were using them now, things that came from the place where her family might be lying dead, without so much as a loving family member to bury them. She had to hold back from breaking into sobs at thoughts like that. She breathed deeply, hoping it would bring her patience.

Toward late evening, the captain went into Hans's study and Illyanne heard the two of them talking. Cooking at the Peshtigo Boarding House had taught her one thing. The manager always made the final decision if there was some disagreement among the cooks. But the manager had to know about the problem. If she could just speak directly to the men who had the power to grant her wish, she could move past the conversation she had with Emma. Illyanne knocked and entered. There were nautical maps spread out on a large flat table. Fishing nets, a helm's wheel, a set of oars and a wooden anchor adorned the walls. Both men were smoking their pipes.

"Pardon me, sirs." She stepped into the room with a little curtesy. "Emma told me you'll be on the lookout tonight for an answer to the Morse Code message you sent last night. But, if there isn't any by morning, I'd like to go ashore tomorrow. Will you be going Captain? I must start looking for my family in Peshtigo."

The men looked at each other with surprise and amused expressions.

"Miss Illyanne," the captain said. "If I go ashore, it won't be on the Peshtigo and Marinette side of the bay. My priority has to be to get word to Green Bay about our running aground. If I go, it'll be to the Door County side of the bay."

"Oh, I see." She turned her focus on Hans. "Since that is the case, sir, Mr. Schumaker, I'd like permission to take one of your rowboats tomorrow, that is, if no reply message comes in tonight."

The captain broke in. "I can't allow it."

"It's *his* rowboat." She laced her fingers together tightly to stop the tiny tremble she felt. She was talking back to the captain, although politely. "I don't mean to sound out of line, Captain but after all that's happened, I don't believe I'm under your authority any more. I mean I think it's fair to say that I'm not really employed right now as the ship's cook." She kept her eyes down, waiting for his possible verbal rebuke.

Hans chuckled and winked at the captain. "She may have you there, Skipper."

She looked up. "So, Mr. Schumacher, what do you say?"

"If the good captain here provides you an escort – ."

The captain stared at Illyanne for a long time. He puffed on his pipe. "Mrs. Eriksson, I and your husband have terribly underestimated you. I'll send one of my crewmen to accompany you."

Hans Schumaker mumbled, "Grace under fire, Cap," and then he chuckled.

"Oh, thank you, sir." She nodded toward the captain also.

"And, that is, *only* if there is no Morse Code reply tonight," Mr. Schumaker added. "If we get word that a salvage or rescue ship is in route, then it's all off."

"I understand."

The captain repeated his caution. "And, my men have to have finished removing all the lumber they can get out and stack. Otherwise, I can't spare a crewman."

"That'll be fine. Thank you." Illyanne slipped out the door quietly.

16

Tuesday October 10, 1871
Two days after the fire
Champion, Wisconsin

PEOPLE WERE ENGAGED in busy work all over the chapel grounds, cleaning, working with the animals, preparing food. Several groups were putting up tent-like coverings in the back acreage, apparently from some spare sail cloth someone had found stored in the barn. Three more families had arrived with stories of having run toward Lake of Michigan. They had waited out the fire in canoes roped together in the chilly night and cold water. All night, they watched the blaze rage on in near despair, fearful that no one or anything would survive it.

One group had come in with a wagon from southern shore of Lake Michigan. They brought big wood barrels full of water and a good stack of farmhouse blankets and quilts.

Anders knew it was five miles by the road but maybe three if you cut straight across the land. "How did you, your wagon and wooden barrels ever make it through the fire," Anders asked.

"The wind carried the fire east. Our land is a little south of the fire line. When the winds moved the fire east, passing us by, we drove to the edge of Lake Michigan, went back and forth scooping up water. We already had the barrels loaded in the wagon."

One of the nuns overhead on her way out to greet them. "Welcome. We are very glad to see you. Thank you for the water. We need it."

"There's another group that will be coming behind us. They're catching fish and will be here soon."

At least God had spared Illyanne. By now, she was probably already in Lake Huron, closing in on Lake Eerie. She was safe out at sea, far away. She probably never even saw the fire.

For a couple of days there was plenty of work on the chapel grounds, organizing supplies, planning meals for the group, caring for the animals, washing clothes. By the second day after the fire more people left to go camp on the north bay shore. Most intended to make their way to their farms and gradually retrieve anything they could and get ready for winter and plan to rebuild.

With a second day of hard work, Anders and Matthew fell asleep under the stars with blankets. "We've done what we can here," Anders said, his back to Matthew's on the ground. "We ought to head out toward Green Bay in the morning. We might be able to jump a ship from there to Peshtigo and still be I time to meet your mother."

Matthew, beside him, sat up for a while, looking up at the stars. "What about Sturgeon Bay and the ferry?"

"The relief driver who came today told the sisters. All the newspaper reports are saying the land burned the whole stretch from here to there. And across the bay, Marinette burned too. The ferry is surely not running. The City of Green Bay was spared, however. The fire began north and south of the city and fed on the dry brush and trees. The wind blew straight northeast in two streaks, so it was like the fire went around the city. We can catch a sail from there or work for a bit if we have to. Better chance of sleeping in a bed somewhere too."

Matthew fell quiet for a spell. "I'm worried about Chepi. I wonder if she made it out all right."

"Probably did." Anders said "I hope Jakoh and Lina had time to see what was coming and got to the water. They're only a few miles from the bay."

"Why do you think Chepi got out, Papa?"

Anders rolled half way over and gestured with his arm and hand. "Sure as shootin', they'd have seen the fire coming. They're right on the Sturgeon Bay. They're on the far side of the inlet in Door County. The fire wouldn't be able to jump across the water. Even if it did, they'd see it coming and run further up the peninsula." He tugged on his blankets and turned on his side again. "I've heard it twice now. The fire didn't go up the whole peninsula. More n' likely the Menominee we saw got well clear of it." He rolled back over. "You're starting to sound like a love sick fool. Now, go to sleep."

Wednesday October 11, 1871
Three days after the fire
Champion and south shore of the bay

They walked around the grounds, school and barn to say goodbye to other survivors and the sisters.

Matthew stood out in front of the buildings waiting for his father.

Anders came out from the chapel.

"There you are. What were you doing, Papa?"

"Just saying a quick prayer for safe travels is all – and thanks for what happened here."

"Well, let's get going, so we don't lose another day."

Word of mouth reports from fire survivors and the relief wagon driver indicated that Peshtigo had been devastated. Anders figured the dock was probably gone. Maybe the ship would have to anchor out and bring its crew ashore in small boats. Regardless of how they reunited, Anders and Matthew intended to be there when Illyanne's ship came in on the fourteenth. "Will we ever have stories to tell your mother when we see her." They had three days.

Because Champion was near the crook of the arm of the Door peninsula, it made sense to head out to the northwest. They planned to cross burned land, hike and camp along the shore line into Green Bay.

Their pace was slow and their path meandered around stumps, fallen branches and uneven mounds of ground. Spindles of burned-out trees still stood tall near fallen ones. Scorched, scruffy brush dotted the landscape among occasional dark shapes which might have been rabbit and fawn carcasses. The ground made a scratchy sound as Anders and Matthew walked over it. Black sandy residue blew around and the grit of it got in their mouths. They had to swill canteen water in their mouths and spit it out several times.

"Watch this," Matthew said, dropping his bedroll and pushing his hands on one of the thinner, burned-out but still standing tree trunks, leaning hard against it. Its roots started to pull up from the ground. He grunted and pushed harder but he could not get it to go all the way over. "Well, that didn't work. See Papa, I'm no good for a lumberjack or farmer." He smiled. "I need to be a sailor."

Anders shook his head, chuckling to himself about Matthew's boyishness and trekked on. Their water supply was going faster than they thought it would. They stopped to drink water from their canteens, often but did not speak much.

At last, they saw blue water and felt the chillier air. They ran toward the Bay of Green Bay and hooted with joy. They splashed Lake Michigan's water on their faces, scraped areas with their feet to sit down and ate their packed sandwiches.

"We're as good as there now, Matthew."

"We'll still have to camp tonight, right?"

"Yeah, but I think we'll get into the city tomorrow. We'll see about getting a train or a boat to Peshtigo."

Lying down on burned ground, they rested face up, making comments about the changing shapes of the clouds like carefree boys of summer. "Let's take fifteen minutes and then we'll go on."

Delay for a few minutes longer seemed worthwhile. Fifteen minutes became a half hour. Then, it was hard to get back up. "Oh, what I wouldn't do," Anders groaned, "for some of your mother's cayenne and ginger oil to rub on my legs,"

"And my feet," said Matthew. They both had taken off their shoes and socks for a while and let the wind dry up the sweat.

They were stiff and tired from the walk over rough terrain. In spite of that, they filled their water jugs in the lake and started again, though more slowly than before.

With another two miles behind them, they could see a strip of earth up ahead, along the bay shoreline, which had not burned. There were tall grasses near the shore and scruffy brush, back a ways from the water but it was all green. The sun had lowered in the sky and it would be dusk in another hour, so they camped. They ate apples for their supper, the last of their provisions. After picking out rocks from the rough ground for a sleeping area, they laid out their blankets. Fatigued from their hike, they slept as if they had gone into the next world.

17

W*ednesday, October 11, 1871*
Three days after the fire
Green Island; Marinette;
Peshtigo River bank

ILLYANNE AND A CREWMAN named Oscar, set out rowing to the Marinette shore on Wednesday. She held up the makeshift sail on the little boat and it pulled them along but they also had to row with the oars. It was much more physically demanding than she thought it would be and it took longer than expected.

Across the bay, making their way up the Menominee River, the scent of burnt wood wafted toward them as they paddled up stream. Marinette sat on the west side of the Menominee River. They could see the city of Menominee, across the Menominee River, across the border, into the state of Michigan. On the Wisconsin side of the river, near Marinette, they pulled the boat up on shore and walked among the deadly quiet. They could make out roads. Where houses and business buildings used to be, there was only blackened rubble, like large remnants of a campfire that had burned for a night. They both stood there surveying the scene of a place that had been.

"This looks very bad, Ma'am."

"Yes, but I have to go. I have to search for my family. My husband and son may have stayed late in Peshtigo and been forced to run this direction."

"You must let me go with you then. We're likely to see – that is, we might come across some sights that will – where people have been overtaken by the fire."

Illyanne only nodded in the affirmative and they set out walking down what might have once been Marinette's main street. In several blocks, they still saw nothing but burned wood, skeletal remains of collapsed buildings and carriages. She could make out the carcasses of two dead horses and turned away. Oscar put his arm around her shoulder in a gentlemanly fashion. They walked on. There was something up ahead. The sound of people. The smell of food. As they got closer, they saw the smoke rising and smelled something coming from a cook fire.

A relief wagon with supplies and volunteers handed out plates of food and blankets, and talked to the survivors. Figures of men, women and some children – perhaps a dozen of them – sat huddled. They were sitting with tin plates of food in their laps. Their fatigued, expressionless faces looked up as Illyanne walked by. She nodded to them and they looked right through her or stared off into the distance. She thought it strange to smell warm stew cooking among the slow movements of these people in the midst of ashes. It felt like she was in a Civil War after-battle scene. The Boarding House men had spoken of a tired, dreary gloom that covered everything as completely as snow-covered land after an engagement. A haunting feeling was in the air here and it moved like a whisper through her, through all of them.

The place possessed a ghostly feeling. Everything had turned black, crusted from the fire. Soot clung to the air. She smelled of ash, like from an autumn leaf burn back home in Sugar Bush. The burnt smell soaked into her, her clothes, her hair, her spirit.

Illyanne and Oscar approached the relief wagon and waited in line. After a woman had served one family, she looked up to Illyanne. "Would you care for a blanket? How about some nice stew?"

"No thank you. I'm just searching for someone."

"Yes, many are. It's going to take time. Why don't you have some food and blanket and rest for now, dear?"

It had clouded over into a pale blue, whitewashed sky, without discernable cloud forms. It has also turned colder.

"Do you have any news about survivors in Peshtigo?" Illyanne asked.

The woman looked away and asked a coworker for help. The coworker finished stacking more empty plates and then looked over toward Illyanne. The coworker wiped her hands on her skirt and came over to respond. "We haven't been to Peshtigo but we've heard it was hit hard. Very hard."

"Will you take me there?"

"No Miss. We aren't going that way. Nobody is going there. We've come down for the day. From out in the countryside, due north of here on the Michigan side of the river. But we've got some news. The reports say that Peshtigo is a complete loss. There's nothing left standing. Homes, shops, schools and churches are all gone. Trees even exploded and their roots burned underground." The woman paused and her eyes were downcast. She swallowed hard. "A few survived but the loss of life was great. We don't have any more details." She shook her head. "The fire spread very far and wide. Some are saying that over a million acres burned. Everything burned. That's all I know. I'm sorry. So sorry."

Maybe there was some way Anders and Matthew had gone to town and seen the fire coming and got away. Or, maybe it hadn't burned as far north as Sugar Bush but she knew the pillar of fire she'd seen on the ship wasn't from buildings burning. It had to be the forest that burned so madly. She felt frantic and her gut stirred. "Isn't there anyone who can take me to Peshtigo?" She realized she had raised her voice and sounded demanding.

"Miss Illyanne." Oscar tried to pull her back from the relief wagon and then she wrestled free of his grasp.

A relief worker man now came over to address the brewing problem. "Look Miss, you probably couldn't walk to Peshtigo here if you wanted. Every inch of it is charred remains."

"What about by boat? We have a rowboat."

The man looked at Oscar for assistance. "It's seven miles by land and near as much by water, Miss. And that'd be rowing upstream against the current. There could be damaging wreckage floating downriver. Then, you'd have to walk inland to Peshtigo. It's very ill-advised. I tell you there is nothing there. Nothing's left. Let us get you settled for the night and you can come up with a plan in the morning." He looked again at Oscar as if to ask him to persuade Illyanne. "That would really be the best thing right now. It's late morning and you would have trouble getting there and back."

Illyanne recovered herself, wiped her eyes and stepped away from the wagon to speak with her Oscar. "I want to go. I see no difference between being stuck here for the night or on the shore of Peshtigo." She cast Oscar a pleading look. "Can't we at least try?"

Oscar didn't answer yes or no. "Let's sit down here and think this thing through." They walked over to a sitting bench which the relief people must have brought. "It could be dangerous. I see smoke coming from that direction so something's still burning. The man's right. Might be uncut logs floating down river. Something big and heavy like that hits us in the little rowboat, it could kill us. And who knows what kind of crazed animal might be in the water."

"What if we keep close watch and skirt the river's edge so we can go ashore fast?" Illyanne had a begging manner.

"It's still inadvisable."

"I want to go. I've already been delayed two whole days."

"All right. Take it easy. I'll take you." Oscar walked band ack to the man at the relief wagon to inform him. He took some wrapped-up bread and blankets, filled their canteens with water for the trip. Illyanne and Oscar walked back down to the spot where they had beached the rowboat and started off on the water. They headed back down the Menominee River out into the bay. Illyanne and Oscar each took an oar and paddled, hugging the bay shoreline.

It was mid-afternoon when they reached an area that was perceptible as the mouth of the Peshtigo River. They rowed upriver a quarter of a mile and pulled the boat up onto land. Both of them were glad to have taken the blankets offered in Marinette. They lay down on the burned ground, exhausted, wrapped in blankets and slept.

Illyanne woke to the gentle snorting guttural sounds of a gaggle of ducks waddling up from the water. Maybe they were poking around for some meager grassy vegetation. She moved gently away from Oscar. She sat up slowly, watching them peck at the ground near her. It was a welcome breakthrough of natural beauty. The sun was low in the sky and the light washed them in a warm brown yellow. She nudged Oscar awake and pointed.

He rubbed his eyes and smiled.

"They're adorable, aren't they," she said. What lovely, remarkable survivors. For a moment she met Oscar's eyes. A silent vein of appreciation flowed through her senses and she thought Oscar felt it too. The ducks looked cute the way they tottered around, close to each other, making baby grunt sounds, untouched by the disastrous fire. It filled her heart with hope even though the poor little creatures poked and rooted about looking for grass to eat and there was none.

"We best start up the river to Peshtigo." It was October eleventh now and the early evening temperature was dropping. They followed the river, rowing upstream, working their arms and backs hard. All the vegetation and trees on the banks of the river had shriveled to black. They rowed in silence. Clouds overhead cast October shadows around them as they slipped through the water.

The tempo of little swishes from the oars dipping into and out of the water relaxed her and her mind wandered. She received a flash memory from her childhood fever dream. Her vision of the bird with the light on its head flew high over the land with no trees. It was so like the ground here after the fire that it gave her the shivers. This might be the time its meaning would become known to her. What did the bird and light mean? She didn't know, yet an upwelling of confidence went through her. The fact that this image had come to her here and now must mean they were on the right path.

It would soon be dark and it was clear they would have to camp for the night. They pulled up the boat again and Oscar climbed up the slant of the river's edge. He called down to her from the crest of the incline. "I don't see any fires anywhere but there's one faint light. It might be a lantern. I'm going to go see. I'll be back."

18

Wednesday, October 11, 1871
Evening
Peshtigo River bank

ILLYANNE SAT ALONE in the chill at the burnt river's edge on the outskirts of Peshtigo. Oh, what hope could there really be in this hellish landscape that Anders and Matthew were alive? But then, Sugar Bush is a few miles out from Peshtigo. Surely, they would have seen and heard the massive fire coming. There was a chance, maybe a good chance, that they had been able to run and they were out there somewhere, just like her in the cold and damp surrounded by ashes.

Oscar had gone to scout out the area over the berm of the river bank. By the time he returned, it was dark and she had fallen asleep again. He prodded her shoulder. "Miss Illyanne. I found some folks alive up there over the ridge. Let's go. They said to bring whatever food and water we have. I have our bags. You carry the food and water."

She followed him up the riverbed incline onto the plateau and another tenth of a mile inland. There was a family, a man, his wife and boy. They huddled tightly together in a natural dugout in the landscape. They sat close together around a lantern. Even in the new combusted shadowy world, the sight of them was heartwarming, a close-knit family sitting around a substitute campfire. A wave of pity ran through her. She also felt a flutter of hope at their survival in the disaster. She sat down on the ground across from them. "Hello. We're so glad to find you," Illyanne said.

The father had a strange look on his face. The family acted like the others she'd seen in Marinette, shocked and dull. She felt compassion for them and being able to be with them. It helped lift her out of her own melancholy. She wished she could cook something for them. Illyanne handed over food and water to them and put her hands on her hips. "We got blankets from a relief wagon in Marinette. Here, take one of ours." She held hers out to the mother, who accepted it without a word.

The father reached out and grabbed the food and water and dragged it toward himself, like a wary injured animal. He took a drink and passed it to his family. He unrolled the napkin of bread, broke off a piece and shoved it in his mouth, then passed it to his family.

Those poor people had been through the fire and no doubt had seen a lot of devastation. Illyanne sat down. The family looked in bad shape. She had an eerie sense that perhaps they had lost a child in the fire. She turned her head up and back to signal Oscar to sit down too. "Have you told him what we're doing and where we've been?"

Oscar told the man, "We came from an island out in the bay. We rowed into shore this morning." Oscar stopped speaking.

Illyanne looked up at Oscar as he was explaining. He stopped suddenly and stared at the man awkwardly. She turned back around to look at the family to say something. She gasped.

The father had pulled out a large knife. He turned it back and forth so that it glinted in the moonlight. She recognized its familiar shape. It was a Bowie knife, which he had hidden somewhere at his side. He stood up holding it. "Thanks for the supplies," the man said. "The two of you best be on your way now."

"But that's all we have," Illyanne pleaded as she stood back up.

"It's more than we've had for three days 'cept for fish and ashy river water." He glared at them both. "Go on now. I don't want to hurt you." He held the knife in one hand and made an underhanded stabbing motion with it. "But I'll kill you if I have to."

For a moment, Illyanne sat still, gaping in disbelief. Oscar took hold of her arm and pulled her away. They walked briskly away from the family. Even as they were away from the danger, Illyanne lifted her skirts to run. She panted hard with each step, venting the anger and humiliation that flushed through her.

"Miss Illyanne, walk fast but don't run in the dark," he called after her.

Illyanne looked back and that's when she tripped and fell flat on her face. "Ugh." The taste of carbon crust got in her mouth and she coughed and spit.

There was enough moonlight for Oscar to see her. He came up next to her promptly. "Come on." He helped her to roll over and sit up, then stand.

She felt her eyes and nose water as they resumed a brisk walk together. How Illyanne now wished she had followed what her mother urged, to carry a three-inch knife wrapped in an ankle or midriff sheath. It was what Menominee women did as they traveled about. Primarily for cutting up fish and vegetables for cooking, cut away brush, sometimes it served as a weapon. Drunk, piggish harassing men could appear in town or out in the wilds at any time. Her mother relayed stories of women out alone who had no choice but to protect themselves.

If only Illyanne had such a knife, she could have at least flashed it around and safely backed away *with* their food. Foolish. Stupid. She wished she'd have listened to her mother. Around here the Indian and white wars were long since over. She wanted to assimilate further than her mother had, to be part of the newer more civilized generation.

Back at their boat, Oscar sat down beside her with his hand on his chin. "At least I still have one of the blankets."

Illyanne sat down and clutched her hands around her legs. Oscar set the blanket on her shoulders and sat down across from her. The stars came out and brought on their mystical ease. Soon, they managed to share a laugh at their misery and bad luck.

They sat in silence for a long while. The bleakness of their situation spoke for itself. It was cold and dark. They had one blanket between them. There was nothing to shelter them if it rained. They had nothing to eat. Finally, Oscar offered a thought. "I'd be glad to fix you a fish and river water supper but I don't think we can even make a fire. There's nothin' out here in this barren land." Oscar sighed and rubbed his head. He stayed quiet for a minute. "We could rip out some of the cross bars in the row boat but we have nothing to cook. Can't catch fish in the dark."

Illyanne did not answer. She tried to think what a Menominee might do. Her people, at least her mother's people, had lived here off the land and waters for hundreds of years. She rocked herself, looked at the stars and pondered the problem. How would the Menominee catch fish and cook it in the dark, in a burned landscape with no firewood?

"You know, in the morning, we'll get into Peshtigo," Oscar said. "Let's hope that there will be at least one of those relief wagons there. We may have to go hungry tonight but –."

"No." She flashed her eyes toward him.

"We have nothing, Miss Illyanne."

"Spear fishing," she said. "We'll spear fish in the morning light. The Menominee do it all the time. Tonight, we use rocks to shave down a handle end of one of the oars into a point. The paddle end will still be usable. We'll spear some in the morning and we'll have to use some wood off the boat to make a fire." She felt better just imagining it.

"I still got my folding knife so I can whittle it some," said Oscar. "And I can gut and clean the fish. It won't be as good as you cooking on the ship but Miss Illyanne, my stomach is growling at the thought of it. I'll get started. You sleep."

She fell asleep to the sound of Oscar whittling. She tried to call up a memory of a home scene with Anders and Matthew but it was a blurry sight in her mind. Unable to force a clear image of their faces to come into focus cut her to the heart. She could not shed a tear however, and fell asleep. In the morning, she felt sick from a cold night. Still, she praised Oscar for his work with the oar. She twisted up her skirts and tucked part of it into her waistband, removed her shoes and waded into the river to start in on spearing some fish.

In her sleep, she had wrestled with the idea of making firewood from the boat. She decided that was not a very good idea. The boat would be unstable and probably sink. They were likely going to have to eat raw fish in the morning. Although bears ate fresh raw fish, Illyanne was not looking forward to it. Just thinking of it, made her nauseous. What would Anders do in this situation? He would probably say something about her plan like, "mighty impractical, Illie. Think harder. Look around to see what you've got to work with."

At least she had brought her little spice bag with her. What might she use to flavor raw fish to make it as palatable as it could be? She had a small bottle of apple cider vinegar. A memory of Beulah talking about a recipe for Ceviche leaped into her head. That was a dish her friend had made in Georgia. Was this the spirits of Anders and Beulah working together, sending her a message about how to survive? One of the guests of Beulah's old master had been an explorer who sailed to South America. He came back with instructions on how to make the dish he had been served there. Beulah made it for a dinner party her master held and she was amazed by it.

Beulah had told Illyanne all about this incredible meal. "Lime juice actually cooks raw fish in a bowl without any fire." She remembered asking Beulah how it worked. She shook her head. "I don' know how, I just know it does. You can add onions and avocadoes, even cut up fruit. You toss it all into the juice, stir it around, let it sit for a while and stir it s'more. Throw in a spice or two. And it's surprisin' how good it is."

Emma had possessed the unbelievable foresight to send Illyanne and Oscar off with a surplus Civil War haversack for help with whatever sort of camping they might have to do. The mess kit worked perfectly for a bowl.

Oscar cleaned the four fish Illyanne speared. He cut up the meat and tossed it into the mess dish. "I don't know about this but I guess we ain't got much choice."

Illyanne poured her few ounces of apple cider vinegar over the fish chunks. That was going to have to make-do as a citrus substitute for limes. She sprinkled some coriander over it, the spice closest to a lemon lime flavoring, as close she was going to get to the original recipe. She stirred it and tipped it from side to side in a motion like panning for gold. She watched it a while, turned the filets over and over and waited. Gradually, she saw the partially translucent meat of the fish transform into a solid white.

She took the first bite as Oscar watched her. He looked very apprehensive, locking his stare on her to get an impression of how it tasted.

She chewed and swallowed. "It's not terrible." She coughed. "It's tart. But not bad." She reached for the mess cup to down some water. "The apple vinegar flavor is strong. It could use a splash of river water. Try it."

"I guess I'm hungry enough to eat a bear. Can't be too bad." He took a mouthful and his eyes went wide.

Illyanne laughed.

He took some more, then ate big bites. "This is all right, Miss Illyanne. You are some kind of cook. I never heard of anything like this before."

"Well, it's my first time making it. It supposed to be lime juice for the sauce but under the circumstances – . I sure wasn't looking forward to eating raw fish."

"Me either. And if we'd have chopped off any more of the wood from the boat for a fire, we'd probably have to swim back to Green Island."

Once their bellies were filled, they needed to sleep. They had paddled up river far enough to stow the boat ashore. Rowing upstream to Peshtigo, against the current, would waste a lot of energy. They would make the remainder of the long trip on foot tomorrow.

19

Thursday October 12, 1871
      Four days after the fire
Peshtigo River bank

OSCAR HAD HIS HAND over her waist when the bright sunlight woke her. Fear rippled through her. Did he misunderstand the simple pleasantries of preparing a meal and eating together? He did seem to have a twinkle in his eye for her several times since they left the island. Oscar was what some might call a big oaf of a sailor, muscular and heavier than most. No telling what his behavior was with saloon women on his travels.

He snored for a while and then fell into a normal breathing pattern. He tugged her more tightly as she lay there still in his grasp. He might well think he could take her for his pleasure. She had heard plenty of Anders' stories of ill-bred, roguish sailors and women. Usually, they drank to excess and then acted like pirates or animals toward barmaids. At least Oscar had not been drinking. Oh, no. After a moment, she realized that made things even worse. He would not be stumbling around. He'd have his full wits about him. And, he was big. Strong. He could grab her easily. She was out here alone. In a burned-out desert. He'd have the wherewithal to act like any sort of brute he chose to.

They were wrapped together in the same blanket, the only one they had left after last night's incident. She had agreed to try to share it as properly as possible under their circumstances. They fell asleep with their backs to each other. But now, she put her hand to her mouth to quiet her growing fear. Her eyes watered. She laid still.

What might she do to help herself? Her thoughts raced. Her head ached. What horror, lying there waiting to become this man's prey. He might beat her. The ravaging would be disgusting. She wouldn't be able to stop herself from fighting back and that might end up causing more injuries. She pictured herself slumped and crying in the next few minutes. Nobody would hear her scream. Nobody would come to her aid. He could even leave her to die there. No one would ever know she hadn't been a casualty of the fire. She made a first move. She tried to wiggle away from him. He was still asleep but he rolled and grunted and his arm cinched her around the hips now.

She felt her eyes moisten again. She froze in place. Perhaps, if she could get away from him slowly. If he tried to rush her after getting up, the spear was not too far out of reach. It could be used as a weapon against him. She would have to kill him or severely injure him to keep him away. What other choice was there?

With her hips, she squirmed sideways the first few inches away from him. He didn't wake. Anders was worlds away, if alive at all. *Help*, she thought, not knowing who she was calling to in her heart.

Oscar muttered something. Dear God, could he be saying her name in his sleep? This was fast becoming a horror upon horror. She began to shiver and took shallow breaths. She had to calm herself. If she jerked away from him abruptly, she could say she felt a snake. No, he wouldn't believe that. Not in this burned landscape. *Please, help*. But, what if she had a bad dream? Yes. She had to try something.

Illyanne screamed, pulled away from Oscar and stood up fast. She flailed her arms all about. She yelled, "Nooo! Get the buckets. Water." She rushed about erratically this way and that. "Anders. Matthew. Help. The barn!"

Oscar bolted upright. "Mrs. Eriksson. Mrs. Eriksson. Wake up." He reached out for her but she backed away with wildness in her eyes. She acted as if she thought he was some kind of demon.

"It's a nightmare. You're all right." He tried to reach out to comfort her but she jumped back from him.

Illyanne pretended to come out her night terror. "Oh, I'm sorry. I don't know what. I, uh – I, uh, whew, I was back at our homestead." She smoothed out her hair and dress, "There was a raging fire. It seemed so real." She folded her arms in front of her torso. She stood far away from Oscar and he seemed to acknowledge that is what she needed. He looked a little afraid of her in the way a person does when they fear another who is deranged.

In the daylight, they began the trek walking to Peshtigo. Illyanne kept a good distance behind him as they hiked. By midday, the sun had climbed directly overhead. Illyanne and Oscar saved a small portion of the apple vinegar fish and they stopped to eat the last of it.

Illyanne stepped down to the river to rinse her hands and splash some water on her face. She removed her shoes and stepped into the river to wash and cool her feet. She saw something bobbing up in the water. The current was carrying it toward her, perhaps two hundred feet upstream. "Mr. Oscar. Come quick. Bring the spear."

He ran down next to her.

She pointed at the thing in the water. "There it is again. Is it some kind of animal or what?"

"Get out of the water." Oscar waded out further in the river and put himself in its path. "You get back." Illyanne scrambled out of the water. Looking back at her he swept his arm, signaling her to get up higher on the river bank. He pulled out and opened the blade of his whittling knife. In another few seconds, he called out to her, "I can see it's a man."

Illyanne looked on, biting her hand, standing up the slope of shoreline.

"He's dead. Stay back, Mrs. Eriksson." As the man floated by, Oscar grabbed hold of the him from the back of his overalls, grunted and lifted him up. He dragged his body to shore and dropped him. He turned him face up. Oscar walked up to where Illyanne was now crouched, observing him from afar. He turned his back on the body and breathed deeper, catching his breath. "You better go down and take a quick look at him to make sure it's not your husband. He's too old to be your son."

She got up and walked down near the body and leaned toward it to get a good look. "I don't know him." She ran back up to the spot where she had been.

"Good for that at least. We're going to have to dig him a grave. I'm going to need your help."

Illyanne did not answer him. She watched Oscar start sweeping away ash about fifteen feet up from the river's edge.

"Get the mess kit. Use the plate as a scoop shovel. And, we'll have to use our hands." He looked back toward the man. "It's gonna be a shallow grave my friend. Best we can do."

Illyanne did what he told her to do. They continued digging for a long spell, fetching and adding mess kit scoops of river water, pouring over the area to dampen the earth.

"That's enough now." Oscar said. "We've certainly been stuck in disastrous circumstances, haven't we? Miss Illyanne, why don't you go down to the water's edge. I'll finish up here."

She walked down. Illyanne observed him from the shore. Oscar dragged the man and rolled him into the grave with little kicks. The body fell in with a thud. Illyanne turned her head and threw up into the river and splashed her face clean again.

Oscar scooped dirt and burned material back in over him with the inside of his foot. "All right. You want to come back up here a minute so we can say a prayer over him?"

Reluctant, she came back up to the heaped disturbance in the soil. "What was he doing in the river days after the fire, anyhow?"

"Dunno. Didn't see any burns on him. Maybe he was starving, got weak, fell in and drowned. Whatever happened, he's gone now." Oscar clasped his hands together and lowered his head.

Illyanne did the same. Some time passed and she looked up. Oscar was still standing there with his head bowed.

Oscar lifted his head. "I figured you'd want to say a prayer and you'd know what to say,"

"Me? I'm not really in a church going way as of late." She flung her arms out. "I've been beaten down by everything, fire, shipwreck, being robbed and separated from my family not knowing it they're even alive." She began to choke up. "Now this. Don't they have to bury men at sea sometimes? Don't you know some regular prayer they say for that?"

"For ocean going sailors, sure. I hear the captain or a chaplain reads something from the good book or there's a special prayer, I guess." Oscar shrugged his shoulders.

"What do you mean, you guess?"

"There's nothing like burial at sea for Great Lakes sailors, Miss Illyanne. He'd just wash up on shore somewhere in the Great Lakes. We can usually get to a port quick if someone dies on board."

Illyanne pressed him, "So, you have no idea what to say?"

He shook his head, no.

"Has that ever happened?

"What?"

"Has someone ever died when you were on board a ship working a sailing run?"

"No Ma'am but I've heard stories."

"Which might be true or might be just more sailor tall tales, right?"

"Yeah."

"All right then," Illyanne huffed. She would try to come up with something to say. Seeing the few survivors and learning what a massive area had burned, death seemed an annoying routine, no longer something profound. "Oh, God, we commit this man to you for the hereafter. Take him into your kingdom. We found him in the river. And, we are doing our Christian duty. We didn't know him but I guess he's our brethren, so we are giving him a proper burial, at least as best we can." Illyanne could not think of anything else to say for the man. He might have been a horrible drinking, gambling, womanizing carouser for all she knew. Or, he might have been a man like Anders, kind and a good father, full of life and energy but now he was just a body from the river. She surprised herself at how little she cared. All the upsets and ordeals of the last few days rendered Illyanne not herself. She just wanted to get this over with. "Bless his soul. Amen. Let's go."

20

O*ctober 12, 1871*
Peshtigo Relief Camp

THEY WALKED THE REMAINDER of the distance to Peshtigo. Oscar took the lead and Illyanne straggled behind. There had been no more suggestive behaviors. She wondered if she had assumed the worst of him unfairly, when she awoke that morning. Maybe it had all been a case of frazzled nerves. Yes, she must have simply been seized with the stress of the situation and not thinking clearly. At least she hadn't called him any names or accused him of anything untoward. Except for the feigned nightmare, which must have seemed real to Oscar, the crisis had happened all in her head. Her embarrassment, thank heavens, was all internal.

Hours later, they first heard the clang of utensils on cooking pots up ahead. Next, the scent of cooking floated over toward them. Perhaps venison stew with vegetables. Soon, a cluster of people and two wagons came into view. People were standing in line and relief workers were scooping up plates of food.

The Peshtigo relief workers set up two cook fires and a third with a big kettle for boiling clothes. Many people had been in the river and had walked into the camp, their pants and skirts covered in ash. The tents looked like canvas Army tents stitched together. The tents formed a half circle around the fires. There were two large dormitory tents with army cots. Between the men and women's tents there was an open-sided kitchen canopy with crude but newly built tables and benches.

A gentleman wearing a full-length cooking apron looked up, seeing Illyanne and Oscar approaching and waved them forward. "Join the line here folks and we'll get you a piping hot meal. We've got a wagon full of blankets, water and clothes. When you've eaten, we'll come around individually and see what other help we can provide you." The cheery tone is the man's voice sounded odd but comforting. "Your fellow citizens have donated most of the aid and our governor's wife honchoed supplies off of trains heading to Chicago. Rerouted them back here.

Oscar and Illyanne responded with a puzzled expressions but they didn't ask what the man meant. Illyanne wanted to explain that Oscar was not her husband but she was so tired, she said nothing. Everyone in line looked worn. They were probably hungry, too and the people accepted mess kits of food silently. They ate with gusto again. An hour went by and they overheard relief workers taking down the names of survivors' known dead. They also made lists of people who wanted small cabins built here to last through the winter.

They sat on camp stools and ate. Afterwards, Illyanne said, "Oscar, you might as well, go and make your way back to Green Island. I'll be fine here staying at the temporary camp for a night or two."

"Are you sure you'll be all right?"

"Yes. They've got tents, cots and food." This relief camp was larger and better staffed than the one in Marinette. "I've got to go on to Sugar Bush and there's no sense in you staying. You let the Schumachers know I'm thankful and I hope to see them sometime. And tell them, sorry about the oar."

"All right Ma'am." He scraped up the last of his stew and handed her his tin. He stood up, tipped his new hat to her and smiled. One of the workers offered to unhitch one of the wagon horses and give him a ride down river where they had left the row boat. Oscar accepted and the two of them mounted up bareback.

"Thank you again," Illyanne said looking up at him sitting on the horse behind the relief rider. "Give Emma my thanks. Tell her I'll write when I get settled again."

She turned back toward the relief wagons and offered to help clean up the dishes. They put her to task on washing dishes. Through the mist of steam rising from a stew, she saw several relief workers. Two tended to pots over the fires and a third worked at the back of the wagon reorganizing supplies. "Pardon me but have any of you relief workers heard anything about people looking for lost family members?"

"Oh, that's about all we do hear from people," the older woman near the wagon said.

"Well, what can you tell folks?" Illyanne asked.

"Not much. There's been some lists put out by newspapers, I guess or the state. They have names of a few hundred who are confirmed as killed in the fire."

Illyanne stopped scrubbing dishes. "Have you got one of those lists here on the wagon?"

"Yes. We've been handing it out to a lot of people to look through. Give me a minute. I've been keeping it in a wood crate in the back of the other wagon."

She returned with a newspaper which had been folded and refolded many times. She handed it to Illyanne, who wiped her hands on the towel tucked into her waistband. She walked off and sat down, bracing herself up against a wagon wheel.

She peeled open the newspaper. It crinkled loudly, brittle from overuse. The front-page story, began listing names which carried over to the inside. Anders and Matthew Eriksson were not on page one. She turned to page two and the long list of names brought tears to her again. There were so many. Her eyes raced down the columns.

Jeremy Stone. Oh, no. He was one of their neighbors, two acres over from their homestead. And, Sarah Stone but nothing of the children. They are out there somewhere, orphans now. Anders and Matthew were not on page two either. She repeated her search just in case.

They were not among the known dead. She sighed and relief surged through her. She bent over and exhaled with emotion. She accidentally crumpled the newspaper. She smoothed it out, re-folded it and brought it back to the relief woman, who was eying her closely.

"Did you find bad news?"

"No. Their names aren't there."

The relief woman touched Illyanne's arm warmly. "I'm so glad for you. We should get updates daily and we'll circulate them but I have to be honest. This destruction has been enormous. I've heard it said, it was especially bad right around Peshtigo. They don't expect to be able to find and identify everyone beyond who's come into camp right here."

Illyanne sniffed but wiped it away.

"I'm sorry, dear. I've had to give this same news to everyone. It's really hard, I know. I'm not saying there's no hope. Good things can happen when you least expect them but you also need to know what might be the worst."

Illyanne only managed a weak-voiced response. "Well, somebody ought to make a list for people who are looking for missing family members. It's common sense. It's the only way families who got separated can find each other. Someone who survived needs to know if somebody's out there looking for them."

Illyanne walked over to the tent and found herself a cot to lie down on and rest. Grief and relief took turns with her thoughts and her guts.

She watched the camp's goings-on. A wagon pulled up, loaded with six empty pine wood coffins for those who might die of their injuries. A relief worker directed the driver toward the back of the tents, where the horses were kept. Her spirit felt so despondent, she could not fight back sleep.

Illyanne woke in her cot when someone jostled her arm and told her, "There's a group that is going to hold a prayer gathering in a few minutes just over there, if you'd like to join us."

She looked up sleepily. "All right, thank you."

"We don't have a priest or preacher but we are going to sing some hymns and say some prayers together, give thanks for survivors, petition for strength in dealing with the effects of the fire."

"I might come over in a little while." She heard the group praying and singing but she felt only numbness.

One in the group started leading the others with the first part of the Hail Mary and the group answered with the second part. It made Illyanne recall saying the rosary with her mother when she was a child.

Her mother used to tell her that it was a very special prayer. As a young girl, Illyanne asked her, "What's so special about it?" She sat on her mother's lap and swung one foot back and forth as she touched the pretty strung beads.

"It brings grace. All prayers bring grace."

"What's that, mama?"

"Well, it's like a special kind of goodness. You can't see it or smell it or taste it."

"Then, how d'you know it's there?"

Illyanne's mother patted her on the chest. "You feel it in your heart. The rosary brings a special goodness because we are asking the mother of Jesus to ask him to help us. He always wants to help her. It's like how you like to help me with cooking or sewing."

"Like when we make bread?"

"Yes, Illie NeeNAH." Her mother tapped her finger on the girl's nose. "That's how it works. And sometimes people feel sad or afraid, they don't say the rosary any more or they forget to do it. But the goodness gets saved up, even from other people saying it. So, when somebody is sick or feeling bad, the goodness can still help them. And, people can ask to send it to other people so they can feel better or get some kind of help they need."

"Like sending a letter?"

"Yes, it's a bit like that, only it gets sent fast." She clapped her hands and a startled little Illyanne. "As quick as a room lights up when you put match to a lantern wick."

"Like magic?" She sprung open both of her little hands and smiled up at her mother.

"Well, yes, almost like magic. The priest at church would call it a mystery. The people who get it don't always know somebody sent it. They just feel better."

Illyanne rallied from the pleasant memory. She got up from her relief camp cot and shuffled over to the group inside her tent. She came closer to hear them praying but remained sitting a few cots away. She followed along with them silently for a few minutes before feeling overwhelmed with fatigue again and returned to her cot.

21

O *ctober 13, 1871*
Five days after the fire
South shore of the Bay of Green Bay

ANDERS AND MATTHEW were up and walking again as soon as the sun came up. Traveling along the shoreline provided a sense of normalcy. The sound of the gentle shoreline splashes felt refreshing. The sight of distant ships in the bay and birds flying declared that civilization survived the fire and they were headed toward it.

Soon, they saw boats on the water's edge up ahead. Rowboats, people and a robust cook fire going with a kettle of something that smelled good. The ground changed over to a mixture of dirt, sand, tufts of grass and small rocks. There was brush in the near distance and gaunt-looking but living trees. As they approached this surprising and pleasant scene, the people shouted greetings from a distance and waved them forward.

"Friends, come and have some bear stew with us." Three men with three small boats on the beach stood around. They wore outdoorsmen gear, heavy boots, coats and caps.

Another man, a woman and a child of about ten sat on the ground eating out of bowls. Each nodded their greetings. They looked haggard and Anders figured they were fire survivors.

Anders and Matthew greeted the boatmen and inhaled the scent of the food. "We were at the chapel during the fire. We're heading back to Green Bay," Anders said. They didn't offer their names nor did Anders or Matthew.

Matthew accepted the bowl being passed to him. "Where'd you get bear out here?"

The boaters looked at each other with a peculiar grin. "You might say we found him," one of the boaters said.

The biggest boater laughed. "We shot him. He must have run away from the fire and gotten lost. He wasn't going to make it anyhow. It was a cub without its mother. A stray. We did him a favor. He would've starved to death."

Anders spoke to Matthew in a low whisper so the boaters could not make out his words. "These men have no honor. The Menominee thank the animal who gives its spirit so man can eat."

"They don't exactly give themselves up, Papa."

"The Menominee still respect their loss of their life and take only what is needed."

Matthew conceded the point with a shoulder shrug. He and his father ate in silence while the boatmen told their stories. They were local men, boaters who said they had been rowing out every day along the shore trying to find fire survivors and do whatever they could. They carried food, potatoes, carrots and blankets. They said they could ferry people to Green Bay.

Anders and Matthew sat on the ground a distance away from the others.

"This stew is delicious," Anders said.

The other survivors nodded in agreement but otherwise they seemed awfully quiet. Anders eyed them and the boaters and ruminated on the situation. Something didn't seem right. He muttered to Matthew, "the blankets those survivors are wrapped in look just like ours from the chapel relief wagon. War surplus. Same gray-brown color, with the U.S. stamp."

Matthew looked over toward the others. He spoke in a low tone to his father. "You're right. They must have gotten them from the relief supplies." He lifted his head and called over to the boatmen, "So are you fellas working with the relief wagon folks? We had one visit the chapel when we were there."

They seemed to look at each other before one of them replied. "No-no, we're just helping out on our own."

When everyone rested after the meal, one of the boater men offered, "Say if any of you folks wanted us to give you a ride into the city, we'd be glad to oblige." He paused for a few seconds. "O' course there'd be a small matter of compensation to settle." He grinned. "We figured a dollar per person would be fair."

The other survivor man said, "Hey, for most people that's a day's wages! You're taking advantage." He stood up, angry. "I haven't got any money. I ran for my life from the field. Don't even know if my wife made it out."

"Oh, that's fine and well, Mister. We're reasonable men. If you'd agree to pay us when we get there, we've got friends with a place to stay and work off the fee. We've got to cover our expenses, get something for our time and effort and the risks we take keeping clear of the shipping lanes."

The man and the woman were not sitting together. They did not appear to be a family but they bent their heads in close together apparently to discuss the matter.

"We'll let you folks talk it over." The boater walked away, out of earshot and joined his two friends at the water's edge and the boats.

"He's a swindler," Anders whispered to the man, woman and child survivors. "Those two are probably making four or five dollars a day out here. And, he probably got those blankets free. All three of them are out here to make money off of desperate people."

The man replied, "But maybe they'll stay true to their promise for transportation, a place to stay and a day's work. I've got half a dollar."

"Got anything more than that?" Anders asked the man. "I figure they'll get it off you before you reach the city. I think it's a bum steer. I've seen their kind before in sailing towns from here to New York. They might do what they say but I don't trust 'em." Anders looked directly at the woman. "I'd have concerns, Ma'am for what they might have in store for you. My boy, Matthew here and I are walking the rest of the way. We'd be pleased to have you along. Expect we'll get there by tonight."

In spite of Anders' warnings, the man, woman with the child agreed to pay for a boat ride to the city. In a few minutes' time, the boaters emptied the stew pot, rinsed it in the lake and kicked sand over the fire. They all took off in the row boats.

Anders and Matthew thanked them for the meal, waving at all of them as they went. "My stars, Papa. You think those men are real fraudsters? They seemed so friendly at first."

"That's their game. That's how they get the fish hook in, son. Their kind's been around ever since men took to the sea – in every port 'round the world, a young dumb sailor gets hooked." He sighed. "It still amazes me how bad people can win you over at first to thinking they're neighborly and helpful."

"Yeah, that is strange. Papa, how'd you get so wise?"

"I've been suckered a time or two by swindlers in seaside pubs and establishments." He shot Matthew a stern look. "And, I've got nothin' more to say on that, son, so don't ask."

Anders and Matthew continued their walk to Green Bay. On ground untouched by the fire, they could see the outline of where the fire had been. It looked like a driving wind blew the fire east and spared the sliver of land along the shore, leading toward Green

Bay. It was now the morning of the thirteenth. Illie's ship was due in tomorrow at Peshtigo.

"Let's get to the docks and try to get aboard any kind of ship heading out. If it doesn't pull into Peshtigo, if we have to, we can jump ship and swim ashore."

On the trek, they saw ships, mostly steamers, leaving and arriving at the port of Green Bay as they walked the shoreline. By the time they walked along the railroad bridge that crossed the Fox River it was dark out. They made their way onto the docks, so first thing the next morning they hoped to find a dock worker who could help them get on a ship to Peshtigo. They slept at the docks in Green Bay city, crouched up against a warehouse wall as a windbreaker. With that and their relief blankets, they beat back the chill of the night. In this spot, Anders felt sure they'd encounter workers come sunup.

22

FRIDAY, OCTOBER 13, 1871
  Five days after the fire
  Peshtigo Relief Camp

ILLYANNE WALKED OVER to the relief camp's cooking fires. She had a pleasant chat with the cook, one Jennifer Fielding. Within minutes, Illyanne was helping her. She was cooking again. The fate of Anders and Matthew remained unknown but the chore of cooking for others cut through the haze of sadness for a while.

She would have another day's rest here and then would try to go on, walk around what remained of Peshtigo and find someone to take her to Sugar Bush. She rested on her cot several times throughout the day. Sometimes, tiredness compelled her to pass hours in mindless, listless inactivity. She thought of the war veterans at the Boarding House told stories of men who had succumbed to bad nerves from being in battle.

Those men spent long parts of their days resting to recover. Illyanne thought the aftereffects of a terrible experience were at least a little bit like battle with all the death and destruction. She had seen women who experienced something similar for a long time after a birth. The best thing was for them to rest as much as possible, even for weeks, if family members could take up the chores. She accepted all the extra daytime sleeping.

Another family had arrived to the relief camp during her nap. It was a mother, a middle childhood boy and a girl who looked about six. They were cold and ragged. Illyanne overheard her telling a relief worker her story. The woman wrapped herself and her children in relief blankets. "We ran for the river. My husband went back to the barn to let the animals loose." The woman broke down and she pulled her children close. She took a moment to recover and she could barely continue. "The barn went up like a dry grass fire. He succumbed." She sniffed. "We stayed in the water most of the night."

Illyanne watched the relief worker trying to comfort her. "I'm so sorry." She embraced her slightly. "Come with me. We'll have you sit down here and we'll get you all some food. Then, we'll have clothes and cots for you."

Later, Illyanne overheard the relief worker telling the woman how sorry she was for her troubles. "I been through hard times, too. Lost a child to the fever and a husband who got crushed to death in a railroad accident." The woman paused and rocked herself sitting on a cot across from the relief worker. "All I can tell you is, if you got faith, hang on tight. It'll carry you through the sadness, anger and desperation. I promise you the sun will shine again."

The widow woman shook her head as if to say no.

"I know you can't believe it now but there will come a time when all this will become past drudgery. And it ends up making you a better person, more steadfast, more helpful to others. If you're a woman of faith, it will be strengthened." The relief worker lifted the blanket and pulled it over the woman. "You get some rest now."

The relief worker was a great curiosity. She had overcome two incredible losses. Illyanne would try to get a conversation with her sometime. Perhaps tomorrow. What she overheard her telling the widow was the first hopeful thing she'd heard since the fire. Illyanne had to cling to hope. But, it felt shaky.

She dreamt of fire and others woke her several times during the night. A boy woke up crying from a nightmare. A relief worker came to comfort him. "A big fire was gonna get me." She stroked his back and whispered to him that the fire was gone and his parents were next to him. Later, Illyanne heard someone weeping in their cot. She did not think of going over to reassure them but she realized her old self, before the fire, might have done so. She rolled over and pulled her blanket over her head with her back toward the sounds. They must have fallen back asleep because she slept until she heard the clink of dishes.

She watched the people eating in the adjacent open air mess tent. All the survivors seemed to move about the camp slowly. They ate breakfast with their heads down, conversing little with each other at the camp tables, like a dreary veil covered their lives. It made her senses feel numb too.

Then, Illyanne heard a familiar voice, coming from the far end of tent kitchen and open-air dining area. She felt a spark of joy. He was visiting, asking people how they were, whether he needed to assist with any new burials. It was Father Pernin, her pastor from the Peshtigo and Marinette Catholic churches. Illyanne got up from her cot and rushed next door. The sight of him instantly lifted her spirits. Someone she knew, lived in spite of the charred surroundings.

Father Pernin was speaking to two tables of children but looked up to see Illyanne. He nodded a greeting toward her. After a few minutes, he finished up with the children and made his way over to her.

"Oh Father, I'm so glad to see you've survived. God bless you." She chided herself internally for being insincere, mentioning God when she had only a dulled belief. She extended her hands and they greeted each other with warm handshakes. She suppressed the desire to hug a priest.

"Mrs. Eriksson, so good to see you."

"Someone said you were in Peshtigo during the fire, Father."

"Yes, yes. It was quite something." He dropped his head. He looked drawn and fatigued. "I got to the river with many others. Even the air was on fire. Horses, cattle, pigs on the land and in the water were screaming. Cut logs from the logging camps were still floating down river right into people and animals. It was terrible." He shook his head, stopping himself from going into any more detail about the horrors of the fire.

He raised an index finger and smiled. "But I managed to carry the church tabernacle with me into the water to save it from the fire." He took her hand and led her over to sit down at one of the dining tables. "I lost it but two men found it days later, completely clean and untouched by water or ash. Truly a miracle. I'm so thankful."

Illyanne wanted to avoid talking to him about her diminishing faith. "I wish I could cook you a grand supper, Father and bring you some rest."

He grinned. "I will rest when I can. I'm trying to keep up praying with the destitute, performing Last Rites and prayers over the departed. I've lost count." He sighed. "I have only this small bible from the relief people." He lifted it from his side and patted it. "The survivors need so much spiritual comfort." He shook his head and sighed. "This may sound like strange thing to say, Mrs. Eriksson, but, it's a wonderful time to be a priest."

Illyanne made a confused expression and Father Pernin laughed. "I'm sorry, I've been so caught up in my own affairs. Where are my manners? Tell me. How did you all fare at your homestead. Out near Sugar Bush, isn't it?"

"Yes. I don't know whether the fire reached out there. I'm trying to find out."

Father Pernin responded with quizzical look. "I don't understand."

"I wasn't home. I was filling in, aboard the schooner, Henry B. Jones as a cook. Anders is healing up a broken arm and he stayed home with Matthew. We sailed the night of the fire. We shipwrecked on the lighthouse island, Green Island. I stayed a few nights with the Schumachers."

"Ah, yes. They attend in Marinette." He nodded. "Lovely people. Large family."

"And I've only now come ashore to search for my family." Her voice cracked and she trembled. "I'm in near despair, Father." She had a lump in her throat. "I only have hope left." She sniffed. "Only hope that they may have survived." She dropped to her knees from the bench she had been sitting on next to him. "I saw the fire from the ship's deck." She looked up at him with water-filled eyes. "I've never seen or heard of anything like that pillar of fire."

He touched her at the elbow and motioned for her get up and sit again.

"All I hear is that everything, absolutely everything has burned. The Boarding House – I worked there. The saw mill and factory burned down."

"Yes, it's true, I'm afraid." He sighed. "Peshtigo is no more. Seventy bodies were found at the Boarding House area." He paused and swallowed. "You must pray. Daily and fervently. The fire spread very far. I don't know about Sugar Bush. The Marinette newspaperman said there was another large terrible fire the same day in Chicago. And, a third one on the thumb of Michigan. Can you imagine that? Three huge fires at the same time?" He shook his head." Anyhow, I have to be going. There are families to minister to. Do not lose hope. I will keep you and your family in my prayers."

"Wait Father." She tugged at his arm and gestured for him to sit back down. "Stay a minute longer, please. You must tell me what you've seen. What survivors are saying,"

"Mrs. Eriksson, it's too dark." He hung his head and shook it back and forth. "Look around. You can see the devastation for yourself, smell the burnt remains everywhere. I don't need to – ."

"But you were there. I want to know. I have to be prepared for the worst as I go searching." She wiped back tears again. "I don't know yet whether Anders and Matthew got away. They aren't here and aren't on the list of the dead. Please tell me how it was."

Father Pernin sat down again. "All right." He paused, leaned forward with his elbows resting on his legs. He spoke without looking at her directly. "I can't tell you all I've seen and heard or I wouldn't make it through the rest of the day." He managed a fleeting uncomfortable smile. "Before it started there was a strange quiet. Birds flitting all over. Poor creatures. Didn't know which way to go. I buried some personal items for safe keeping. I called out to others to do the same. Most of them did not take heed and were found later. Couldn't get my dog to come out from under the bed. Found him burned to death, afterward." He sighed. "The distant thundering fire came fast, so loud I had to shout at people to take cover. When the circling, whipping wind and dust came, some people stood still in the street, praying, looking up, just struck dumb. I pulled three people into the river with me.

"Many people died, Mrs. Eriksson. Running away, jumping into wells, digging themselves into the dirt and jumping into the river. Some drowned, too exhausted to continue treading water for hours longer." He paused for a while, holding back his own emotion. He looked up briefly. "Are you sure you want to hear these horrors?"

Illyanne nodded. "Yes. Tell me. Please, Father."

"The air was noxious to breathe. It stung my eyes. I was blinded for two whole days after it all. I've seen people at the river bank reduced to charred skeletons. Unfortunate souls. Human beings shrunk down to a third of their natural size." He choked up for a moment and kneaded his hands. "The fire consumed every drop of moisture in their bodies." He closed his eyes for a moment. "Some families could not even lift their loved ones into a coffin or into the ground because the bodies crumbled into cinders. God help them, in one family, the parents even took their own lives and their children's lives to spare themselves from the fire."

Illyanne could not break her gaze from him. She noticed deeper furrows in his face than she had seen before.

"The heat was like a furnace. It melted sand at the river's edge. Turned it to glass. I went into the river with many others and waited it out. The grumble of the ravenous flames on shore went on and on all night. It mixed with people's screams and the cries and grunts of animals. Pitiful beasts. Cattle, pigs, chickens trying to stay alive in the churning waters. Fire surrounded us and globs of it fell out of the sky. Logs rolled around the whole time from up river. It was hellish. And draining."

He slapped his thighs and sat back to an upright position. "Well, at least now I can offer people their faith again."

Illyanne cocked her head at him. "What do you mean, again?"

"Oh, well for years and years I've been preaching for people not to neglect their faith, not to let all the business success around Peshtigo take over their lives. Lumber, railroads, shipping, homesteading. The numbers at Sunday Mass just kept getting smaller and smaller." He caught her eyes again. "You probably know many did not heed that word. There was much drinking, gambling and carousing with ladies of the night."

Illyanne flashed a shocked look toward him.

"Oh, yes. I knew about all of these things," he said. "One might say, people began worshipping their golden calves – land, money, industry, building legacies. Many working their land were too tired to come to church on Sunday." He shrugged his shoulders. "They all made their faith a secondary concern, and failed to teach their children. "The ferociousness of this fire has humbled us all." He paused with an odd smile on his face. "And now, people need God again."

Illyanne felt a surge of guilt. She and Anders had been so busy for years working to build their home, clear land, plant and reap the fields, getting the homestead settled. But they did teach Matthew and came to town to attended Mass – most of the time. They were faithful, even if she now had only remnants of spiritual feeling.

Illyanne grabbed the Father's sleeve as he stood to leave. "Oh Father, you don't think this was all God's punishment, do you? Killing people? Destroying everything?" Her eyes flared. "It's been eating at me. I mean the bible's pillar of fire was supposed to be God's protection, so . . . what can it mean?"

"Mrs. Ericksson, we cannot know God's mind in relation to some natural disaster." He hesitated for what seemed a long time.

Illyanne wasn't sure if he was feeling overcome with emotion. She kept her eyes fixed on him, waiting, trying to be compassionate for what he had endured. But she was dying for an answer.

"It's true that there is destructive fire in scripture." He looked up, searching his memory for details. "Elijah. Sodom and Gomorrah." Father Pernin wrinkled up the space between his eyebrows and shook his head, no. "But the burning bush, the pillar of fire for the Israelites, the tongues of fire at Pentecost are all different." He shook his head. "Fire can be a blessing or a punishment." He sighed and paused a moment. "You really mustn't worry yourself about this. There are so many other things to be mindful of now."

He saw the concern in her face. He grasped her hand, laid his over her and patted it. "We can only return to the faith we do know, help each other and seek comfort from our Heavenly Father, carry our crosses." He let go and sighed. "I've stayed too long and really must go." "You've helped me today Mrs. Eriksson."

"Me? I can't imagine. How?"

"You might say you've been my priest for a few minutes." He made a little laugh. "I feel renewed at having unburdened myself to you. God bless you and your loved ones. I will pray that you find your family in good health." He made the sign of the cross over her.

Illyanne in turn, crossed herself. Making that little motion had some effect. She recalled it represented a confession of faith, a baptismal renewal and a defense against the devil. Admittedly, she felt a small boost of hopefulness.

23

Saturday-Sunday, October 14-15, 1871
    Six & seven days after the fire
City of Green Bay

ANDERS HEARD VOICES on the Green Bay dock in the gray morning light and he nudged Matthew. He groaned, raising himself up stretching from sleeping against the sidewall of the dock warehouse. Luckily, the building had cut the wind and the relief blankets proved to be life savers. "They're here, Matthew. Get up. You wait here and I'll go talk to them."

Matthew watched from afar as his father walked over to some dock workers and spoke with the dock men. They pointed him further down the dock. Matthew could see the masts of several docked ships in the dawn mist. Anders walked further away and Matthew could only faintly see him talk to a cluster of other workmen in loose trousers and pullover sweaters.

In a few minutes, Anders returned. He looked upset and didn't say anything. He pressed his back up against the building and slid down to a sitting position against the warehouse wall.

"What happened? What did they say?" Matthew asked.

"I gotta think." Anders breathed hard and stared straight ahead. "They laughed at the idea of jumping aboard a ship and getting off at the Peshtigo dock. Said we'd drown for sure in the water. It'd be at least a five-mile swim to land. If we didn't drown first, we'd freeze to death. And anyhow, there's no ships going into or coming out of Peshtigo."

Matthew stayed quiet for a moment, trying to understand their situation. "What'll we do now, then?"

"I don't know. Let me think. A wretched sensation seeped through Anders, a doom of uncertainty. For the first time, he realized his secret travel might keep Illyanne from finding him and Matthew again. Dear Lady of Champion, lead me home to Illyanne. And show her the way back to us.

Anders and Matthew remained bewildered, watching the dock workers. The men stood out there on the open dock, milling about, waiting for their daily assignments, in gaggles of four or five, chatting and laughing, men with homes and jobs. The bosses who carried ledger books with them went back and forth between the groups. One of them was the boss Anders had spoken to earlier. The man pointed toward Anders, then spoke to the other boss. They both turned and looked at Anders and Matthew.

"Hey, Papa, that man's coming back our way."

Anders got up and walked out to meet him again. In moment, he was heading toward Matthew with a big smile and quickened pace motioning to come forward. "Let's go."

"We've got a job for the next few days. The man felt bad for us being from the Peshtigo area and he's short a man today and two tomorrow and maybe a third day after that. He'll give us two dollars a day to work as unloaders. He told me where we can get a quick breakfast and then we head back here to work. They start work in an hour." Anders rolled up his blanket and pointed at Matthew to do the same. "Later, he'll tell us where we can bunk tonight too. That'll give us time to figure out what to do next."

"What about mother?"

"Will her ship come in here?" Matthew's eyes watered.

Anders felt the burden of their situation. "Don't know. Keep her in your thoughts and prayers today." He went silent for a moment, choking up and blinking back tears. "We'll keep asking around. One thing's for sure, she won't be docking in Peshtigo." He re-tied his shoes and tucked in his shirt. "The way the man put it, there's nothing there but burned down buildings and ashes." He sighed. "Let's go find something to eat."

Matthew stood up and grabbed his valise. He took a moment to close his eyes. A quick intention flitted through his mind for God to bring his mother back to them and for Mother Mary to intercede too. Please help us find my mother again. And, if it's all right, please, Chepi, too.

The flapjacks with maple syrup and sausages held them for the long day of hard labor, moving dollies and handcarts of sacks and crates. They shoulder-carried boards of lumber right off train cars alongside the dock that must have been sitting there, maybe the last train to leave the Peshtigo Northwoods before the fire.

By the end of the first day, exhaustion set in hard. It was still a few blocks walk to the bunk house. They passed several pubs already buzzing with day workers drinking. Anders thought it was like hearing his own past. He detected the German and Swedish accents among them. They were happy men, with jobs, with money in their pockets and men who had a place to sleep for the night.

At the bunk house, they stood in line and ate the stew and biscuits with the other men. Little conversation filled the room where men sat at tables with crude benches. Lying down for the night in a room jammed with eight bunk beds, Anders said, "Wish your mother well wherever she may be tomorrow at the arrival time."

"Who knows, Papa. Her ship might pull into the port of Green Bay and dock right in front of us. I'm hoping for that."

The two of them slept as if one of those big steamer ships had plowed right over and flattened both of them. The cramped quarters of sixteen men to a room abounding with snores, belches and an abundance of bad smells didn't even bother them.

Before dawn, the bunk house proprietor woke up all of the thirty-two residents who's stayed the night and provided them a hefty breakfast. Most of the men worked the docks and it was part of his business to see that the men got off to work on time.

Going through the breakfast line, Anders saw the woman from the beach cooking in the back of the serving line. "Hello, Miss." He waved and she looked over toward him. "Good to see things worked out all right for you."

She forced a smile and a nod. "I should have listened to you. I've got to work through the week but I guess it's all working out all right."

Neither Anders or Matthew had an opportunity to speak to her again as the staff hurried the men through breakfast and shooed them out the door.

24

Saturday, October 14, 1871
Six days after the fire
Peshtigo Relief Camp

THE NEED TO FIND ANDERS and Matthew felt even more pressing after Illyanne's talk with the Father Pernin. The fire in Peshtigo had been worse than she imagined. She was sure now that something that intense would have reached their homestead in Sugar Bush, just five miles outside of town. Still, she had nothing else in the world to do but to try to find them, even if the fire had overcome them.

Today, the Henry B. Jones was due back in port in Peshtigo. There was the smallest of chances that somehow Anders and Matthew might make their way to the scheduled time and meeting place. Going down to where the dock had been, just to be certain, would be a long trek there and back, perhaps three miles or more. She had to try.

Illyanne convinced herself that it wasn't really going to be stealing a horse, just borrowing it. The relief workers had gathered their horses far back behind the kitchen tent, about two hundred feet, so as to minimize any noise or smell from them.

In the faint light of the morning of October fourteenth, Illyanne walked slowly and gently to the cluster of horses. One of them whinnied and Illyanne stood still for a long time, waiting to see if one of the relief volunteers would be coming to see what the trouble was. No one came after a full minute.

She untied one and after getting far enough away walking with it so no one could hear the horse's movements, she jumped on it bareback. She brought with her a small wrap of her cornbread dish and tucked it beneath her blouse, in case any desperate wandering people might try to steal from her. She found a military canteen at the supply wagon and carried some water with her. She would wait where the dock had been until midday and if there was no sign of Anders and Matthew, she'd make her way back.

She followed the river as her guide. The quiet sloshing of the water along the river's edge was the only sound. There were no trees, no insects, squirrels or rodents about. Even the birds had not returned since the fire. The landscape remained black and charred though light winds blew the grit around like sand. It laid in swirls here and there like the kind of ice crystal snow that sometimes fell in early winter, what everyone called a dusting.

It took less than an hour for her to reach the mouth of the Peshtigo River where it emptied into the bay of Green Bay. For a while, it was relaxing waiting there. It was a crisp but sunny October day. She tried to sleep lightly with her face in the sun but was unable to do so. She sat for a while, then went up the ridge of the river bank and walked along the river shore.

Soon, the unnatural oddity of being surrounded by nothing but the burned environment unnerved her. There were no people, no ships, no rooftops in the distance. The dock and warehouse had burned down. She could make out a blurry far away image which she thought was the Green Island lighthouse but here on shore, she was alone. There was not even grass or brush for the horse to nibble on. Illyanne started to feel chilled and nervous. She got up and paced.

She stroked the horse and spoke to him. "I'm glad you are here with me. No one would help me but your spirit was willing." She laid the side of her head just down from his withers and continued to pet the horse. "I am thankful."

There with the remnants of Peshtigo behind her. Looking out into open water, she wondered what happened to the other ships. Surely, a number that had offloaded their cargo somewhere. There would have been a number who should have returned with empty cargo holds in the last few days. Maybe they had sailed on to the port of Green Bay. Maybe that's where Anders and Matthew had gone hoping to meet her. If they survived the fire, today they would learn that the Henry B. Jones did not come back. And, they would not know where she or her ship was. They might even wonder if she was alive. This disaster created a confounding snarl of what-ifs for Illyanne. Fortunately, being out in the fresh air helped her from falling into another despair.

After a brief time, the horse turned its head and nipped at Illyanne's torso.

She giggled. "All right, my friend." Illyanne hugged the horse's head but it jerked free of her. "Oh, you're like Matthew, aren't you? When he started to get bigger, he didn't want his mahsa hugging him all the time, either."

She wished Oscar was with her. It had been different having a companion. There had been a strange primal bonding between them. He turned out not to be such a bad sort. She felt sure now that she had misread him in her earlier emotional state. When the sun reached the position of approaching noon, she felt she had made a sufficient effort. Several hours had passed without seeing any nautical activity.

She spoke to the horse again. "Does your spirit know that Anders and Matthew will not come?" She walked around to put herself face to face with the horse and stroked his nose and neck. "Is this how you tell me by this unsettled feeling? Hmm? I think so."

She rode him back to the relief camp, figuring someone might notice and take her to task if she stayed away longer than a half day. She tied the horse up alongside the others and gave it water and fed it handfuls of oats. She started walking back stepping very lightly so as not to be heard.

"Oh, there you are." Jennifer Fielding, darted out in front of her.

Illyanne got startled and flushed while trying to regain her breath.

"I've been looking for you all morning."

"Oh, I've been out getting some air, trying to think."

Jennifer fluttered with excitement. She grabbed her by the hand and started pulling her along. "I've got a driver for you tomorrow after all. He'll take you to Sugar Bush early and bring you back. Come, let me introduce you." She led Illyanne around the tents until she finally came upon the man, ready to introduce them to one another.

It was all arranged. After breakfast in the camp, the driver, Mr. Tom Cooper would take her to Sugar Bush and back. "There's just one catch."

Illyanne stopped and looked at her, "What ever could it be?"

"You have to agree to help me with breakfast," Mrs. Fielding said with a big smile. "It would be wonderful if you could come up with something different. I'm not getting to be any better of a cook and I think folks would appreciate something new and really good." She let her arms fly open. "You have free reign over the supplies."

"It will be my pleasure." Illyanne made a mock bow and curtsey.

"Excellent. First things first then." She led her to meet the driver and speak with him briefly about the ride the next morning.

"Now, let's go take a look at what you've got so I can plan something," Illyanne said.

Illyanne followed Jennifer to a supply wagon. Jenniefer lifted the tarp and Illyanne cooed over the stockpile of food and blankets.

"All thanks to Mrs. Fairchild, the governor's wife."

Illyanne listened as Jennifer chattered on and scanned the provisions. There were drug good ingredients, flapjack mixture, dozens of eggs, dried fruits, fresh apples, spices, bread, a ten-gallon milk can."

"My gosh, there's plenty here for me to make two different things for breakfast. "I think I know what I'm going to cook up." she told Jennifer Fielding. Flapjacks and perhaps an egg quiche pie, in honor of Father Pernin and thanking him for his taking time to talk with her. She was going to have a nice time preparing a stick-to-the-ribs breakfast for the relief workers and fire survivors.

Illyanne went back to her cot to rest. She overheard one of the relief workers reading a newspaper column aloud to one of the other workers in the dining tent.

"'Northeastern Wisconsinites have to look far back in time, to Pompeii's volcanic eruption in 79 A.D., to find a place that fared worse at the raging, fiery hand of nature. That ancient Roman city lost two thousand when fire rained down on its residents, burying them in volcanic ash. The Peshtigo Fire death count will likely come close to that. Devastation will linger here for decades after survivors rebuild. The truth is the destruction is so extensive – to homesteads, fields, animals and industry – that some people will likely never find the remains of their loved ones or ever learn of their last moments.'"

The newspaper crinkled as the woman abruptly let it drop in her lap. She looked at the other worker to whom she was reading. "I can't imagine there'd be any hope if somebody hasn't found their other family members after a whole week."

Overhearing that put her in bad humor. The camp worker resumed reading but Illyanne stopped listening. However, she fixed in her mind that she had until October sixteenth,a week after the fire to find Anders and Matthew. But now, she needed to walk. She had not yet walked Peshtigo's roads.

Illyanne walked alone. The roadway still crunched with each of her steps. With horses and modest wagon traffic, it had begun to look like a roadway again. It was enough for Illyanne to get her bearings and remember where buildings had been. It was strange to look out at a place burned completely to the ground and only have an overlay visual memory of where things had been.

She came to an intersection looking for the old Boarding House remains. No, this rubble isn't it. It must be the next block over. She wanted to see the place where she had once worked as a cook, where she really had the joy of experimenting with so many different foods, recipes, spices, cooking methods. It was also the place where she had developed a good friendship. It was Beulah who had taught her so much, who loved cooking as she did. She admired Beulah so much for her resiliency. Born into slavery in Georgia, she came north and flourished. Beulah lived at the Boarding House and there was every reason to assume the fire took her life right here. It was Beulah with whom she laughed outside of the homestead. Together, they breathed a kind of fellowship in the love and language, smells and tastes of cooking.

She was like an older sister. She didn't bother too much about her slave past. "What's past is gone and done with. Gotta live for the future." Illyanne told Beulah she always wanted to leave the impression with people that she'd be no trouble. She knew well enough that some settlers looked down on Indians and had very disagreeable and occasionally even violent confrontations with them. She learned from her not to worry what others thought about her Menominee heritage. "It just is," Beulah told her one day. "You takes what you can from your past. You cherish it and use it as best you can. An' you goes on living in whatever way you do. You ain't all white and you aint' all Injun neither. Ain't nothin' more to it than that."

Finally, Illyanne found the location. The Peshtigo Boarding House took up a whole city block. There they were, burned but the still unmistakable large outlines. Toward the far end, where the kitchen and dining room had been, there were the misshapen lumps, the remains of the big iron ovens which had melted in the blaze. The wood building burned down to nothing all around them. It was clear the burial teams had come in here and shoveled up what human remains they could find. They probably wouldn't have all the names. So many of them were new immigrants, single men, who had come here for jobs. A maximum capacity, the building could house two hundred.

Illyanne stood still and closed her eyes, standing adjacent to the ash and lumps of what had been the bustling Peshtigo Boarding House. She could almost hear the dishes clanking, feel the heat of the stoves. No one was around so she felt free to speak out loud, though in a low tone. Her dear friend must have died here. The relief workers had said it was almost a sure thing that anyone who survived at least stopped into the relief camp for something to eat, medicine and clothes and blankets. Nobody had seen a black woman in her thirties. "I'm so sorry, Beulah. You were a fantastic cook. You taught me a lot. I had great times with you. I will think of you every time I make bourbon pork chops." She teared up and sputtered a laugh. "And I'll always remember the way you bargained with the bartender to get some other liquor for your recipes. We had happy times, didn't we?"

She sniffled a little and began to walk the perimeter of the remains of what had been the large wood structure. "You should have been able to live, get a little house and live your life here. I know you always said, there ain't no man for you 'round here but I think eventually, there would have been. Beulah, you deserved so much better in life." She fell quiet and numb.

The fire dumped so much death and disaster on Illyanne and others. That hollowed-out feeling she had most of the time was just about the only feeling she had these days. She hoped that Beulah would have collapsed from the smoke so that she didn't have to suffer the horror of the fire itself – or, good gracious – have endured the building falling down on top of her. "Whatever happened, my friend, that pain is all gone, now. You're at peace. I wish you were here to talk to me about keeping my faith strong, because I'm in a weak way right now, a very weak way."

Illyanne did not know any Menominee prayer or ritual to do for Beulah but she wished she did. Her mother's distancing herself and her daughter from tribal life had its consequences in the settler's world. She recalled an honor ceremonial practice which she could perform only in her mind. Illyanne imagined Beulah's spirit smiling at her while she wafted the smoke of burning sage toward her with an eagle feather. Illyanne had heard some Indians used this practice but she didn't recall whether Menominee did that or whether it was a proper thing to do for the dead. It might have been Ojibwe, Potawatomie, Winnebago, Oneida or from one of the other tribes who'd live near Green Bay over the years. But this thought would be her Christian prayer for her friend. If the idea was not traditionally correct, God and Beulah's soul would know her true intent and appreciate it.

"I hope God blesses you and that we'll meet again someday." She made a cursory sign of the cross, turned away and walked on.

25

O*ctober 16, 1871*
Monday

DOCK WORK PROVED TO be strenuous. Anders had to remind himself that they were in their second and last day of working. It was the sixteenth already, eight days since the fire. Train loads of lumber had arrived in Green Bay and been sitting idle for more than a week. After the regular workers offloaded lumber to the deck, Anders and Matthew loaded it onto a steamship. Two days of heavy work manifested in their bodies as sore muscles all over, especially Anders' arm. It was getting better. He had stopped using a splint. Two long socks with the feet cut off, pulled up the arm and over the elbow served as support braces but his arm still throbbed with hard work. Anders and Matthew both moved more slowly, spoke less on breaks and each of them complained of strained and aching backs, arms and legs.

"All right, Anders, you and your boy can knock off a little early," the dock boss said. Here's your pay. It's the least I can do for you. That's for the both of you." He handed Anders six bills and a little extra.

"Thanks," Anders said. "We're not sure what where we'll go or what we'll do now. Got any ideas, boss?"

"Well, you get a last night at the bunk house." He pinched his ledger book under his arm. "Sorry about Peshtigo and your situation.

There's been folks wandering into town for days, from out that way, looking for work. I wish you the best. If you want to stick around and have a steady job, c'mon back and find me." He started walking away but turned around promptly. He pointed an index finger toward Anders. "Don't forget to check with the Lumber Room about your wife's schooner. If there's any kind of transport going to the Peshtigo or Sugar Bush area, they'll know about it." He raised a hand to wave. "Good luck to you."

Anders and Matthew ate at one of the pubs they'd seen the night before and treated themselves to steak, potatoes and bread. They walked back to the bunk house. Anders told the desk manager, "We'll be leaving tomorrow but we aren't going back to work so we'll sleep in. Don't wake us for breakfast."

"We're not running a hotel here. Everybody gets rousted for breakfast at the same time." The man behind the check-in desk might have been a former dock worker. "You don't want to eat, that's your business. But everybody's out the door by eight."

Anders and Matthew tensed at the old curmudgeon's words.

"I can push it to eight thirty but that's it. Then, out you go."

26

BEFORE DAWN, ILLYANNE was preparing breakfast at the camp cook fires. In the dark, she had dressed beside her cot and tip-toed outside the tent, so as not to wake the other women and children and the few men who formed only two reunited families. She would get to Sugar Bush today. Home. Warmth spread through her like the heat from a shot of homestead brandy. She might find Anders and Matthew alive. Seeing so much death in the last few days, she had come to terms with it. If they were dead, she only hoped she'd find them so she could bury them properly on their land.

She whipped up a new breakfast concoction with cornmeal, sausage, bread, apples and eggs. She pan-fried sausage in pinches and tossed in the apple cubes. The smells mingled wonderfully but two teaspoons of cinnamon and a dribble of vanilla finished it off. She combined the meat, fruit and cornmeal and it baked to a nice cake over the fire in a Dutch oven. While that cooked, she poured and fried up flapjacks with blueberries and raspberries in the mix.

Jennifer came by just in time for her to go get ready for her ride to the homestead. She had a blanket around her shoulders. "I see you are really in your element here."

Illyanne looked up from her cutting board. "You know, that's really true. When I'm cooking, it really is my little joy on earth." Illyanne handed her the flour sack pot holders, her apron and a serving spoon. "It's all yours. The flapjacks here with a towel over them to keep them warm. Syrup's on the table. Pull the casserole off the fire in another five minutes. I'm off to Sugar Bush." As Illyanne walked away, she could see the smells of her cooking had already rousted a few hungry ones forming a line for breakfast.

The days had flown past and it was already October the fifteenth, a full week since the fire. On the surface, Illyanne felt a surge of cheerfulness at finally being able to go home. A storm of doom roiled beneath however, making her stomach feel queasy. She worried at what she might find. No one had been able to tell for certain her whether the fire reached as far as Sugar Bush. Maybe there was a chance the homestead had not burned down.

Tom Cooper stepped down to help greet her. "Good morning, Mrs. Eriksson." He tipped his hat to her. "I haven't been out to Sugar Bush myself so I'm not sure what we will find. It might be good news but you should know, it could be the worst. You've already seen that, having stayed in Peshtigo relief camp a few nights. "

"Mr. Cooper, I understand." She met his eyes and held her gaze for a long time. "But this is a trip I have to make."

"Just want you to steel yourself is all, Ma'am."

Illyanne knew what he was thinking. She might find the charred remains of her beloved husband and son. If she found them dead, the instant wave of grief would slice right through her. "I appreciate your concern but I'm ready."

They traveled in a buckboard wagon. She tossed two relief blankets in the back in case she found them. Thomas Cooper came around the side of the wagon and helped Illyanne step up and get seated on the bench. Illyanne felt comfortable in his presence.

He took his spot next to her and took hold of the reins. He leaned back and pulled up a folded wrap tucked behind the bench seat and handed it to her. "If you'd like a lap blanket."

The wagon was the smaller one, drawn by a single horse. He wended the wagon around streets where relief wagons had now worn a visible path. They passed the remnants of the Peshtigo woodenware factory, another very large structure in the town. The clip-clop of the horse's hooves and the sway and jerky movements of the wagon traveling over rough ground made her weary. Somehow or other, it soothed the harsh reality of the scorched sights.

Numerous shovel marks and footprint disturbances in the black grit along the road, showed where the burial teams had done their work. Among the scorched buildings Illyanne saw a number of bent metal objects.

"What *are* those strange things sticking up here and there?"

"What they used to be is the better question. They used to be the metal hoops for barrels. They made a lot of wood barrels there. This must be where the famed woodenwares factory stood."

"I wouldn't say famous exactly," Illyanne said. "But it did supply many states with wooden pails, broom handles and such. I heard it quite often from the men eating at the Boarding House. They shipped things all the way to Europe." She felt silly for saying this. It was so trivial. What did it matter now? She hoped the driver would understand it was just empty chatter borne of shock and worry. It was only something idle to say as she tried to ease her own discomfort at the alien landscape, knowing people had lost their lives there.

Illyanne forced herself to be quiet. Hearing of the barrel hoops and the sight of the burned land triggered a somber feeling in her. It was eerie, like looking back in time at ruins of some place where a society once lived. Yet, she was from that society.

Soon, they were out of the city's streets and on the country road which she and Anders had taken a thousand times back and forth into own. Once a familiar roadway with farms in view on both sides of the road had been reduced to flattened, crusted black areas where there used to be clumps of trees and heavy brush. As they increased their speed, something rattled around in the back of the wagon.

"What do you have in the back?"

"Tools, water and some light provisions in case we get stuck somewhere. All the supply drivers have been carrying them. In case we come across –. If we see someone who we need to take care of – . We don't have to dig with our bare hands. We can cover them."

They both fell silent for a few minutes. To avoid any awkwardness, Illyanne tried to keep a little conversation going. "That fire was the most incredible thing."

"Yeah, people have been calling it a firestorm."

She made quizzical face. "What does that mean?"

"The way I heard it put to me is that the fire turned into a tornado."

"A tornado? She turned toward him. "How could –? Isn't that from a rain and wind storm?"

"Yep, but in this one, the fire made the same motion as a wind tornado. It grew so fast with all the dry trees, brush, lumber and sawdust everywhere. It got very, very hot, as hot as a furnace for forging steel. That intense heat rose up just like fire climbs up curtains when a lantern gets turned over. Only it was one huge flame scrambling up trees and buildings. It was so big, it sucked in more air from below. It burned so high that it also started sucking in more air from higher up. That's what made it such an inferno. Witnesses said that they saw the fire turn into one, crazy, spinning shaft of a blaze."

"Yes. That's what I saw from the ship's deck." That cursed pillar of fire, but she didn't say it out loud.

"Uh-huh. It burned and burned like a fiend that gorged on everything there was. Just fierce, a tornado of fire." He shook his head.

Illyanne's stomach tossed around and she remained quiet. They did not encounter any other wagons or people walking.

"I think I recognize this area, Mr. Cooper, from the lay of the land. A number of farms were along this stretch of road.

"Better close your eyes then Ma'am to what's coming up. The burial teams didn't come out this far. I'll let you know when it's all clear again. I was in Antietam and Gettysburg with the Wisconsin Iron Brigade during the war. Saw men turned into raw sausages." He swallowed and paused. Illyanne looked over at him. "It won't be as bad as that. But, I can tell you from personal experience, nothing comes of seeing such death and destruction. Nothing but misery. It sticks in your mind and torments you in your dreams. You're alive and that's all you need to know for now. Trust me on this. Close your eyes, Ma'am, until I tell you to open them again."

Seeing the blistered landscape did carry a punch. "I am tired from being up before dawn and cooking anyhow." She shut her eyes. She let the thrum of the wheels and the brittle crunch rolling over the sandy cinders work as rough lullaby and she dozed. The familiar and ordinary sound of the horse clomping and the gentle rattle of the harness and squeaking of the seat spring somehow comforted her.

"We're well out of town and getting close to Sugar Bush now. You can look now."

Illyanne's eyes popped open. She sat up straighter. The familiar tall grasses and brush that reddened and yellowed in the fall were gone. The trees had vanished and there was no tree line in the distance, just a dark expanse. The horizon was like what Anders used to describe as being out at sea at night without any other ships in sight, a beautiful and frightful stretch of water. The black, bald line of land felt so strange and alone. She had known this patch of road well. Now, she could only barely discern their whereabouts from the lay of the land. "Mr. Cooper, I think our homestead is just up this way."

He drove a short way further until she saw the remains of a stone fireplace. "This is it."

"Whoa," Tom Cooper pulled on the reins and helped her down. "I'll wait here so you can be alone with your thoughts. I'll water the horse and I need to stretch out a bit too. We'll be right here."

"Thank you, Mr. Cooper. I am obliged to you for your sensibilities." Illyanne nodded but did not look toward him. Dead silence blanketed her land. The homestead always had the sound of rustling leaves on trees but that was freakishly absent now. She stood still and took several deep breaths, straightened up her spine and began walking on the black dirt landscape toward what had been her home and barn. Yes, this was the spot. The iron feed trough was there, misshapen in the heat but otherwise intact. She saw black encrusted bumps and protrusions scattered not far from it which she supposed was the bones of their cows and goats. Poor dears. Illyanne did not see anything initially suggesting Anders and Matthew were in this burned shambles. But she needed to be thorough. She walked on.

Illyanne's stove, distorted by the fire, sagging in its middle, nevertheless remained standing where her kitchen had been. The heat must have immediately been drawn higher up, instead of staying low and completely melting it. Curiously, it did not look as bad as the stoves at the Boarding House. Might it even be somehow salvageable? She could almost see the ghost of herself baking bread there nearly every day for as long as she could remember.

The stones of the fireplace remained mortared in place for the most part, though blackened and cracked in spots. The top portion had fallen over into a pile of rocks. She paused again before walking the perimeter of the remnants of the house. So much labor went into building this house with Anders. Here, the memories of her life were now all debris, nothing more than a thing of the past.

She felt a little of the dull trance that Boarding House veterans described after a battle. It was surely less severe than a war but at the sight of what had been her home nothing could be said. It paralyzed. Yet she had encountered many other people in the relief camp who suffered scenes like this, and worse. So, Illyanne drew a modicum of strength from having seen such survivors. She had to know the fate of her family. Were Anders and Matthew here? She felt her knees wobble, stopped, breathed deeply and pressed on.

Illyanne felt disconnected from her own steps, almost like she floated along. Her eyes searched in earnest for anything, which might be her loved ones from their size and shape. She had learned in this grim new world that incinerated human skeletons could be recognized. She picked up her pace, scanning left and right. The rifles and pistol that had been near the front door were now cooled molten puddles. The water well pump had melted and folded over in half on itself. She finished the entire home perimeter and breathed with relief at not finding Anders and Matthew. Yet, there was the little cellar to check. They might have tried to take refuge where she stored her provisions in the winter.

She walked back to the driver. "I have not found them but there is one more place they could be. If you bring your tools, we can check the cellar. I can show you where it is."

Tom Cooper grabbed the pick and shovel and followed her back to the ashes of her home. She found the familiar spot where flat floor stones made a perimeter around the cellar trap door in the ruins.

Illyanne stood back while he lifted the pick and slammed it into the burned remnants. Ashes and charred bits flew up. He struck it several times and then there was a big hollow thud and crash. Debris fell into the opening of the cellar.

"I'll go in." He sat down at the edge and jumped in.

She heard glass break. Her Mason canning jars. All of her work, boiling fruit down into jelly, pickling cucumbers and preserving tomatoes, corn, beans and squash for winter meals, was gone. He tossed up a crusted piece of lumber, then another and another from what had been shelves. The sun was bright but gave only indirect light into the cavity of the stone-walled cellar. "They're not in here," came his shout.

She came closer and looked down at him inside the cellar. "Are you sure?"

"I can help you down in here if you want to look for yourself. There's not a lot of room in here. No place to crawl away from the disaster that would have been happening to them. There are no human bones. I'm sure. They're not down here."

Illyanne spun around so her back was to him. She walked away so he would not see her fighting back tears. Thank God. But, where were they? If they were not here maybe they had run off the homestead and died somewhere out there. If they did, she might she never find them. Or, had they somehow escaped and survived?

Tom Cooper climbed out of the cellar opening. Illyanne helped him stand.

He groaned a little and stretched his back. He rolled his head around, then made arm circles and leg circles. He started brushing himself off from black dirt on his pants, and coat. He straightened up, swiveled his head and flexed his shoulders to throw off the anxiety of the moment.

Illyanne fussed over him, sweeping her hand over his shoulders to help brush off the dirt. "This stuff is like coal dust."

As they rode, the feeling of silent, unburdened goodwill took hold in both of them. "I feel so much better but I still don't know where Anders and Matthew are."

She felt sociable now. She set her hands in her lap. "Why don't you tell me something of yourself."

"Well, I live in Green Bay. I work for the railroad now. It's lumber industry management. Before the war, I worked as a lumberjack. My back isn't so good since the war. I was in a field hospital convalescing for a good while. Anyhow, I knew part of the lumber business so now I track rail shipments and deliveries."

"And you volunteered to come to the relief camp?"

"Yeah, all the businesses are doing what they can to help out. Like I said I've seen war devastation before. Seemed to me the after effects of this fire might be similar. The company asked for volunteers and I figured I could be of help."

"Well, you are. You are so right. Who else would go down into a cellar and get all full of ash to help out a survivor looking for her family?'

They exchanged smiles.

"And, do you have a family?"

"No, Ma'am. I'm a widower but I expect to marry in the Spring."

"Oh. I am sorry and it's wonderful that you will be married soon. Mr. Cooper. I am so happy for you."

They fell into quiet again for the longest portion of the ride back. As they approached the Peshtigo relief camp, Illyanne decided to voice her thoughts. "I'm not sure what to do next. My husband and son might have survived but just as easily, they might have succumbed while helping a neighbor, being out in the fields or going fishing. Their names were not on the list of the dead. I don't even know where the relief people got that list."

"It likely came from Green Bay. The fire went around Green Bay and it's the center of a lot of lumber transport, by rail, steamers and sailing ships." He paused while the wagon jostled along the road. "You know, maybe the Lumber and Shipping Center would have some information and lists for you to check."

"The Lumber what?"

"Oh, I don't know what the official name is. Everyone calls it the Lumber Room. It's a commerce center but it has a nice lobby and restaurant. It's a hotel too. The big businessmen in the lumber, railroad and shipping industries made so much money so fast, they wanted a place to show off, bring in more trade and industry. If you ask me, they aimed to worm into the public's good graces and impress other industry barons who might come to visit. It's real fancy."

"Have you ever eaten there?"

"In the restaurant? Once. I took my betrothed there. We became engaged after dinner."

"How was the food at this Lumber Room place?"

"Expensive but delicious. We had pheasant."

"Hmm. That's not something most women don't know how to cook." She muttered to herself, "It has to soak in a brine first." She spoke again in a normal tone. "And, you say this Lumber Room has a place that would keep lists of survivors?"

"Well, yes. I can't promise anything but if there's any place that has information about what's going on, the commerce desk at the Lumber Room is it. They track all kinds of information on lumber production, marine and rail shipments, labor lists, weather. All sorts of things. Men come in there looking for work and they connect them to ship and rail business people."

"I must go then. Will you be driving back to Green Bay soon?"

"In a day or two. I'm not supposed to take passengers though. I was pushing the limits of my duties to bring you out here to your Sugar Bush."

Illyanne went quiet. If she went to Green Bay, she might find something about her family or Sugar Bush survivors. "I've got to do something. I might be able to work there as a cook. I am a very good cook."

"Like I said, I'm not supposed to be giving rides to passengers. I guess I could bend the rules a little. I can take you to the city travel office, put you in a horse drawn cab from there to the Lumber Room. I shouldn't be seen taking you straight there."

27

O ctober 16, 1871
Seven days after the fire
City of Green Bay

ANDERS AND MATTHEW slept-in until eight thirty. They found their way back to the place where they had eaten breakfast a few days earlier. They both ate the fried skillet breakfast with eggs, cheese, bits of pork and potatoes.

"Well, that was filling, Papa. Let's walk some of that off."

"That's a good idea. I need to think about what to do next anyhow. Maybe we should stick around here for the winter, keep trying to get some news."

"What about Sugar Bush?"

"If we can't get there, what can we do? I don't know, Matthew. That's why I just want to walk and think."

They walked the city streets and wandered in and out of a few shops. One had fur hats, pelts and tobacco. They paused in front of a ladies' dress shop. The dress on display was a pretty green, with ruffles and a matching parasol. Anders longed for Illyanne. "Wouldn't your mother look fine in that."

"Sure would. But you'd have to bring her here to some fancy thing happening. There's no place to wear that in Peshtigo. It would even be too much for church."

"Maybe one day."

They walked on, past the new post office, several pubs, a bakery and a machine store. Horse drawn wagons full of sacks and goods came down the street heading in the direction of the docks. They made a few turns and encountered a residential area with grand Victorian homes. It became interesting to walk by them and chat about their size and their amazing and different features. "This must be where the shipping and railroad bosses built their homes," Anders said.

They strolled and talked about the Victorian styled homes they saw. They had never seen such homes. Large two-story houses, some painted two colors, with lots of windows of all different sizes, circular castle-like towers and vast porches with railings and spindles.

"They're huge, Papa. I'll bet three or four families could live in one of them. Wish we could see the insides."

"Matthew, seeing this makes me wonder if the home building business might be something for you to think about."

They walked some more and found a park near the mouth of the Fox river opening into the bay. It was a perfect place to rest and watch the ducks and geese. And, it allowed Anders time get lost in a favorite pastime, watching ships come and go in and out of port. They sat silently on a park bench together for a long time letting the sky and water soothe them. The three days of working the docks left them both quite subdued. A steamship's horn warning reminded Anders of a sad and lonely foghorn and he missed his wife. "We should get going and get back to the Lumber Room."

"To get a train home?" Matthew asked.

"If there is one. A couple of dock workers told me the railroad tracks got melted by the fire. But maybe we ride as far as the tracks go and walk the rest of the way to Sugar Bush. I don't know. Let's talk to the Lumber Room people to see what information they have."

"What about mother's ship?"

"We'll ask about that too. I have to wonder if the ship wouldn't get word of the fire and the captain keeps the crew in Cleveland for a while. Or, if Green Bay dock is all backed up, she gets sent down south to Milwaukee. The Lumber Room ought to have some kind of news."

It was getting to be late in the day, the sixteenth when Anders and Matthew arrived again at the grand Lumber Room. A number of people stood in line at the information desk. The clerk looked up and motioned for them to have a seat and he would get to them as soon as he was able to. Anders had Matthew sat down on a bench in the atrium and looked around at the well-dressed men and women and a few workmen.

"It feels good to sit down after all that walking," Matthew said.

After a few minutes, Anders elbowed Matthew and pointed his chin at the woman dressed in shiny light blue silk. "Get a load of that." She sat alone with her back to the atrium, apparently, dining alone. "The citified ways they got around here. A lady sitting all alone in a fancy place like this. I never!" He shook his head. Of course, if a guy like Karl had a wife, she'd probably act all uppity like that, dress up and sit alone in a public restaurant just because she wanted to."

"And, look over there," he elbowed Matthew. "Look at that fella with the bushy mutton-chop sideburns," Anders whispered.

"That's not a beard or sideburns, Papa. It's a double fly trap." The two of them snickered as quietly as they could, aware of the echoes of their voices in the cavernous atrium.

"Lord, help the man if that fella ever worked as a sailor," Anders said. "Imagine getting that thing caught in the rigging aboard ship. Ohhh, ouch. They'd probably have to cut off his beard with a sharp knife to get him free." They chuckled together in low tones, aware that voices could carry in the high open ceiling.

Anders saw that the information desk clerks changing shifts. The one taking over at the big counter told the next patron in line to wait a moment while he set up. He fussed with arranging papers and books in front of him and then waved forward, the man who had been waiting. It must have been a quick easy question because the clerk was now signaling Anders to come forward.

He stood up and turned back to Matthew whispering, "All right, you stay here and stop laughing." He had to shake off his own chuckling and cleared his throat twice as he approached the information desk.

"You a man looking for work?"

"I might be – but mainly I want to ask about getting aboard anything stopping into Peshtigo. Ship, rail or stagecoach, anything."

"Peshtigo? What for?"

"Me and my son over there are from Sugar Bush, right near Peshtigo and –."

The clerk had a dead serious expression on his face. "You wouldn't even get as far as Little Suamico. The railroad tracks are unusable, melted, twisted. I am so, very sorry for your troubles. All of us clerks have seen survivors come through here for over a week. And, my heavens, how have you gotten by?" The man leaned forward to examine Anders from head to toe but not seeing any fire-related injuries.

"We're all right. Haven't been back to the homestead so don't know what we're gonna find."

"Sir, I'm sorry. I thought you knew, would have heard by now."

"Know what?"

"The extent of the fire. It went burned through a huge area." He pointed to a large wall map behind him. "See those reddened areas?" There were two great, diagonal blotchy streaks across the map. "Peshtigo and the surrounding areas for miles burned. Everything was destroyed. Everything." The red looked like haphazard swipes made with a very wide paint brush.

Anders looked at it. "I heard that the fire went around Green Bay. But when you see it like that —." He couldn't think of the right word to express the stunned feeling he had.

"Uh-huh. They're saying it was the strong winds from the west." The clerk said. "It blew the fire in those two huge swipes."

Anders stood still, processing the likelihood that his beloved homestead had been destroyed.

"Those are all confirmed reports of burned areas," the clerk said. "I'm afraid Peshtigo is, well, Peshtigo is no more. The newspaper said the fire might have gone through as much as million acres of land."

Anders cocked his head and looked at the clerk as if he didn't understand him. His eyes watered.

"Yeah, I'm sorry. Reports are that Sugar Bush was burned down, too. As far as we have heard, nothing is left standing. We've got reports from sailing ships that have gone up and down the Peshtigo River in the last few days. All they could see on either side with ship's binoculars was sheer, flat devastation everywhere, black as pitch. There is a huge relief effort underway all over to support any survivors."

Anders looked away. He stepped back from the counter feeling like a slap of lake water hit him from a wave that came over the bow unexpectedly. He couldn't think. He turned briefly back to see Matthew looking at him. He faced the clerk again. "What jobs did you say you had?"

"Got a lumber salvage ship going out right away today. Setting sail as soon as they get enough men for the job. Ship ran aground the night of the fire and they offloaded a cargo load of lumber on Green Island. Should be about a two-day job. You can head right down to the dock this minute."

"We sail back here?"

The clerk nodded a yes.

"What's happening to ships that are due in to Peshtigo? My wife's aboard a schooner, filling in as a cook for a week run to Cleveland. It was due back-in two days ago. Have you got any word about the schooner, Henry B. Jones?"

The clerk shook his head no. "They might come in to dock here but I doubt it. I don't know for sure. You really want to get to Peshtigo? You'll have to walk or catch a ride with a relief wagon."

"There must have been some survivors."

"Yes, but there's only relief wagons going up there to bring people out or set up camps. It sounds like the dock is gone."

"What's the salvage cargo?"

"Lumber. About fourteen tons of it."

Anders stood dazed. What should they do now if they can't get home? Going out for the two-day sail would give them a place to sleep, eat and get some more fast money. Maybe Illie's ship would set anchor just past the mouth of the Peshtigo River and he'd find her aboard in a few days. With his arm, could he work a full day of lifting lumber well enough? It had been a full month since he injured it lumberjacking. He could pace himself. Worst scenario, he figured, if he got fired, he'd still be back here in day. "Sign us up," he told the clerk. He turned and waved Matthew to the information desk.

28

October 16, 1871
Eight days after the fire
Peshtigo Relief Camp; Green Bay

TOM COOPER PICKED ILLYANNE up before first light at the Peshtigo Relief camp and they rode to Green Bay together. With several stops to rest and water the horse, they arrived at the city coach center depot in Green Bay in early afternoon. There had been some pleasant conversation along the way but for most of the trip, Illyanne had remained quiet and lost in thought.

"I'll be dropping you off at the city carriage depot office."

"Oh, that'll be fine."

Tom Cooper reached into the back of the wagon and carried Illyanne's carpet bag for her. He led her up the steps to the depot office, near the train station. She thought the place resembled the Peshtigo telegraph office, though twice its size. It was a simple structure, raised up on a boardwalk with a partial roof over it and hitching posts out in front. Two outdoor benches nicely painted green rested against the exterior walls on either side of the entryway. She presumed that in good weather, travelers waited there for their city carriage cabriolets. Tom told her the city was talking about laying tracks for trolley cars in the near future.

They stood outside the coach office on the boardwalk. "Well, I guess this is it, Mrs. Eriksson."

"Illyanne, please," she said. "After all our time together, it doesn't seem right you should be so formal."

He nodded in reply. "Why don't you sit down here." The day was sunny but cloudy and rolling bands of sunshine washed across the street. She did not sit down.

Tom made a motion as if to say, he would go inside and check on a ride to the Lumber Room for her but he could tell she did not want him to go inside yet.

"I don't mind telling you, I feel strange and nervous."

"You'll be all right. Let me go inside and get you a driver and give him directions."

"That's not what I mean. I'm not worried about that."

Tom shuffled his feet and gave her a quizzical look.

She felt she was on the edge of a precipice. She knew she had to jump off it to continue the search for her family. For her, the silent torture of not knowing their fate had gone on for so long, there was now a distorted comfort in not knowing. If they have died, and she failed to learn of it, she could pretend to keep hope going. Illyanne stepped toward him. She lowered her head.

"Illyanne, what is it?"

He sat down and motioned for her to follow suit.

She looked over at him in a penetrating expression. She knew he could see her tearing up. "I might be a widow this very minute." She gulped. "I just don't know it yet."

"I know." He touched her forearm with tenderness.

"And I might also be a mother who's lost a son."

"Now, you don't know that. You have to keep up hope."

Illyanne cleared her throat. "I am so much obliged to you for all your help."

"Don't think a thing of it. We're all just trying to help out everyone recover from this awful fire."

Illyanne choked up with emotion and Tom Cooper was also moved at this difficult time of change for her. Her first time in the big city. The disaster at hand. Still not finding her family. Seeing her homestead burned.

A shaft of sunlight broke through the clouds and moved down the street. Men hurried across the street between the passing horses and wagon traffic. Tom got up and went inside to transact the business of Illyanne's cab ride to the Lumber Room

"The driver will be out in a minute." He sat down next to her and they remained quiet, businesslike, looking out into the street, like ordinary townspeople waiting for a coach.

"I wish you well with your marriage, Mr. Cooper."

"Thank you."

"You have made me feel more hopeful but I do worry so." In a forced goodwill farewell, she added, "Still, I feel it's likely before long, I'll be reunited with Anders and Matthew." She did not completely believe her own words but she could not burden another person with the depths of her angst. So, she mustered the most congenial conversation she could. "I just had a bout of bad nerves is all. We'll be back working the homestead in no time."

Tom's eyes turned a bit glassy. "Now, you're talking sense. I'm sure of it."

Neither of them had noticed the driver, who now stood alongside them, holding his hat in hand, looking at the two of them. "Ready to go?"

"Yes," Illyanne said. They both stood up again.

The driver stepped down to a cab in front of the boardwalk. He climbed up to the driver's seat.

Tom held out his hand to usher Illyanne down the steps. He took her hand for balance as she stepped up into the carriage.

"Goodbye, Mr. Cooper. Thank you again."

"You take care of yourself, now." He looked at the driver, nodded and handed him the advance payment.

The carriage pulled away. It took Illyanne several minutes for the full-bodied eerie sensation she had all over to subside.

The carriage had two seats, facing each other. Its folding hood was down so a rider had an open-air, full circle view of the city. Illyanne told the driver, "It's the main commerce desk I need to visit. And Mr. Cooper told me it's quite a place to see, so I'm looking forward to that."

"Oh, yes Ma'am," he brimmed. "Everybody knows the Lumber Room. It's really something." He turned his head sideways to speak to his passenger.

"The boom 'round here's been going on now for better'n a full decade, I'd say. The Lumber Room is like a celebration of prosperity. It's got a nice restaurant and a big lobby that is decorated like nothing you've ever seen."

"What does it look like?"

"It has real high ceilings. It's got benches all around, like indoor park benches in all the different kinds of Wisconsin woods, Aspen, Birch, Maple, you name it. Big wall paintings with scenes about logging, railroads and shipping. Lots of regular workers come in there to sit and eat their lunches."

"It's all only temporary, too."

"Oh?"

"Well, I heard anyhow that they're looking to build a mansion with a grand ball room and business meeting rooms all together in a resort. Right now, it's inside a bank and office building." The carriage stopped outside of a large building three stories high. "Well, here it is, Ma'am."

She had started off with Tom Cooper shortly after dawn. The last hours of the business day had arrived now after her journey. The place took up a full city block. Its stone exterior communicated strength and certainty. Brass plates affixed to the brick outer wall sat on either side of the in and out sets of double doors. Elegant engraved letters identified this place as *The Lumber Room*. Further down from that in much smaller lettering in two concentric semi-circles, the place was titled, *The Green Bay Area Lumber, Railroad and Shipping Exchange.*

Carriages and wagons laden with people and supplies were in sight up and down the street. The sounds of conversations and passing horses and wagons all blended together. From somewhere behind buildings, Illyanne heard trains click-clacking along tracks. Men in suit coats and ties walked by busily on the boardwalk in front of the building. A few women walked by on the arms of a father or a husband. Some of their dresses were made of fine fabrics with ribbons and lace trim, with bustles in the backs. Some had high collars they adorned with cameo pins. Some passersby looked at Illyanne and her plain homestead prairie style dress and whispered about her. She had only a small relief blanket to keep around her shoulders and a plain little straw hat.

Illyanne got out of the buggy and stood still, taking in the largesse of the place. She realized she was staring and turned back to thank the driver for the ride and his time. He tipped his hat and smiled as he urged the horse to start off again.

Inside, the atrium commanded her gaze upward. Many people walked about in this cavernous area, their business voices echoing in places where there was marble flooring. Plush rugs of many colors absorbed some of the sound in the center. There were people in suits and bowler hats, working men in baggy woolen pants, jackets and newsboy caps. Others wore what looked like miners' denim work pants, all of which Illyanne had seen in Marinette newspaper advertisements. Everyone seemed to be going somewhere, meeting someone.

There were Roman columns with scrolls at the top with a cream white, light brown and thin striping in gold. Hanging gas globes softly lit the interior. Illyanne had to step out of people's way several times and then decided to seat herself on one of those wood benches. She felt an odd mixture of distress and fascination as she looked around.

On one entire wall, the establishment had displayed large illustrations and photographs and painted murals of trains, lumber being cut and transported and loaded onto ships. A gentleman guide situated in a corner chair and podium, came forward to deliver a short talk when visitors stopped to view the wall more closely. He appeared to be speaking to a small group of auxiliary ladies from some society club.

"Good afternoon, ladies. Welcome to the Lumber Rom. A number of industry moguls co-founded this facility. They drew upon architectural influences from the New York Stock Exchange, big city train stations and European palaces. They hired top craftsman to paint the murals and maps which you see here and at the commerce desk." He pointed a hand toward the large tall desk further back in the room.

She craned to catch the details about the restaurant. It was "first class cooking" the man said and it was open for three meals a day. They must need a lot of cooks for that. There was a hotel up the grand staircase, mostly for business men but "occasionally women too. Governor Fairchild's wife is expected this week, for example, for a fire relief fundraiser." He went on. "Unfortunately, ladies I cannot take you upstairs." He made a forced sad face and adopted a faux French accent. "Ladies, may not visit *des chambres de hommes*, that is, the men's bedrooms are off limits for you." The ladies tittered.

The group moved off to one side of the large room and Illyanne lost interest. On the opposite side of the atrium, from afar, Illyanne could see into the restaurant tables topped with white tablecloths. The distant sound of patrons' clinking china plates and glasses mingled with the swirling scents of good cooking.

In the center of this bustling room was a chest-high grand desk. The front of the desk had a painted map of all the Great Lakes with markings of railways, saw mills, and shipping ports. It showed Peshtigo as a main center of lumber and shipping. Illyanne felt a boost of pride. She stood up and walked to the desk. Several suit and tie clerks answered questions for visitors from behind the desk. Other smaller desks extended behind the counter with more people working there poring over papers and log books and monitoring data chalked onto large slate blackboards. Behind the desk, she observed a man pulling a ladder to one side, climb up and write chalk numbers on a slate board, come down again and push the ladder along a trolly track back where it had been.

She approached and waited for one of the clerks to finish with someone else in front of her. "Good afternoon, sir. I am from Peshtigo."

She saw his face turn crestfallen instantly. Gone was his pert manner as a compassionate willing demeanor came over him. He extended a hand toward her. "Oh, I'm so, so sorry. What a terrible, terrible thing."

"Yes, it was. Thank you. Some of the relief workers told me that this building might have a list of survivors. I'm looking for my husband and son." She went on to tell him she had been aboard the schooner, Henry B. Jones, as a cook and asked whether they knew it has shipwrecked on Green Island.

"Shipwrecked? Oh my!"

"Well, run aground. Isn't that the same thing? I thought you would have heard by now. They were due back into Peshtigo two days ago."

"No, the telegraph lines have been down and no other ship has reported any Morse Code messages. We've had no communications at all. What happened?"

"The night of the fire, we set out late and there was so much smoke we couldn't see and she ran aground. The Green Island lighthouse family took us in."

"And the cargo? What was the cargo?"

"All lumber. They pulled out as much as they could and it's sitting stacked up on Green Island."

"Heavens. Where's the ship's captain?"

"I thought he would have made his way here by now. I rowed over to the north shore at Marinette and then went to Peshtigo looking for my family. Anders Eriksson. He's a sailor. He often worked aboard the Jones but he's been out with his arm in a splint. Do you have a listing of the dead or family members searching for survivors?"

A concerned look came over the clerk's face. He walked to the side and swung open what looked like the lower half of a Dutch door. "Please step up inside here so that and I can take down the details of this incident."

Illyanne followed and as sat down in the chair he pulled aside for her. She folded her hands in her lap. The clerk sent one of the other workers to go and get her a cup of tea. He directed another to fill in for him on the front desk.

"I'm sorry, I've forgotten your name."

"Illyanne Eriksson. My husband is Anders Eriksson and our son is Matthew."

The clerk pulled out a sheet at his adjacent desk. He dipped a quill pen in the ink well. "Since the ship's captain has not reported here and under the greatly unusual circumstances of the fire, I'd like to ask you some questions about this shipwrecked vessel."

Illyanne wiggled in her chair. "I'm glad to tell you whatever I can."

"Mostly this is for insurance purposes and to advise the owner or owners. We serve as a clearinghouse, you see and this information may be vital for the insurer, if there is one. It's also helps us collect general maritime information. There's interest in establishing laws to govern ships' seaworthiness and establish a registry." He chattered on. "Shipping on the Great Lakes is buzzing but there have also been a lot of shipwrecks. Bad weather mostly, the likes of which amazes salt water sailors. I'm so sorry, I do trail off sometimes."

Illyanne simply blinked at the clerk. People in Peshtigo did not talk so fast.

"Now, you say this schooner's cargo was lumber. Do you know what kind? How many board feet it was carrying?"

"No, I'm sorry. I don't. Lumber was stacked all over the deck and in the hold too. Several different shades and grains to them."

"Any idea of the tonnage of the cargo?"

"Well, I once overheard one of the men say something about fourteen tons of lumber. Could that be about right?"

"Yes, excellent." He marked the figure down with his dipping pen. "What date and time did you leave port? In Peshtigo, was it?"

He peppered her with more questions about what time the ship left port and what the visibility conditions were prior to the wreck. The clerk scratched away information on the sheet of paper he had, dipped his pen in the ink again and went onto a second sheet.

"I had gone below deck but heard a terrible loud blast and came up. We were all topside, as they say, when the fire back at Peshtigo really flamed up. I'm guessing we were a few miles downriver. We were all on deck and watched that horrible pillar of fire go up. I remember the captain ordered the sails up and then down because there was a strong wind. He told me the smoke was the thickest he'd ever seen and the ship was going too fast and they couldn't see where they were going. I'm sorry I can't be of more help than that. I went back below and worked on the evening meal."

"Do you know what kind of damage did the ship sustained?"

Illyanne kneaded her hands, uncertain what kind of answer the clerk was pressing her for. "The men dived underneath the next morning. One of them said he thought she broke her back. That's how the crewman said it."

"Oh, my word, the keel broke?" He arched his eyebrows.

"And, you say the lumber is stacked up on Green Island?"

"Yes, as much as they could get off the ship." Illyanne fidgeted in the chair. "I don't know how much more I can help. If you please sir, is there a list of Peshtigo survivors you can check for my family? And, could you start a list for family members who are searching for their loved ones, too?"

"Well, Mrs. Eriksson, you see, that isn't quite how we manage the information. Right now, they have only printed lists of the confirmed deceased and injured. I'm only an employee clerk here and I can't go off and start my own list as you like. Though I do see your point and I quite agree with you but it's beyond my power to do anything. I can make a note here in our daily diary that the other clerks read when they come in. That much I can do but not much else, I'm afraid."

"I've been searching everywhere for days." She wiped her eyes. "I was in the shipwreck myself, banged my head, got drenched in freezing water and fainted on the shore." Her voice became creaky from emotion. "I've rowed a boat to the mainland, slept on burned ground, been held up by a man with a knife and a starving family, buried a dead man floating down river, traveled to my homestead in Sugar Bush. It's a field of black cinders now. I've lived in a relief tent, talked my way to visiting this place. And now, you are telling me you can do nothing. I'm simply, I don't know. I feel I am out of options, sir."

"I'm so very sorry. As we all are." He seemed to be genuine. "At what you people have been through." He hung his head and shook it and there was silence and tensed up feelings between them. "There's one more idea I might offer you."

Illyanne looked up with hopeful desperation. "Anything, please."

"It may not end up helping you but we have had bits of information come in here over recent days form returning relief wagon volunteers. There's been reports of a lot of people who gathered at the Mary chapel and got shelter and treatment there. In Champion." He pointed to the wall map behind him. "Here. It's about fifteen miles up the peninsula."

Illyanne looked at the clerk, with a perplexed expression.

"I know it seems like it goes against the grain of common sense, going east and then north on the Door peninsula, when they are from Peshtigo across the bay. But there is good reason." The clerk explained that Green Bay didn't have a relief camp at all the first week after the fire. All the land west of the city is Oneida Indian land. He again pointed to the area on the map. "South of where we are now, there's the docks and the Fox River. So, the chapel grounds, a known trading post, really was the only place to send fire survivors for temporary lodging. The fire went through there too but we got word within a day, that the building and land there was spared."

He could see that Illyanne was surprised but also processing the sensibleness of what had first appeared to be a contrary idea.

"If your husband and son came through here the first week after the fire, we might very well have sent them out there."

Illyanne mumbled to herself. "I just can't imagine how Anders and Matthew would have for any reason, gone all the way over to the other side of the bay."

"I've spoken with a number of the relief workers, Ma'am in the last week and I can tell you, people are missing all over. They ran any direction they could, by any means they could. A lot of them ended up in places you wouldn't expect them to be in. So, should I sign you up to ride out there tomorrow on the relief wagon?"

She was stymied for a moment and he kept talking. She might regret it if she didn't try searching in Champion. Winter and the first snows weren't far off. Some folks might be getting shipped out soon to Milwaukee until spring. I really recommend you look there."

"All right then, sign me up for it, please."

"Very well. Let me get you a room for the night."

"Oh, no," She lifted up and open palmed hand.

"It's complimentary. No charge. All the businesses are doing what they can to help out. And, as luck would have it, we've received two more telegraphed cancellations from Milwaukee travelers. Everyone wants to see successful recovery efforts before business goes further."

"That's so generous. I don't know what to say. I'm very grateful." She blushed.

"I'll see what I can do about getting you a new dress and have your clothes washed an ironed, too." He ran his eyes over her from head to toe and she felt shamed and dirty. It was from the cinder dust on the road, of course, but that look cut through her. The man was kind and demeaning at the same time. Was it her Indian heritage that showed? Or, that she was the wife of a sailor? Or could it be that she was not one of the ladies of money and fine dresses? A feeling of resentment stirred in her which she had never known before. This must be the feeling Beulah had once tried to explain to her. She was beholden to this man. Yet, he must have meant well.

"And, I'll put your name on a list for the restaurant so that you can have a complimentary meal as well."

Illyanne thought she ought to say 'God bless you' to the man, but it would not come up and out of her mouth. She felt too weary. "Thank you, sir. You're very kind."

"You're welcome. We've been offering two rooms a night for couples or singles at our discretion." He cupped his hand and whispered, "longer if you need it." He resumed his normal speaking voice. "It's just lucky that we still have one available tonight. All the businesses are helping out. I do need to get back to work. The cost of lumber is assured to go sky high and I'm going to need to contact the ship owners — probably have to organize a salvage ship and crew right away." He handed her the room key. "Good afternoon to you, Ma'am. It's just up these stairs."

29

O*ctober 16, 1871*
The Lumber Room, Green Bay

WHEN SHE ENTERED THE room which the porter had led her to, she gasped. The porter looked at her with alarm.

"It's just so beautiful."

He smiled.

She stepped into the room. A luxurious puffy covering lay over the bed. The room's color scheme included burgundy, cream and orange accents. There was side a vanity set with a water pitcher and washing bowl. In front of the small fire place sat two low upholstered chairs. Some reading books sat on the mantel by Dickens, Fenimore Cooper, and Alcott. On a side table there was a copy of *Harper's* magazine and a newspaper, the *Green Bay Press Gazette*.

"What is that big metal bin for over there?"

"Ma'am, that is a bathtub."

She stood still with amazement for a moment scanning the room. This place was fit for a queen.

"I can prepare hot bath water for you."

She stalled a moment. How unbelievably indulgent. It was absolutely decadent, though it was a marvel. She couldn't – but she was filthy from traveling. "Yes, please."

She walked to the window, framed in velvet burgundy drapes. The room possessed a magnificent panoramic view of the mouth of the Fox River emptying into the Bay of Green Bay. The sun was falling lower in the sky casting the richest pigments. The vast blue of the bay reaching to the horizon cooled her senses. She could imagine Peshtigo nestled in the distance. Steamers and sailing ships carried on their work as they floated along on the water.

Within the hour, the porter returned with several others who poured hot water into the large basin. "Your dress for the evening, Ma'am." The porter laid it on the bed. She would leave the dress she had on for the women to launder when she went downstairs for dinner. All was provided at no cost.

When she washed up, combed her hair and donned the dress, she lingered in front of the looking glass. What incredible finery. The light blue silk dress had a small bustle. What would Anders would say if he could see her now? It was a little excessive but what harm was there in it? She would enjoy the dress, the luxurious surroundings and tomorrow she would be on her way to continue the search for her family. And, anyhow, they certainly weren't going to allow her to go sit and eat in their dining room looking like a burned-out nomad.

She sat at the furthest table from the main dining tables. To be as unobtrusive as possible she seated herself with her back toward the lobby.

It was still early but the waiter greeted her with a "Good evening, Madame. Will anyone be dining with you this evening?"

Illyanne had to take a moment to process this, almost as if she were translating in her head. "Oh, sorry. No, I'll be eating alone." She had felt awkward dining in a restaurant alone. She had seen men, newcomers at the Peshtigo Boarding House sit and eat by themselves. She did need to eat and so she hoped to quietly mimic those men and pretending it was completely ordinary to do so.

She reached out to accept the menu the waiter handed her. There were three selections for the evening. Ham and sweet potatoes; Beef Bourguignon and Turkey Chikhirtma.

"I'll have the Chikhirtma. I've had that before with chicken but this looks interesting." She declined to have any wine but accepted water. "Is it all right if I look through this magazine while I wait."

"That is fine Ma'am but the meal will come right away. Your selection is a slow-cooked recipe which has been cooking all day. I only need to dish it up so I'll have it out to you quickly."

In short order, the waiter set a beautiful wide and flat ceramic bowl in front of Illyanne. Large pieces of turkey set atop of rice with plentiful amount of sauce poured over it all, decorated with green flecks of some herb. The aroma was delicious and a small curl of vapor rose over the dish. "This looks good. I thought it was a soup dish but thank you. I'm famished."

She began cutting up the turkey and eating bites of it with the sauce and rice. Rich and full of flavor, it took her mind back to the kitchen at Peshtigo Boarding House. Chikhirtma was a Beulah recipe, another one of her Georgia things she brought with her. It was a wonderful replenishment for her stomach and her state of mind. When the waiter returned, she asked, "Would I be able to come back to the kitchen and chat with the cook? I am a cook myself and I want to ask about the recipe."

It was allowed. After she finished the dish and sat for a few minutes and sipped some more water, she nodded to the waiter that she was ready to be led to the kitchen. The familiar kitchen heat and clink of dishes hit her ears after coming through the cooking door. How she missed the activity and the atmosphere.

"Mrs. Fletcher cooked that dish for tonight, Ma'am. She's right over there."

Illyanne walked further into the kitchen where assistants were putting orders on plates to go out on the waiter's big trays. She called out, "Mrs. Fletcher? Oh, Mrs. Fletcher, may I have a word with you please?"

The woman with her back to Illyanne, finished stirring something on the stove. She wiped her hands on her apron and turned around to face Illyanne coming toward her.

"Beulah! You're not dead."

"Illie? My God, if you ain't a balm from Gilead to heal my sin-sick soul." Beulah threw her arms out wide.

They ran to embrace each other. They laughed and cried and stood back to look at one another and gasped in amazement at each other being alive and being where they were. Illyanne felt a strange rush go through her. It was like a sugar surge she'd get when taking test taste of maple syrup after the pot of sap had cooled down. She fanned herself.

"I thought you died in the fire, Beulah. I looked for you. I came back to Peshtigo. You wouldn't believe how burned to the ground it is. I could barely find the outlines of the Boarding House. How did you –?"

"Escape?"

"Yes. Almost everyone was overtaken."

"Easy. I wasn't there at all. Just like you'd always told me to, I took a few days off and came down here. I left days before you did."

"Then, who did the cooking for the Boarding House?"

"Middle of the week, another bunch of new workers came in on a ship. Turned out two of 'em had worked as ship cooks before so, they temporarily got hired on."

"I heard about this place and I came to talk to them about trying me out the next time I could come down. Little did I know, I'd never be going back to Peshtigo at all. So, I been here now going on two weeks. What about you and your sailing adventure? I heard you were going out."

"Oh, my, it didn't work out well, I can tell you that."

"You sure are looking fine. Somethin's gone well for you. Look at you. all lady-fined up."

Illyanne felt silly. She was not dressed as the person she really was, not the person that Beulah knew. She slapped her hands on the skirt part of her dress. "Oh, this dress isn't mine. They loaned it to me here. I'm just staying here for tonight."

"Like I said." Beulah made several exaggerated head nods. "Doing all right for yourself."

"It was only by the kindness of a clerk who arranged it. It's at no cost. For the Peshtigo survivors. Can you believe it? That's what they're calling us now. Anyhow, I've been searching for Anders and Matthew now for over a week. No sign of them yet. At least they aren't on the newspaper death list. But, Beulah, I don't know whether they're injured out there somewhere, or if they're alive at all." She dismissed her own complaining so as not to sound desperate. Some of the other kitchen help were looking on. "But never mind all that. How about you and your work here? Oh, and that dish tonight. That was fantastic."

Beulah looked past Illyanne and whispered. "I think I better get back to work. I'm getting the evil eye from the manager. I'm in the servant's quarters, turn left when you go out the front entrance. One block down. Ask out front at the desk. I finish up at eight and we can talk then. Can you come by?"

Illyanne caught a stare from a kitchen worker behind Beulah. "Well, it was a wonderful meal and the seasonings were excellent. I must have you write down the recipe for me. It was very nice to see you again, Mrs. Fletcher. Thank you." She turned and followed the waiter standing by to escort her out.

Seeing Beulah worked like a hypnotic on her spirit. Beulah was alive. And right here. Illyanne was anxious to get together with her again and ended up pacing in her beautiful guest room. She no longer cared about the extravagance of the suite. Sitting on a log around a campfire would have suited her just fine. A few minutes after eight she walked past the front grand desk, telling the clerk at the desk, "I'm just going to go out for an evening stroll." She held up a folded sheet of Lumber Room stationary from the suite desk. "And, I have arranged to get a recipe from one of your cooks. Could you tell me where their quarters are?"

When Illyanne arrived she and Beulah hugged again. She stepped into Beulah's small, dark one room apartment. "I wish I could have you come up to my room at the Lumber Room but –." Illyanne looked down.

"You know they'd never let me."

"Oh, I know but I wish you could." She looked around. "This is small and quite basic." There was a small pot belly wood burner, a single bed, a chair and an older settee with a side table and lantern.

"Yeah, but it will do for now. I was planning on going back to Peshtigo and then coming down here in the spring. Guess you could say now, I'm already moved in. I think I'm going to be able to build me a cabin out of town in a year. Money's good and they like my cookin'."

The women chattered on, reminiscing about recipes they remembered cooking and certain restaurant patrons that were interesting, funny or terrible. "Peshtigo really did bring in all types, didn't it, Beulah? And you're cooking as well as ever. That dish tonight was delicious."

"Oh, C'mon." She lowered her voice and spoke close to Illyanne. "Someone might hear through these thin walls. I dunno if you remember I made that once before. Chicken Chikhirtma. It's a stew soup. That stuff is nothin' but good old slave food." She put her hand over her mouth to muffle her laughter. "'Round here, they think it's divine." Her eyes rolled. "I changed it, made it with turkey instead o' chicken, thickened up the broth for a gravy sauce. I piled up some meat on a bed of rice and smothered it with the sauce and chopped up some herbs for the top. And because it was turkey, I added sage to the sauce. That's it. Simple and they act like it's king food." Beulah doubled over laughing. "Oh, it just kills me, Illie. I mean, it's so easy to make. You put the stuff together. There's a few steps but then it just simmers for hours while you go have a walk outside, take a nap or go work in the garden."

Illyanne had her go through the steps again and she wrote them down. There was no telling when or whether she'd ever be cooking for her family again. Still, cooking was her only real emotional tether to this world, the way things were at present. She had found Beulah alive. It felt like plunging into the cold-water Peshtigo River in summertime, refreshing all over. It rejuvenated her whole mood, making her feel more hopeful. Someone she knew and cherished was still in the world. No matter what she would find about Anders and Matthew, Beulah was an anchor.

"You know, Beulah, it feels like a godsend, a good omen that I found you again."

"How do you figure that?"

"It just makes me feel like Anders and Matthew are out there somewhere, alive."

Beulah fell quiet and stood up. She crossed her little room and adjusted the filament on her oil lamp.

"What's wrong? Did I say something wrong?"

Beulah came and sat down next to her again. "Listen, Illie. I pray you find your husband and son; I really do." She sighed and held Illie's hand. "I just want to say, you gotta be prepared is all. 'Cept for the war, this fire's the biggest, worst thing anybody ever heard of happening anywhere. Ever! It's good to have hope but there comes a time. You gotta realize Illie, there's a chance they didn't make it out."

Illyanne pulled her hand away and turned her head and sobbed. Hearing this truth hit hard, though she'd known it all along.

Beulah handed her a kerchief and waited in silence.

"I don't think I could go on living without them. I'd be so, so miserable." She doubled over, crying. "I really don't think I could manage. My kin are all dead. I wouldn't know what to do, where to go, how to live. The homestead is burned, the house, barn and animals are all gone. And I don't even know my Menominee people."

Beulah just hugged her for a while. "I know you don't think you can go on but you can. You can. I've seen pain and heartache like nobody's ever seen. Chil'n sold off away from their mothers. Men dyin' from battle and disease, others overworked in the fields. It hurts. It hurts real, real bad. But, b'lieve me, that passes. It gets better and you goes on. You're young, got your health and you can earn a living cooking, Illie. There's lots who don't even have that."

Illie began drying her eyes and sitting upright again.

"Besides, we're only talking about being prepared for the worst. You oughta come work cooking with me. Always makes a body feel better doin' something for somebody else when they's down hard in the dumps."

"I just might do that. I'm going looking for them in Champion tomorrow."

30

October 16, 1871
Aboard a salvage ship,
Green Bay; the Bay of Green Bay
Green Island

ANDERS AND MATTHEW came aboard the salvage ship and a crew member took them below deck to show them the galley, berthing space and crew mess and lounge. They saw Karl right away. Anders laughed as he spoke. "So, this is the business you had to attend to in Green Bay?"

"Ah, no. Not exactly but I expect like you, another business opportunity came up and here I am."

"Sure, Karl."

Matthew nodded at Karl and made his way around him in the below deck space and continued to follow the crew member giving him the two-cent tour.

The ten men hired on for the salvage job had nothing to do but sit and wait as the ship sailed to its destination. The schooner's captain put out the word to the regular crew that they were on board for the salvage work, nothing more. It was at least a short sail to Green Island.

Most of the salvage crew stayed on deck as they set sail to watch the ship leaving harbor and taken in a view of the adjacent shores. At first, the land appeared normal, trees, green and houses visible.

But as the ship moved further out into the bay, it quickly turned to blackened landscapes on either side. In the distance, it looked like horizontal stroke of pitch that someone brushed across a seaside painting.

Despite the shoreline destruction, the sun shone on open water. The water sparkled and the striking blue sky returned. Out in the bay, the ship picked up speed. The breeze delighted the men who took up viewing spots along her gunwales. The men lifted their faces to the sunlight and their hair streamed in the wind. As always, the scent of open water delivered its timeless quixotic feel to the sailors. Busy commerce remained in evidence as they watched other schooners heading into port.

"Pretty as a picture, Matthew. Look at that." The wind filled the schooners' sails and they gleamed in the sun. One of them passed by close enough for the sailors aboard both to wave and shout a passing greeting to each other. The ships moved with fast grace, light in the water with empty holds, having offloaded their cargo in some other port. "That's beauty in motion." Anders broke off momentarily from his sun basking and opened his eyes and to look at Matthew. He nudged him. "This is the thrill of getting underway. You feel it your bones and in your blood. Nothing like it anywhere."

Soon, they passed the port traffic and the shoreline was no longer visible. Only water surrounded them and the men, one by one, went below to play cards, tell sea stories and doze. It was a hallmark of the seafaring life that even among men who had not met each other before, sailors could easily confide in each other, eat, sleep and work together.

Below deck was well-lit as several deck prisms embedded on the main deck bent the sunlight and scattered it around the interior deck. One of the men, called Bobby, was a bit older and thicker than the rest. Someone said he had been an ocean sailor in his past. "I've got a good one for you boys. I once saw the Flying Dutchman out in the great Atlantic."

Three of the other men groaned. "Aw, Bobby, don't go scaring the young lad."

One of the others looked at Matthew and said, "Never you mind. He's trying to pull your leg." Some of the men booed, some chuckled but at the same time there were rallying calls for Bobby to tell the story.

The crewman named Davy looked at Anders. "If the boy's gonna follow in your footsteps you might want to let him get a listen." He shrugged his shoulders. "It's part of the sea life."

Anders turned to Matthew and said, "I think it is all claptrap, nothing but a sea story son but Davy here's got a point, so go ahead Bobby, let's hear your tale."

"All right then, young gent, first thing you gotta know is that the Flying Dutchman is a ghost ship from a good hundred years ago. She's doomed to sail the seas of the world for eternity. If you ever catch sight of her, you'll know it. There's nothing in this world like it." Bobby paused and his voice went low and whispery. "She glows." He took a breath. "Yes, that's right boys, she glooows. There's a spooky light that comes from her insides. And if she's spotted on the high seas, well, it portends doom, mates. And laddies, I've seen her. Such a shiver down my spine I can tell you I've never felt in my whole life."

"Don't listen to him, Matthew," one of the sailors said, who was whittling, sitting further away from the rest of them.

Davy threw a bunched-up shirt at Bobby and got him by surprise in the face. "You're all wet Bobby. How come you're here if you saw her and it was a signal of doom?"

The men laughed.

"Well, that's because of my most excellent sailing skills and I steered us out of the danger."

Loud and good-natured belly laughs filled the space below deck. A pause of several minutes transpired while smaller conversations went on.

The small Asian crewman named Haru stood up and broke in. "I saw a freak wave once sailing on Lake Michigan."

All the men's eyes turned toward him, waiting for details.

"It was very big, like the *Great Wave of Kanagawa*. That's a famous wood block print by a Japanese artist."

"Kana-what? And, what's a wood block print?" Someone among them asked.

"Kan-a-ga-wa. It's a place in Japan. And a wood block is a carved drawing. The artist brushes it with ink and presses it onto paper." Haru saw in the men's faces they did not understand. "It's like a stamp." He motioned by slapping one open palmed hand down on top of the other. "Like a printing press but a picture instead of letters."

"The Kanagawa wave picture shows fishing boats with men rowing and riding in the troughs of giant waves. It is so tall and water is splashing everywhere. In the picture, the top of the wave looks like it has fingers." Haru stood up, hunched his back, raised his arms overhead in front of him and wiggled his fingers to imitate the droplets from a breaking wave.

He smiled at the men as they laughed.

"The wave is curling and is going to fall on top of the fishermen and their boats." He motioned great wave arcs with his arms. "I saw a real rogue wave like that crash over the bow of a schooner. In Lake Michigan. About five years ago. Whew. The wave I saw was just like that Kanagawa art print my mother has on her dining room wall. Still don't know why it didn't kill us." Haru shook his head. "It was one wave. Just one. If a second one would have come along, we would surely have died."

Anders asked, "How tall was it?"

"Oh, easily twice as tall as the top of a schooner mast."

The men reacted groaning both at this impressive height and in disbelief. One said, "And how big was that fish you caught last week?" A roar of laughter from the men followed.

"So, Haru, did you ever see waves like that in Japan?"

Haru shrugged his shoulders. "Heck no. I've never been to Japan. Even my dad was born in California." That got a refrain of howling laughter from the men.

At one point, Karl trotted out to center stage to brag about the business world. "You want to have a good life? Fellas, save up your sailing pay and get into business like I did. Fine things await you, men. I travel. How'd you like to sail as a paying passenger instead of a seaman? I have a nice house, carpets, a carved wood dining table, fine china, a few animals and acres of farm land. And the best part is, you become a man of influence."

Anders chimed in. "You gonna tell them all about how your grand holdings just burned down to the ground?"

Karl frowned at him. "Naysayers. They always get left behind. Too bad. When I get back, I've got some rather important industry men to approach at the Lumber Room where I know they are meeting for a very important business luncheon. The governor's wife is coming and I know some of the men attending." He pulled out a small note pad and flipped through some pages. "Day after tomorrow. I have some money-making ideas to discuss."

The men looked askance at him. "You're a grimy sailor just like the rest of us."

"Today I am. But, in two days, shipmates, I'll have money to buy a new suit and you won't know me. I'll wear the same suit for when I go to meet Inga."

Anders scolded him. "Karl," but it only egged him on.

"Indeed, I have to spruce myself up to go meet the beautiful Inga. Her fiancé was my neighbor but he died in the fire. She's on her way here now from Sweden. She's gonna need some major consoling boys, if ya know what I mean."

Some of the men snickered.

"I'm going to have to man-up to the task of breaking the news to her *and* comforting her sorrows." Karl turned his back to the men, wrapped his arms around his own torso and pretended to be kissing a woman in his arms.

The same few men tittered in unison like drunkards in a pub, roaring in cycles at one embellished lewd story after another.

"She won't be able to get enough of me." Karl went back to acting, sat down on a sleep rack with a bedroll and then laid himself on his side. "Oh, darlin'." Karl stood up and laughed along with the men.

Anders stood a few feet away and threw down a broom he had been using, making a loud crack when it hit the deck. "Knock it off, Karl."

Karl looked back at him with a smirk. "What's eatin' you?" Karl forced his face inches from Anders. "I'm just kidding around. Sailor talk."

One of the other sailors, Louie, stepped in. "Hey, hey here fellas." Louie pushed his way between Anders and Karl. "Let's see who'll be the king of arm wrestling" There were two long tables and stools which had been tucked against the bulkhead. "Pull those out here, men. Whadya say we pick the two biggest men? Bets of a dollar of our pay for the winner of your choice?"

The cheers went up. "Yaaay."

Anders would definitely sit out arm wrestling with his good arm. "I'm saving myself for the salvage work." He walked away from the cluster of men to lay down in one of the bunks.

The group selected two among them with the biggest biceps. They group became loud and rowdy, like horses near a fire, ready to run wild.

Louie called out the ground rules for the opponents. "No touching the players. No standing up or lifting off from your seat. Elbows have to remain on the table top. Wrestlers cannot talk. All right?" He took the bets without taking any money or writing names down. "All right, let's get down to it."

The two wrestlers sat down across from each other. The contest began. Animated sailors hollered, clapped, whistled at their man and hurled insults at the other one.

Half a minute in and one of the men slammed the other's arm down. A huge argument broke out. Several claimed they had seen the winner lift his elbow for a half a second. Several of the men came close to fighting and the racket they made brought trouble.

The ship's First Mate pushed in and separated them from each other. Men shrunk away to the periphery of the mess and lounge area. "What in blazes is going on board my ship?" He stood in the center of the deck room with his feet spread far apart and his arms on his hips. He looked back and forth from the two sets of men who came closest to blows. Karl was among them.

None of them answered.

"Anyone?" The other men turned back toward their own bunks and busied themselves.

One with his back turned spoke up. "It's just the age-old things, First Mate. Cheatin,' muscle, pride and money."

"Well, I don't give a flyin' fig about your little spats. There's no fighting and no gambling on my ship."

"No money exchange hands, First Mate, honest." a voice in the crowd said.

First Mate spun around. "Now you men, get it through your thick heads. No gambling. None. Including promise of future earnings. Got it? I figure you're here because you love the sea, the sail and adventure, have the skills to salvage and want to make some fast money." The First Mate was red-faced as he paced. Only the soft wood creaks of the ship's hull could be heard as she moved in the water.

He scanned the lounge staring at each man. "I don't want to hear anything more about any disagreements. Or so help me, I'll throw the first man over the side myself and you can swim the five to seven miles to shore." He waited for a minute and they were all quiet. "Get your salvage work done and done right and you'll get paid what's your due. No more contests." The room remained silent and First Mate stood in the center of the area for a long time, then went back up on deck.

The men played cards, talked and slept over the several hours it took to sail the nearly fifty nautical miles to Green Island. The dawn revealed the wrecked schooner listing on the shoals and the lumber stacked further up the slope of the land, both strange sights for sailors. The salvage ship pulled in front of the damaged schooner and anchored there.

The First Mate called all the men topside. "All right, men gather round. If you weren't below deck for our little incident and don't know it yet, I'm the First Mate. To you, my name is First Mate. We got fourteen tons of lumber to recover. Listen up. Here's how we're gonna do it."

He went through his plan step by step. The crew would let down the flat-bottomed barge they had towed. Teams of men would paddle the barge close to shore. Men on shore would hand off lumber to the barge men. Once the barge is full, the barge men will row back to the ship and rope up the boards in groups of twenty-five. The salvage ship's deck teams will pull them up with the help of pulleys and a swing arm mechanism. The below deck crew will stack the lumber in the hold and on deck.

"It's hard work men. Get down to the mess deck and fill up on grub. We start in twenty. The teams will take short breaks at noon and six if it's going well. Get to it mates. We work until the job gets done. Into the night if we have to. We have the lighthouse to show our way."

The men ate a heavy breakfast first and then spread out into teams. It was demanding and sweaty work but the sun was out and the temperature, in the fifties, kept them cool and productive. In the first two hours, the men loaded a couple of tons of lumber. Anders and Matthew started out working on the land. Karl was assigned to the deck team. The teams got to work and quickly found a rhythm. After four hours, the First Mate called them in to rest, drink water and get more grub.

The teams resumed and a good portion of the stacked lumber disappeared off the land. Anders and Matthew picked up boards and passed them to men on the barge. Anders could easily lift two or three boards at a time with Matthew on the other end of them. As they cleared stacks of lumber off the land, the salvage ship pulled up anchor and moved from the front of the wrecked ship to its stern.

That's when something went wrong. The wrecked ship blocked Anders' and Matthew's view of the salvage ship but they heard the clatter of lumber hitting the deck and men yelling. Still on land, they ran around the back end of the wreck to see the salvage ship. All of the men had stopped work.

The men in the empty barge came close to land and waited and watched with Anders and Matthew. "What happened out there?" Anders asked. They explained that an entire bulk of boards had come loose and fallen onto the salvage ship deck and injured someone. It turned out to be Karl.

"A load like that could kill a man," Anders muttered.

The barge men began talking loudly. The deck team and the barge team blamed each other for not handling their part of the job properly.

31

O*ctober 17, 1871*
Nine days after the fire
Green Island, Wisconsin

FROM SHORE, FOR THE first time, Anders noticed the name of the wrecked ship on its stern. The cargo he'd been working with for hours was from the Henry B, Jones. Illie's ship. Earlier, when salvage ship arrived, he could not see the name on the bow because of sun glare. He turned around and looked up the land toward the lighthouse and home. The salvage crewmen were squabbling with each other about the accident. In the confusion and work stoppage, an impulse struck him. Anders suddenly ran like a wild man, up the rise in the land toward the lighthouse residence.

Several of men on shore called after him. "Where you going?" and "What are you doing," but Anders kept running. "First Mate's gonna have your hide."

Anders ignored them. As he ran, he yelled, "Illie, Illie."

Emma saw him from her kitchen window. She muttered to herself, "What now?" She walked outside and stood in front of the house. She heard him more clearly now. He was calling for Illyanne.

Anders stopped in front of Emma. "My name is Anders Eriksson." He was huffing and trying to catch his breath. "I'm looking for my wife, Illyanne. She was on that ship."

"You're her husband?"

"Yes." Anders stepped closer and his eyes were wide with hope.

Emma moved toward him and he could see she was moved. "You're alive. She's going to be so pleased."

Anders felt confused. "Is she alright? Please, have her come out, right now."

"She's fine but she isn't here. She left days ago." Emma grabbed him around the upper arm and started leading him inside. "Got a little knock on the head but she's fine. She's just fine. She'll be awfully glad to see you. Come in and sit for some tea."

"Is the captain here? Let me speak to him."

"He and the crew went ashore out back, to the Door peninsula side of the bay. They headed for Green Bay to get help. Isn't that how you got word to send a salvage ship?"

"I don't know anything about that."

Emma pulled out a chair for him. Anders sat down, pulled off his hat and hung his head. He pounded a fist on the table. She poured some tea and some bread and sat down across from him. "I know she was headed to your homestead in Sugar Bush. She rowed ashore several days ago to Marionette. Captain sent a crewman to accompany her. She went looking for you and Matthew. Is he with you?

Anders got a distant unfocused look in his eyes but he nodded a yes. He sipped some of the tea and tore into the bread. "The man at the Lumber Room said there was nothing left of Peshtigo and the surrounding areas. Everything burned. Everything. She won't find us there."

"Well, I have a strong feeling about this. Somehow or another, there will be a light to show the way for the two of you to find each other after this thing. I'm sure of it."

"Look, I've got to get back. The First Mate's gonna have my head. Much obliged to you, Miss?"

"Emma Schumacher. Pleased to have made your acquaintance. Call me Emma. Your wife and I had a pleasant, few days together, talking and cooking for the crew."

Anders smiled, put his cap back on and ran outside and down the land's incline. Matthew and the two other crewmen saw him coming. One of them said, "What got into you?"

"Oh, I uh, had to make a mad dash to the outhouse, that's all. Sorry. Is the injured man all right?"

Anders decided not to tell Matthew about Illie, right then. No sense in worrying him any more than he already was.

Soon, a crewman on the salvage ship deck hollered out that the injured man was fine but would work below deck. The teams started up again. They got a dinner break and rest and worked into the night. The salvage ship hold was filled up by the end of daylight. By the light of the lighthouse, the crew began stacking lumber on the upper deck for another hour and a half.

All of the men had spent their energies. It had been a physically exhausting day. They worked the job and that was it. Each man found himself a niche somewhere among the stacks of lumber on deck for the sail back to Green Bay.

The First Mate made rounds checking-in with each man. He came across Anders and Matthew nestled among piles of lumber on deck, where they were playing cards by lantern light. "So, you've settled down, I see. Worked all the fight out of the men." He started walking away, laughing again, shaking his head. "Nothing like channeling men's energies into something productive."

After a while they put away the cards and snuffed out the lantern. "We might as well sleep right here," Anders said. "Nice night and I doubt there's an open spot below deck." They wedged themselves between layers of lumber with their relief blankets and gazed at the night sky's stars.

Anders exhaled loudly, tucking his hands behind his head and resting on his back. "It's total peace and wonder up there. Never get tired of looking at it."

"It has a calming effect, doesn't it, Papa?"

"Yep. Nothing like it in the world, the rocking of a ship on a clear night, looking up at the remarkable heavens. Takes the bite out of any man's troubles."

"Look, Papa, a shooting star." Matthew laid his head back with his fingers laced as a pillow. "It's like the ocean, isn't it? How they say it draws the venom out of anything to just sit and watch the waves for a while? And, mother could be out on deck looking at the same star we are."

Anders sleepily grunted agreement. He turned on his side with his back toward Matthew. "About your mother. That was her ship we salvaged. She was on the island a few days and went ashore looking for us."

"What?" Matthew sat up quickly. "Why didn't you tell me before?"

"I'm telling you now." Anders spoke with his eyes closed. "It wouldn't have made any difference except you would have worried and maybe slipped up on the job."

"Oh, my gosh. Papa."

"I meant to tell you at supper but couldn't find a way with all the men around. Anyhow, there's nothing either of us can do. We can only trust in the Star of the Sea to keep watch over her. Go to sleep."

Anders fell off to sleep and Matthew slept shortly after him. At first light, they would be in port in Green Bay again and collect their pay.

At the pier, Anders and Matthew disembarked together.

"Papa, should we wait your friend to get off and come down the dock, so you see him off?"

Anders only replied with a low grumbling sound.

"He was your sailing mate. He did welcome us into his home." Matthew set down his blanket roll of belongings and Anders did the same.

"Mostly to show off all his possessions."

"Well, I'm going to stand here 'til he comes by to say thanks, wish him good health and good luck. Here he comes."

"Well, all right then," Anders said. "A sailor once told me it's a wise man who raises a son to be better man than himself."

"And then the father follows the son?" Anders asked.

"Something like that."

Karl came down the gangplank and approached the spot where Anders and Matthew had stepped aside from the main walkway.

"Hey Karl."

He stopped and turned toward them.

"Just wanted to say thanks for putting us up."

Karl nodded.

"You going to be all right after that knock on the head?"

"Yeah. Knocked the wind outa me for a bit but I'm already recovered. First Mate was just being careful to keep me on board ship." That big grin spread across his face. "Can't keep a lion down for long."

Anders made a snorted laugh and nodded. "Oh, and Karl. Listen, about Inga," Anders said. "I thought about that. You had a good point. She won't have any money and she'll be sad. You'd be helping her out to have her stay with you in the city. It would avoid scandal if you got married. So, if you did marry her, I'd wish you all the best."

"Thanks, mate. I was just kidding around but who knows, eh?" Karl made a lazy salute with a couple of fingers. "Fair winds and following seas." And he walked down the dock.

32

October 17, 1871
Nine days after the fire
Champion; Green Bay

AS ILLYANNE RODE ALONG in the relief wagon through the outskirts of Green Bay, the landscape reminded her of the halcyon days before the fire. It was the peak color of autumn. The sun illuminated the red and orange trees and the dark blue skies intensified the colors. She felt comfortable in the outdoors and back in her newly laundered prairie dress. Geese and ducks honked and quacked in the crisp air. For part of the trip, she was able to gaze upon the pretty deep blue water.

Soon, the driver crossed into another scorched earth area on southeastern side of the bay. The full truth of how far and wide the fire had raged shocked Illyanne. Black shapes of burnt trees littered the land the further they went from the city. She smelled annihilation again, from Green Island to Marinette to Peshtigo, the city of Green Bay and now here on the Door peninsula. One big horseshoe search trail. The sobering view made her eyes water. She could not escape the wretched sadness. Everything she saw, felt, smelled and revolved around the devastation of the fire. The scent of burnt wood and the feel of sandy black cinders on the breeze continued even after days of traveling.

"Miss? It's an awfully sad sight, I know," the driver said. "I don't know if you have ever been to a funeral but that's the feeling this disaster brings out. It's like somebody let the blood right out of you. But it does pass. You've come through."

She tried to clear the lump in her throat. "I'm not so sure about that. I may be here in the flesh but it's all just so draining. I feel like a fish."

The man spurted a laugh. "A fish?" He turned his head cockeyed. "How's that?"

"I've gutted and cleaned a lot of fish in my time, for cooking. This whole fire and the damage everywhere make me feel like a fish being gutted."

"Oh, I can understand that."

She hesitated a second, trying to gather her thoughts. "I just cannot imagine how God would let all this horror happen."

"Well, I think the Almighty has his own purposes. That's the way President Lincoln put it, anyhow."

"Lincoln? What's Lincoln got to do with any of this? He's been gone better than five years now, hasn't he?"

"Oh well, sure. He wasn't talking about the Peshtigo fire. Something far worse."

"What's worse than this?"

"The War between the States. Brother killing brother by the thousands. So many wounded. Terrible suffering and dying. Widows and children without fathers. I know you aren't positioned to hear right now, but that was surely worse."

"Were you a soldier in the war then?"

"Naw. I was too young but I lost an uncle in '63. Chattanooga, Tennessee."

"I'm so sorry."

"Thank you. We were close." He swallowed hard and his voice thickened with emotion. "Went fishing and hunting together a lot."

"Can't say as I knew that devastation but I've heard plenty of veterans talk. They often mentioned the sadness at losing men. Oddly enough, they seemed to dwell on it."

"I think it's a way some men deal with the bad memories."

Illyanne turned her head toward the young man with an inquisitive look. "You seem to know a lot about the war."

"Oh, I read all the newspapers. My family saved them all. Some call me a war enthusiast. I followed all the battle reports. Can't get enough of it. Anyway, like I was sayin', something Mr. Lincoln said in his reelection speech got me thinking about today."

Illyanne looked at the driver. "What did he say?"

"He couldn't understand why the Lord would let the war go on so long. Eventually, he figured there was some kind of grand settling of scores going on over the country because of us having held people in bondage."

"President Lincoln said that?"

"Yeah. He had fancier words but that was his point. And I figured that might be true of a lot of things we can't make sense of, like this fire. Kind of makes a shiver go up your spine, doesn't it?"

Illyanne pondered this for a while as the carriage rolled along. "Really. That is an amazing sentiment. I must say, though I don't understand it." It sounded like the driver was saying the president thought the war was God's will. Which sounded absolutely crazy. Was this driver a wishful boy soldier or a bit touched in the head? The Peshtigo fire was a horror that fell upon everyone. There was no enemy. How could people losing their lives, their work and their homes be the divine will? She could only follow the driver's meaning so far and then it tuned into a tangled mess of nonsensical thoughts. The idea annoyed her but she didn't want to become cross with the man. So, she pulled up her lap blanket to signal that she did not care for any further conversation and she stayed silent.

She nodded off at moments and when she stirred again, she saw more of scorched remains of animals and the occasional homes which again dampened her spirits.

"There it is up ahead, all safe from the flames, just like I told you, Ma'am."

Illyanne had been slumped in the bench seat but she straightened up and peered into the distance. It was an astonishing site. The building had not burned. An amazing small white steeple pierced above the blackness. She heard only the horse's footfalls and the squeak of the wagon bench seat bouncing around over the parched road as they continued their approach. Then, as they came up a small incline in the land, she saw the full spread of the field. Wonderful brilliant, lustrous green! Sheep and goats grazed there inside a white picket fence. The distant perimeter of striking burned black ash surrounded this gem. Illyanne choked up as if she might cry at the simple beauty. She dabbed her eyes in a manner she thought was discreet.

"Ma'am? Are you alright?"

Illyanne cleared her throat. "Oh, yes. It's nothing." She stared at the chapel and its yard up ahead. Something about it struck her as incredibly serene. A feeling emanated from this place like invisible light penetrating her whole being.

The driver pulled up and stopped at a gate in the fence line. "Here you go, Mrs. Eriksson." He stepped down and reached up taking her hand as she descended.

She pulled her shawl tighter over her shoulders. "What's this place called again?"

"This is Our Lady of Champion Shrine and School. You know the story of Sister Adele. She –."

Illyanne nodded and flapped a hand, "Yes, yes. I know. I know. Years ago, she saw the Virgin Mary in a vision here and built this place." She reached into her small bag and dug for some coins and handed them to him. "I'm much indebted to you, sir. Thank you for bringing me. And thank you for the thought-provoking conversation."

He got back up on the wagon, took hold of the reins and tipped his hat to her. "Hope you find your kin in there or at least get some word of where they might have gone."

Illyanne stood at the gate as the driver started off. "I'll just be getting some water for the horse around back and let him rest for an hour after I unload the blankets and supplies. So, if you want to go back today, you know where to find me. There will be another wagon tomorrow."

She nodded in acknowledgment again. Something made her feel hesitant, standing outside the white picket fence. Illyanne stood still at the exterior of the little swing gate, looking at the chapel. She did not know where to go or what to do if she did not find Anders and Matthew here or some word of their whereabouts. She would be like one of those crusted tree trunks with the life sucked out of them. She felt that she would not survive losing them. She imagined she might be found wandering around somewhere, a half-Indian woman gone crazy from loss and mourning. Winter was coming. The nights had already started turning chilly. The burned land at Sugar Bush offered nothing. A terrifying fleeting thought about dying alone ran through her. Yet, she felt a thread of hope standing here. If they were here, she wanted to look her best. She smoothed her hair and took a deep breath. She lifted her head and shoulders and swung open the gate of the little fence. Her heart swelled.

33

October 17, 1871
  Nine days after the fire
Champion, Wisconsin

A SHEEP BLEATED AND scurried away as she came through the gate. Illyanne smiled to herself. She walked toward the chapel and opened the door into a quiet cavern, dimly lit with candles. People in the pews knelt and prayed. She heard a group near the front reciting the soft cadence of the rosary. She had never seen it before but she recognized the sunburst display stand set out on the altar from her mother's descriptions. Eucharist adoration was in progress. Illyanne remembered that was a consecrated host in the little glass case set into the ornate carved wood stand. God incarnate right there, humbled for human beings to come to Him – at least that's what the Church taught. Illyanne wasn't sure she believed it at all any more. The recent days had so stunted her spirit.

Still, she knelt in one of the back pews. She crossed herself and pulled her shawl up over her hair. God, if you are there, help me. Lift this dark cloud of burned everything. Help me find Anders and Matthew. I'm so, so afraid they may have died in the Peshtigo fire. I don't know what I'll do if they are dead. Illyanne once again felt her eyes well up and spill over her cheeks. I need to find my family. Please bring my husband and son back to me. Please. She hung her head and meditated on her pleading prayer, her hands clenched. Thoughts of the biblical agony in the garden, the Lord sweating blood in distress drifted into her head. She knew her torment was nothing compared to that but it was still nearly crippling for her. If her worst fear were to come true, she prayed for the strength to endure the loss of Anders and Matthew.

If she didn't find some hint of them soon, maybe she would go to the reservation and seek help. Perhaps trying to reach God in the form of the Menomonie Great Spirit, Mecawetok might somehow work out better.

It seemed mysterious that in the next instant, that old sea shanty came into her head. It was the one Anders used to recite, the ode that the sailors on the Henry B. Jones had been singing that first day in the all the smoke.

Oh Mary, Star of the Sea,
Light of all waters,
Guide us through all dark and stormy seas
Protect us from being lost at sea.
Lead us to that haven of peace and light
Back to our home port,
Found only in Him
who calmed the sea.

It felt right to appeal to Mary. This was a Marian place. She really was the star of the sea. She was the heaven-sent one, like the fixed North Star. Mary watched over mariners and guided them back to port and back to her Son. The sisters built this chapel to remember her appearance here. Illyanne's mother used to say, Mary was one of a kind, a special helper, an after-apostle spiritual mother for everyone. "God sends her to us," is what she used to say. "She's up there, praying for us and standing by to talk to her Son for us to help out." And, she came and appeared here, to this little patch of farm and forested land. Here. There was something piercingly basic and alluring about that. Being in this place made it feel more real.

The second stanza of Anders' little sea shanty, the one which she could not recall when she was on the deck of the Jones, seemed to erupt inside her head now as if someone was reciting it to her into her very soul.

As we set forth
Upon the Great Lakes
and cross the deserts
of our time,
Show us, Oh Mary,
the fruit of your womb,
for without your Son
We are lost,
Aimlessly casting about
Adrift at sea.
Guide us back,
Back to safe harbor
Where we can rest,
Rest again in Him.

It made her smile to hear the men singing it in her memory. She could see Anders in her mind's eye, singing it on the homestead as he chopped word or bailed hay.

She repeated Anders' prayer sea shanty in her heart and cried quietly there in the pew for some time. Though she reached for God, she could not grasp Him in the midst of everything that had transpired. She could not see or hear or feel Him. She only felt the familiar acid wrenching in her gut for Anders and Matthew. Had they survived? Where were they? If she didn't find them here or catch word of where they might be, she would be at the frightening end of her search.

She did not notice the sisters finishing their rosary and leaving the chapel. One of them touched her elbow gently and startled her. It jolted her out of her fervent haze.

"I'm so sorry. We need to close up the shrine for the evening."

"I came here looking for my husband and son. Anders and Matthew Eriksson? Do you know them?

"I'm sorry. No. Come with me where we can talk. I am Sister Therese." The sister led her out a side door and into a small church-school office. The sister sat behind a desk. There were crudely cut wood shelves all around with some books and papers on them. Four chairs formed a semi-circle in front of the desk.

"Please have a seat." The sister shuffled some papers around, laying them out in groups to be attended to later.

Illyanne bunched up her hands and sat down leaning a little forward. "Have you had a lot of visitors? I've heard many took shelter here the night of the fire. I'm hoping someone wrote down names so families searching for people can find them."

"We had many visitors, yes. It was a hectic night." The sister set her big black sleeves on the desk top and folded her hands. "Many had trouble breathing and had burns. Hands and feet mostly. I'm sorry. There is no list of names. May I ask your name?"

"Illyanne."

Sister Therese wrote it down. "Oh, how beautiful. It sounds French. Is it?"

"Oh, I don't know. Maybe. There were still French fur traders around when I was born."

"It's a pretty name anyhow." The sister cocked her head and smiled, the black veil and white wimple rustled as she moved. "It's like a combination of Ellie in Elizabeth and Anne, the Virgin Mother's cousin and mother. Lovely."

Illyanne gave the sister a perplexed look, having never heard this before.

Sister Therese peered at her with curiosity and calm. "I feel certain the Blessed Mother has had you under her protective mantel and she brought you here to this place."

Illyanne didn't want to scoff openly at that. But, she certainly didn't believe she'd been under anyone's protection since the fire, the shipwreck and her arduous trek through burned-out lands.

"And you have a wise mother," Sister Therese turned toward her with a warm smile.

"She's gone now. Passed some years ago."

"I'm so sorry. But I sense she was wise. And, devout too, no?"

"Yes, Catholic. Many Menominee are, from the French missionaries. She taught me traditional beliefs too, saying it was a new way of understanding the old teachings. The upper and lower worlds, good and evil spirits and all."

A young girl came in wearing a long bib apron. "Sister?" She looked at Illyanne with surprise and bowed her head toward the nun apologetically, she guessed for interrupting. "Shall I bring some tea?"

"Yes, Patricia. And, we'll likely need a place tonight for our guest." She left promptly.

"Oh, no." Illyanne stood up. "That won't be necessary. I only came to see if my husband and son were here, or some word of where they may have gone. You don't have a list so I'll be on my way." She stood up. "The driver said he would be out back. Thank you. If you'll show me the way."

"Please sit down, Illyanne. I'm afraid the relief wagon driver has already left. He was here less than an hour but you were in the chapel for much longer."

"Was I? Oh, my." Illyanne flushed and held the back of her hand to her cheek for a moment.

The girl named Patricia came back with a tray of tea and some little cakes.

"Actually, that smells wonderful, sister. Thank you." Illyanne sipped at the tea and ate several cakes quickly. "I guess I didn't realize how hungry I was."

"You'll stay and eat a meal with us. We don't serve supper for everyone. We live in a farming community where many people work late. We hand out bread and apples in the evening for families who send someone to pick them up." The sister looked down for a moment and swallowed. "Not as many as usual have been coming since the fire. Our big gathering meal is breakfast. And, there's really no place else for you to stay the night. I assure you it's no trouble. We've taken in over a hundred this last week to sleep in the chapel. Many have gone now.

"Our sisters are all out over the grounds and barn now. In the morning, you'll see everyone who is still here at breakfast. You can ask them if they've seen your husband and son. Maybe someone crossed paths with them."

Illyanne chimed in. "I still can't imagine how they would have come here from Sugar Bush."

"But, fear not, Illyanne, we will inquire. Now, Patricia will take you to a place where you can rest. It's nothing special. Just a child's bed for when someone doesn't feel well at school. You can rest and we'll wake you when we are passing out the evening rations."

Illyanne nodded in approval. Patricia led her to the school child's room. It was small but cozy. There was a pitcher and wash bowl. Illyanne cleaned her face and hands and laid down to rest. The walls were rough logs and rustic plaster and a small crucifix on one wall.

Worries of Anders and Matthew interfered with her desire to sleep but she finally fell off. She dreamed of Anders. She was lying in his arms, beneath heavy blankets comforted by his presence. It must have been late autumn. They were in their bed at Sugar Bush and the morning light was streaking in. The breeze outside rustled the leaves of the trees. She wanted to wait a minute more before getting up to start the fire. The rooster crowed outside. The scene was blurry but the feeling was deep and warm. She heard Matthew calling for her. "Mother, where are you?" It was unmistakably his voice, and she snapped back awake.

34

October 17-18, 1871
    Nine - ten days after the fire
Champion, Wisconsin

"MISS ILLYANNE? EXCUSE me, Miss Illyanne?" It was the girl, Patricia standing in the doorway.

Illyanne sat up. "Yes."

"Sister sent me to fetch you for evening rations. Would you come with me, please?"

Illyanne wiped her eyes and followed Patricia. She led her out of the school part of the building into a connected structure, the living quarters. There was a long table in the kitchen and people came by and picked up bread and apples in flour sacks and walked back outside.

Illyanne helped pass out food alongside one of the sisters. The sister who had brought Illyanne in, explained to her. "I have told the other sisters you are searching for your husband and son. We will all be praying for you."

The nun with the scarred eye looked in to see how the food distribution was going. Somehow, Illyanne knew this was Sister Adele, the one who had the vision years ago. An extraordinary sense surrounded her.

Illyanne recognized another striking similarity to her heritage religion. One day her mother showed her a keepsake box. She remembered that it contained an eagle feather, a deerskin patch decorated with colored porcupine quills, a shell necklace, and a little drawstring medicine bag. That led to Illyanne's questions about what the pouch was for. Her mother told her that the Menominee had a medicine man, who was something like a priest, a Mukakee Ogima. Illyanne's mother told her he gave people these bags as a kind of a reminder of their faith. She said "The people treated the medicine man with great respect. Only he could speak to the spiritual world. Whenever anyone was around him, a strong warm feeling that came out of him." This sister Adele was like that. Illyanne was in the presence of a person who experienced a direct visit from heaven – if she believed the story. For the time being, she saw nothing wrong with taking their word for it, that the apparition had really happened, and right here.

"If you sisters need someone to help in the kitchen, I have worked as a cook." She thought of mentioning her Saturday night dinners at the Peshtigo Boarding House but realized this might sound unclean to them. "I would be glad to help. To repay you for your hospitality."

Something about being in the company of these women felt uplifting. The sister who first spoke to her led her back to the bed in the school. "I'll be up early and will come to the kitchen to help cook breakfast."

"Really, it is not necessary."

"Please. It will give me pleasure. I love to cook."

The sister nodded and then went away. In an hour or so, Illyanne heard all of them singing in the chapel. First, a female voice sang something in elongated tones which echoed in the upper regions of the chapel. The group of the other sisters, sang a response in melodic unison. It sounded praising and mournful and pure. She walked to the door of the chapel and the young girl, Patricia, was standing there by the chapel door with it cracked open a little to listen.

"What is going on?"

"It's Vespers, the last prayer of the evening. The sisters sing it in Gregorian chant in the evening."

The both fell quiet for a minute, listening as the voices woo them.

"It's beautiful," Illyanne said. "I've never heard anything like it before."

"Well then, you can see how it lifts up the soul."

Illyanne barely heard her, momentarily entranced. "Oh yes, I guess so. Evening vespers. "What is it from?"

"It's hundreds of years old. I think it's from old monasteries in Europe."

On the way back to her school child's room, she asked Patricia about the apparition. "When Mary appeared here, what did she say?"

"She didn't speak the first two times. She just smiled and vanished. She appeared three times. It was twelve years ago on October eighth."

"The same day as the fire?"

"Yes, we always recognize the day with some special prayers at Mass," said Patricia. Anyhow, Adele was about my age when she saw the Virgin Mary, outside along a pathway. The lady told her she was the Queen of Heaven. She was to teach the children the faith and pray for the conversion of sinners. Without penance, she said her Son would be obliged to punish them." Patricia made a little laugh and continued. "I always took that to mean that Jesus let her visit people before he has to do something drastic – like send a flood."

Patricia's comment brought on a fleeting dread. Could the fire be some kind of punishment? But for what? Could she and other people have done something wrong without even knowing it?

Illyanne got up early and made her way to the kitchen where two other nuns were already starting breakfast. They put her to work chopping up potatoes for frying. Thankfully, the sisters had onions. She cut up and fried three onions and then set them aside while she fried the remaining potatoes in oil, flipping them to get a brown crusting. The skillet was large but she had to fry up three pans separately as the sisters and guests would be nearly twenty people. She tossed in salt and pepper and some paprika and stirred the fried onions back in. The potatoes filled a large bowl that would be passed around the table.

As she was cooking, Sister Catherine, next to her in the kitchen was breaking eggs into a pan. Sister Margarette, standing next in the assembly line of cooks, busied herself dicing up a small amount of ham. Illyanne chatted with her, explaining she was living near Peshtigo and had seen the fire flash up there. "Honestly, it reminded me of the pillar of fire in the Bible."

All of the nuns were amused at that. They smiled and nodded and went back to their work.

"That really scared me," Illyanne said. "Don't you sisters think that's a little strange that something so terrible would be like the Bible's pillar of fire?" She shook her head as she continued to cut up potatoes. "I just can't imagine what that means."

The one named Sister Jean said, "Pfff. It doesn't mean anything. There's rain and floods and volcanoes that pour down fire but it's not like they are like Bible stories happening again. It's nothing. Just nature doing what it does."

Sister Catherine added, "Anyway, out here, the fire crept up burning through fields. It was more like a low wall of fire and a night sky of reddish-brown smoke."

The other sister said nothing but listened to their exchange and shrugged her shoulders. Illyanne wondered why these sisters would not be more concerned. Surely, they knew the Bible. How could they just shrug off the fact that the devastating fire arrived in the form like the Chosen People's pillar of fire?

Ten guests came to the breakfast table and six of the sisters sat down too. Illyanne asked, "Where are the children. There's a boarding school here isn't there?"

Sister Therese, the nun who had greeted her yesterday, and who seemed to be her guide answered. "Oh, most are all home with their parents. The few that are still here are orphans. Near the harvest, the children stay home to help out their families, gathering apples, pumpkins, potatoes and smaller garden greens."

The sisters added the diced ham to the scrambled eggs and her potatoes served as the perfect compliment. There was also bread and raspberry jam.

As people arrived, they remained standing in front of empty plates and place settings. When Sister Adele came in, they all prayed over the meal, Illyanne mumbling along with them. They sat down and began eating and talking and passing the serving bowls of food around.

Illyanne asked the guests if they had seen anyone fitting the description of Anders and Matthew. The only replies she received were that nobody had seen them or they weren't sure. They could have been in the group is all she could find out.

One of the sisters saw how deflated Illyanne's reaction was. "You have to remember; it was total chaos here. Families came running into the chapel. Children were crying. Some had burns, trouble breathing. We were all busy taking care of the injured, making bandages, getting food and water. There wasn't time for polite chatting." She half-expected that she would find no trace of them. Someone would have told her something yesterday if there had been any chance they'd been there.

When the relief wagon came again mid-morning, Sister Therese told her, "May God be with you on your search and may your heavenly mother light your way. We'll pray for you."

Her mind flew back to a day when she would have smiled kindly, thanked her and returned some little salutation like God bless you, too. But Illyanne did not feel this urge. She simply nodded and held her head down in a little bow and she walked out to meet the relief wagon. Illyanne felt numb on the ride back to Green Bay. What ever would she do now? She might have to go on alone. Widows had a bad enough time getting along. Being half-Menominee, she expected it would be even more difficult.

35

October 18, 1871
Ten days after the fire
The Lumber Room,
Green Bay Relief Camp
Near old Fort Howard

WORKING AT THE DOCKS and on the salvage run put significant money in their pockets, all together almost fifteen dollars. Anders didn't know what else to do except check back at the Lumber Room to see if there was any news on transportation to Peshtigo.

The information desk was busy with a line of people standing there. Anders and Matthew sat down on one of the wooden benches and people-watched.

The line dwindled and Anders inquired about getting a ride to Peshtigo or Sugar Bush.

A different clerk was manning the desk than the one who was there two days ago. He clerk shook his head no. "The only people going out that way are the relief wagon drivers. They haven't got room to take riders. They fill up with supplies to hand out. Now if you want to work as a relief team, I can have you speak to someone."

"No, thanks. Are there any relief camps near here?"

The clerk advised them of the one near Fort Howard, which had been an old military outpost, just outside of the city on the north side. "It just started up a few days ago. You could get a carriage or walk it in about an hour and a half."

Since they had money, they hailed a carriage outside the Lumber Room. They arrived at the Green Bay camp. One of the fire survivors showed them to two cots in the men's tent where they could stay. Supper had already been served and the relief people had cleaned up and left for the evening. That night, Anders and Matthew ate some bread left on a cart for any camp late arrivals.

They dropped their packs and laid down on the cots. Some men played cards nearby and others talked in a small circle. Outside, someone had a harmonica and Matthew headed out to sit by the fire. It was a big fire with a mix of people, families, children and two young men. Some were telling stories and singing songs.

Matthew sat near the young men and edged into the conversation about going out West. The fellow called Ralph was itching to go to California. "I'd do my bit panning for gold and if that didn't work out, I'd head up north to San Francisco. There's lots of shipping work there and all kinds of new businesses."

Matthew offered a comment in reply. "Yeah, a week ago, I would've considered heading out there with you. But my Pa," he pointed his thumb toward the tent and lowered his voice, "he wants me to take over the homestead. I got a taste for sailing and shipping. Trouble is, now I like this girl who's here."

The two young men groaned in a teasing manner. They shoved at Matthew's shoulders. "Aw, she'll wait for you," Ralph said.

"No, no, I've got it," Tony, the other one said. "You go out first and look around for a good six months, get settled. And iff'n you don't find another girl who catches your fancy –." Tony slapped Matthew on the back, "You just send a letter back home here with the fare to sail to Chicago and take the train all the way to out West. Have her come out to you."

They all laughed. "Yeah, but what about my Pa? And the homestead?" Matthew picked up twigs from the ground and tossed them into the fire. "I just can't imagine disappointing him." He hung his head.

The talk stopped for a minute and then Tony said, "Well, you can get into sailing and shipping right here – that is, if this fire hasn't entirely killed it off."

Matthew got up and told them he was going to visit the latrine pit. They were nice fellas but he was glad to go off and to have his thoughts to himself. He didn't know what the fire may have done to the homestead and the whole logging and shipping business. Would it be functioning after the fire? Would he even be able to really try sailing? And if he did get the chance to go, how would he ever break it to his father?

Along the dark path, out from behind some brush, someone stepped out in front of him in an impish manner. "Matthew, hello."

He looked up and for a moment he was dumbstruck. "Chepi? Chepi Redleaf, it is you?" Matthew stood still for a moment. He reached out for her and she reached out and they grasped each other's forearms. She was laughing.

He placed his hands on her shoulders. "The fire. What did you all do?"

She nodded. "We got into the canoes for the night. We paddled toward Green Bay along the shore. Came ashore where the burned area stopped. We camped there a few nights. Then, the relief people in a wagon told us to come here. We camped and walked through Oneida land to this place."

Matthew kissed her on the cheek and they hugged each other tightly. His thoughts about everything else melted away. He had found her. There was only the two of them in the midst of the charred world. But they were together. It must be a sign that she was indeed his fate. The timing of the encounter with Chepi right after he had been talking about her Matthew took as a mystical sign that she was the one for him.

Someone approached, coming toward the latrines. Matthew pulled Chepi aside some distance into the shadows. "Is your uncle here with you in the men's tent?"

"No, we all were here for one night. We ate the relief food but we stayed outside of the tent. My uncle and the other Menominee with us in Sturgeon Bay went back to Menomonie lands. He told me to stay here to help with the relief workers for many days."

They sat down near a large tree trunk in the moonlight. Chepi laid her head on his chest and nestled under his arm. They remained this way for some time in silence, their hearts united. They breathed in the quiet joy of having found each other alive. It had seemed so unlikely. A sobering sentiment circulated between them about what could have happened to each of them in the fire.

"How did you find me?" Matthew asked.

"We saw the fire was on both sides of the water. You told us you were going near the chapel. Everything up the peninsula as far as Sturgeon Bay burned. We found out that people who went to the chapel were soon sent to a new relief camp, here. So, if you were alive, I knew you would probably come here in a few days. I thought I could find you on your way to the outhouse. So, I waited. I've come out here and waited many nights, hoping to find you."

Matthew chuckled and hugged her closer. He got up. "I *was* on my way there. I'll be right back. Stay here." He returned in a few minutes.

"You are a smart girl." He smiled and stroked her hair which glistened in the pale moonlight. "My dear Chepi. I'm so glad you are all right. I'd better get back. My dad will be wondering where I've gone off to."

Chepi leaned in and set her cheek against Matthew's. "I will be helping with the breakfast tomorrow. I will see you and your father then." She jumped up and went into the night.

36

O*ctober 18, 1871*
   Ten days after the fire
Champion; Fort Howard Relief Camp near Green Bay

DESPERATION TO FIND Anders and Matthew had compelled Illyanne to visit the chapel. It ended up making things worse. In traversing about one hundred miles, from Green Island to the little chapel in Champion on the other side of the bay she had not found her family nor any hint of their whereabouts.

Hope had now thinned out. The light inside her dimmed. Her hopeful deadlines of October fourteenth and sixteenth had both passed. The possibility of never finding her family was fast becoming a likelihood. She would probably go and cook with Beulah and have a good lifetime friend. Perhaps, if Beulah ever married, Illyanne might become a favorite auntie to her children. That way, she would at least have a shell of a second life, an adopted second family. Illyanne came to realize on the relief wagon ride back to Green Bay that, like so many others, her old life may truly have burned away in the fire.

When she returned to the city, she went to visit Beulah, who always lifted her spirits, at least for a while.

"What you gotta do now, Illie, is get work and find some place to lay your head. Why not try the Lumber Room? You sure can cook. I can recommend you to them, however good that might do."

"Well, I suppose."

"Absolutely. You oughta go back there. You still got that fancy dress they loaned you?"

Illyanne shook her head up and down. "Yes, it's back in the room."

"I say go back there and change into it and go on down there right now and talk to the restaurant manager. They'll be cooking and getting ready to serve the evening meal."

It was only when she was alone again with her own thoughts that her dour outlook on everything started up again. But, Beulah was right. Right now, there was nothing else for her to do but start working and then figure out how to keep looking for Anders and Matthew.

Illyanne changed clothes and descended the Lumber Room staircase. The grandeur of the plush rugs, tall columns and elegant paint and lighting helped buck her up. Taking Beulah's advice to heart, she straightened up and raised her head. A different clerk was manning the information and commerce desk than the one she had sat and spoken to a few days earlier. "Good afternoon, sir. I wish to apply for a job here as a cook. I have experience cooking at the Peshtigo Boarding House. My friend is a cook here and she recommends me."

He directed her to wait in the dining room. She sat down at the table she'd eaten at the night before. She fidgeted in her chair. Thankfully, in a few minutes the manager came by. They chatted for a while. "We do have a job for a cook but it's on the road."

"I don't understand."

"In conjunction with other businesses, we're sending a cooked dinner meal to the fire survivors at the relief camp just north of town. The job is meal preparation, loading the food and utensils and driving a wagon to the camp, serving the meal, returning and doing the cleanup."

"I can do that."

"It'll be simple recipes. Stews, biscuits and bread."

He asked her some cooking questions and then said, "If you can start tomorrow morning, you're hired."

November 1871

A month after the fire

Green Bay

As a Lumber Room employee, with income, she was no longer entitled to stay in their hotel. She rented a room in a boarding house, another block down from Beulah. She began working the next day. The first week went well but day in and day out, she felt her family almost disappearing, except in her heart. Illyanne began to live her new life, which she hoped would be temporary. Work lessened her strife but it left her tired. If she didn't find Anders and Matthew, she wondered if she would ever really rest again.

The last few days of October arrived faster than Illyanne could have imagined. The cooking work was good. She had a bit of independence in creating recipes so she tried new kinds of bread and stews. Cutting up meats and vegetables and seasoning the stew kept her mind busy. It took two or three hours to make the food, two hours to drive the wagon to the relief camp and back and an hour to serve the meals, and then clean up and prepare for the next day.

She began falling into new routines. Seeing the old cleaning man mopping up in the kitchen every morning when she came in was pleasant. They shared the same conversation every day with small modifications, and all the while amused at themselves.

"Good morning, Mr. Cleary."

"Top of the morning, Miss Illyanne. What are you going to cook for my supper today?"

"A little more of the same old vegetables and meat. But today, I'm going to make something new in the sauce."

"Oh, my tummy's growlin'. Well, I guess I oughta get cracking on this floor."

"All right, Mr. Cleary. I'll see you later."

The cooking job helped her fight the sadness, most of the time. Yet, a full day's work drained her energies, helping her sleep. Illyanne saw many unfortunate people every day at the relief camp. They wore clothes that didn't fit. The people whose homes had burned milled about and stayed mostly quiet. She saw them living in old soldiers' tents, spending their time gathering wood and sitting around campfires and lining up to get a meal which she dished out for them. People came and went but she saw some of the same faces, day after day. At least Illyanne had a job and a rooming house place to stay through the winter.

For several days, two children regularly lifted her mood. A brother about ten and his sister who was a few years younger, stood in line to get their portions and smiled. She learned that their mother, who was still missing, had told them it was important to find something interesting every day. Whatever that was it would be talked about at their family dinner table. The poor things were always dirty and ragtag. Coming through the supper line one evening, the little girl informed Illyanne cheerfully, "Today, we saw a fox."

The older brother put his hand gently over his sister's mouth. "Well, we might have seen a fox. It was early in the morning when this we were coming back from the outhouse. Something with a bushy tail was out there."

"It was a fox. I saw him," the girl said.

Illyanne opened her eyes wide. "Well, it might have been a fox. It's a good thing your brother was with you. But don't try to catch him." She switched to whispering. "If you do, I'll have to cook him. And as a cook, I happen to know that fox stew tastes terrible." She winked at the older brother. They both giggled and took their plates and moved along in the line. What a boost she got from interacting with these children every day.

She saw Beulah in the mornings but they only had time to briefly greet each other and get to work. It was still encouraging to see her. Beulah had coached her to go on when she despaired so. "I knew of plenty of folks in the war who never got to see their loved ones ever again. And they didn't necessarily get any letter about how they died either. But they had to go on. Had to. Ain't no other choice but dyin'. You're gonna be fine."

Whenever the dreary faces of the fire refugees holding out their tin pans got to her, she thought of Beulah. Then she knew to stop feeling sorry for herself and "cook them people the best darned meal you can fix up for them, just like they was Anders and Matthew themselves." In those moments, Illyanne felt thankful that she had survived and was able to do something she enjoyed to help others. But the struggle went on and on, daily, even hourly sometimes.

She exchanged greetings with Ruby, who lived in the room next door to her. She was older, a widow who worked as a housekeeper and had trouble with her feet. She often said things like, "Thank God, the day's over. I can't wait to put my feet up." One day, she was carrying a package and seemed to have more trouble than usual.

Illyanne helped her carry her package and get her sitting down in her chair and propped up her feet. "I can rub your feet for you if you like. I've got some ginger oil that might help."

Ruby agreed and Illyanne ran next door to get her bag of natural medicines. "Get your stockings off. Do you have a bucket? You need to soak your feet for a few minutes." She heated some water like she would if she was making tea and poured it into the bucket with some cold water, so it evened out as warm. Illyanne dried one foot at a time and rubbed the ginger oil into her hands and them massaged each foot.

Ruby thanked her over and over for how much it helped. It felt good to help someone else.

"I'll try to make some more at the kitchen for you. It smells strong though and I'll have to come up with a recipe with ginger so it smells normal. I know a chicken with ginger recipe. I'll see if I can get it onto my week's menu and I can cook it. I'll bring you some ginger oil soon so if I'm not around, you can use it yourself."

Life was different without her family but Illyanne carried on. Some of it was nice and Illyanne felt she had become more outgoing around other people than she had been before. The down moods still came but perhaps they were less frequent now.

The first few days of November, Illyanne was again scooping up rations of stew for a line of people at the relief camp. She got so dispirited from it, some nights she delegated serving to one of the relief camp women who'd had helped often to clean up. It gave Illyanne a chance to take a stroll. Often the outdoors felt refreshing but at times the gloom took over. She could not change her perception of the people — the long noses, dark eyes, blond hair, dark hair and almost always, pale skin. They all bore the weary look of defeat.

She forced herself to talk to them with cheerfulness. "This is a bit of chicken stew tonight, with corn and mushrooms and potatoes. I seasoned it just right. This one will stick to your bones. And we have bread with a nice crust and cheese tonight." It was as much for them as it was for herself.

When she was cleaning up the pots and plates, packing up the wagon. Some children in the camp piqued her curiosity. They were playing a form of tag, running about the camp and singing the sea shanty about the Star of the Sea . . . light of all waters, guide us through all dark and stormy seas. She called after one of them and a boy stopped. "Where did you hear that shanty?"

"From some sailors. They taught us."

"Sailors here?"

"Yes, Miss. They said they sing it when they raise the sails."

"What sailors? Do you know their names?"

"No but there's a young one and an older one. They were here in the camp. We were all singing songs to pass the time."

"Did the older one have light-colored hair? Are they still here?'

"I don't remember their hair and I don't know if they're still around."

"Would you go and see if you can find them and ask them if they know my husband, Anders Eriksson, and my son, Matthew? I have to finish loading the wagon."

"Sure, Miss." The boy ran off.

He returned in a few minutes. "Nobody answered to those names. Maybe they moved on."

"Well, I'll be back tomorrow. I appreciate it if you ask around. If you find out something useful, I'll give you an extra biscuit."

"All right, Miss."

After her one day off, she didn't see those children again.

There were plenty of sailors among the camp survivors. She might get some word of them. And, she might not. Beulah's words about the possibility of not finding her family did not really keep her head level. Instead, throughout her days, she swung back and forth from feeling hopeful to utterly despondent.

Several nights later, Illyanne had regressed into one of her bad states again. She set up for distributing the evening meal and camp survivors were lining up. She couldn't find her helper. She did not care about anything while dishing up the platefuls of stew and bread. She did not really look at the people. They seemed faceless, all part of the unending line of hungry, needy, downtrodden camp people.

That night she had a talk with Ruby in the next room in her quarters. Ruby had lost her husband before the fire and Illyanne asked for her advice on how to persevere.

"Well, you cry an awful lot." Ruby laughed. "Soon enough, there's debtors who come to collect on things. We had a small place with a few chickens and goats, grew a little corn. Thank heavens I didn't have any children to worry about." She sighed. "The world doesn't give you much time to mourn. You have to get on. I couldn't keep the place myself so as soon as I buried Sal, I sold and came to the city to find work."

"How did you ever get over your gloom?"

"Who says I'm over it?"

"You seem to get by all right. You're not sickly, lying in bed all day." Illyanne motioned for Ruby to put her feet up so she could massage them again.

"It does get a little easier in time. But, you go on because you have to and seeing somebody who's worse off – I'm sorry to say – helps a bit too. I haven't lost a child like some have. When there's no choice, you scrap to find every little joy you can and you go on. Life just makes you put it behind you."

Illyanne got a faraway look in her eyes. "I am coming to believe my husband and son are gone and I will never know where they were or how they left this earth." She did not tear up. A wave of tiredness simply swept over her. She patted Ruby's feet and let them down.

"That's a bad shake," Ruby said. "I'm sorry for your grief. There's many a woman and man out there in your situation. I don't want to add to your sorrow but you're young enough that you could find another husband."

"Oh no, Ruby, I couldn't even think of it." She got up from the chair in Ruby's small room. She felt a rush of guilt and confusion. "I'm awful tired all of the sudden. Thanks for the talk."

In Illyanne's own modest rented room, she realized Ruby and Beulah had given her roughly the same advice. It sunk in hard now. She would have a little pack of misery on her back now to carry all the time. The load would lighten sometimes but it would continue with her and never leave. She began saving money for whatever she might do after the coming winter. She'd have to sell the homestead.

She wanted to do something in the short term to feel better, something for others who were worse off. Maybe she could bake bread for the firestorm widows who sought help from the church.

37

November, 1871
Green Bay

ILLYANNE LOST TRACK of the weeks and days. It was already the middle of November. It turned colder and it could start snowing any day. One day when she arrived at the camp with supper, she saw relief teams sawing and pounding away to construct some small cabin homes.

She asked one of the women holding out her plate for stew, "Is that going to be where you all live this winter?"

"Some of us."

"What about the rest of you?"

"They're saying families can get free transport on a steamer to Milwaukee."

"Milwaukee? That's awfully far away."

"They say they'll bring us back in the spring. There's homes that'll take us in for the winter. I've got two youngins." The woman choked up a little. "Don't really want to go but it might be the best thing."

Every day the relief teams kept building. The relief workers ended up joining six cabins together for multiple larger group homes. There was a common kitchen center with a big fireplace and another in each of the cabins. She arrived early one day and approached the head man of the construction team – volunteers, fire survivors themselves. "Sir, I wonder if you could build one of these group houses with a big barn door in the center. Looks like I will be coming here all winter. If I could pull the horse and wagon inside, everybody would stay a lot warmer." She smiled. "Including the horse."

"Well, I don't know. That'd take a lot more wood and time."

"Long as I'm here cooking and dishing up, I can make sure all your workers get fed."

"Ma'am, I b'lieve we've struck a bargain." He held out his hand to shake on it. "It'll be ready by next week."

The remaining camp dwellers totaled around thirty. With the colder weather, the trip wasn't too bad from the Lumber Room to the relief camp near Ft. Howard and back. It was just under four miles one way. The Lumber Room had already provided her a Mackinaw six-point blanket coat made from the thickest Indian wool blankets. It was next best to bear skin to fend off the cold.

The change in the weather drove home the reality even further that Illyanne would probably never find Anders and Matthew. So many other people suffered the same fate. There would be a slim chance to find them when spring came. But now, people needed to be hunkering down wherever they were. The daily routine and having made some acquaintances helped and gave her the basic necessities to survive. Still, misery sometimes plagued her. She served up ladle after ladle of stew onto plates held up by expressionless faces. New faces still appeared. Old ones reappeared after being gone for days. Others never showed up again. People were probably finding relatives to live with while others found their way to the camp.

Sometimes, Illyanne fell into thinking of feeding these people like feeding the livestock back at the homestead, an empty obligation to fulfill. If she did not buck up, she would descend into the state that she saw in these people's faces. So, she forced herself to look into the eyes of hungry homeless people holding out Army mess tins for their supper. She uttered little pleasantries to them and tried to smile. One of the men who stood before her, waiting for his supper was lost in the same gloom she had been in a minute before. His face resembled Anders. She looked back at him again. He really looked like Anders. No, actually, he didn't just look like him. "Anders!"

He looked up and for a few seconds he did not believe his eyes. He dropped his mess pan. "Illie! Illie-NeeNAH! Oh, thank God."

Illie said, "Thank God," too. She felt a rush of emotion and she knew that this time she really meant it.

She dropped the ladle abruptly and some of the gravy splashed out from the big pot onto the next fire survivor standing in line.

Anders and Illyanne both came around the bread table and rushed toward each other. Their bodies made a thud as they threw themselves into one another. They hugged and kissed and cried and laughed, remaining clenched together for a long time. Illyanne's heart flew. She leaned against his chest, needing to catch her breath.

She whispered "Thank God," again.

Cradling her head against his chest, Anders said. "And the Lady of Champion. Finding you is like another miracle. I prayed that she would lead me to you."

"I can't say that I really prayed much." Illyanne said. "I was so crushed by everything."

"I prayed for both of us."

The dreary camp dwellers standing in line watched, most without expression, some with smiles breaking through their melancholy. A few clapped.

She glanced over at the people in line. "Sorry. Please help yourselves."

Anders and Illyanne slowly fell down on their knees, on the dirt camp floor while still hugging each other. They stroked each other's faces and hair for a long spell, then they stood up together again.

"I can't believe it. You are alive. And well." She pushed back from him to take him all in. She ran her eyes over him from head to toe, ran her hands over his shoulders and arms. "Your arm has healed up all right, then?"

"Not entirely. Anyhow, it's been six weeks. It's good enough for dock work and burial teams."

She refused to let that little reminder dampen her spirits. "That shirt needs a little mending. But, oh, you look good." She saw that he needed a shave and a bath wouldn't hurt him but everyone needed a bath. She hugged him again tightly. "You got away. You got away. You're all I've hoped for."

Hearing the commotion, Matthew came forward. The three of them twirled as they hugged each other tightly.

The flurry of questions came. The fire, the running aground and Green Island.

"I know Illie. We were there. Matthew and I went out for a day with a salvage crew to load up the lumber."

"What were you doing on a salvage crew?" Illyanne asked. "Then how did you get here? Were you at the home when the fire came? I've been back there so —."

"We were near Champion, on the peninsula when the fire hit. Wait. You've been back home? How was it? Did anything survive? Is the house still standing?"

"Why weren't you home? Either one of you?" She squinted her eyes and gapped her mouth, questioning. "Look, there's so much that's happened." She held a glassy-eyed trancelike smile looking at him. "The important thing is we found each other now."

"Yes, Illie-Nee, by God's grace and his Star of the Sea." Anders threw open his arms wide.

Illyanne couldn't stop smiling at whatever Anders said. "There's a thousand things I want to ask."

She served them two plates with a larger than usual helping. "It's my venison mushroom stew. I cook at the Lumber Room now. That's where this is all from. I'm hired on as a temporary cook to aid the fire survivors. You two, go sit over there and eat. And don't move one inch. I'll finish up here and join you."

Anders and Illyanne talked and talked sitting together after dinner. Matthew walked off after a bit and returned and stood up in front of Illyanne. "Mother, there's someone I want you to meet. I have met a very special girl. Her name is Chepi Redleaf." He motioned the girl, standing out of sight to come forward.

Illyanne looked up not fully understanding.

The young Indian girl stepped toward Illyanne and bent her head. "Pleased to meet you." She wore a buckskin shift dress and leggings. She wore her long dark hair down but it was wavy from recent braiding. Illyanne recognized a bead design on her dress. It had a vine leaf and flowers, a bead pattern that was distinctly Menominee.

"You are Menominee?"

"Yes. And Algonquin but raised Menominee."

Matthew came up and stood beside Illyanne. He whispered in her ear. "This is the girl I plan to marry, mother."

Illyanne's eyes flashed toward Anders. "You knew about this?" She turned back to Matthew with a pleading whine in her voice. "You are only fifteen." At the same moment, she felt the mystical pull of kinship. If this Chepi Redleaf and Matthew did marry and have a child, it would have more Menominee blood than she herself had. The thought pleased her.

"But in a year, Mother, I will be old enough — the age you were when you got married."

Illyanne stayed silent for a while. "It's been quite a day. I'm feeling lightheaded." She went weak in the knees but Anders was there to hold her up.

He called for someone to bring her a camp stool to sit on. She breathed deeply and in a minute was fine again. "Chepi Redleaf," she called to Matthew's girl and stretched out her hands to her. Something in the young girl projected a feeling of a good spirit. "You're lovely. I hope to have some time with you soon to get to know you better. I am NeeNAH, after the Menominee mission town on Lake Winnebago, near Appleton." She paused for a moment. Their eyes met in congenial recognition of tribal commonality. "And, my English name is Illyanne Eriksson."

38

Excerpts from the diary of Illyanne NeeNAH Eriksson
Discovered by Chepi Redleaf Eriksson in a trunk at the
Sugar Bush, Wisconsin homestead of Matthew Eriksson in 1882
Eleven years after the fire.

DECEMBER, 1871

When I found Anders and Matthew a month ago, we were all dirty, tired, and in a state of shock. Still, I sobbed with joy. We ate together and slept on the ground. We took simple pleasure in talking for hours. The stars pulsated magically that night.

We walked for three days to the Menomonie reservation. We crossed the burn line from a Netherworld of ash into fresh air, glorious trees, brush and animals. We caught lake fish. Chepi showed us how to cook it in a dugout hole lined with a scrap of deerskin form her tunic. Heated rocks dropped into water in the deerskin boiled the fish and rice. We learned that Chepi's name was from an Algonquin fairy spirit of the dead who whispers knowledge from ancestors to medicine men in visions.

The Menominee welcomed us and helped us build a tree bark home for the winter. Father Pernin visited and convinced me to teach catechism to the children with Chepi, who knew both languages. All of his helpers were lost to the fire. He gave me a book for notes and for my own writing. It turns out I like writing and the children are a joy.

. . . <u>May, 1872, seven months after the fire</u>

We returned home to Sugar Bush. Relief wagons and workers came on their rounds, with blankets and food. They built us a cabin. We have begun turning the soil. Some Menominee stayed to help.

The sight of seeing Matthew in the fields with his father in the early morning light is so warming. Chepi, still close with Matthew, also stayed. She and I gather the crops and stay busy all day, cooking bread and stew.

. . . <u>July 1872, nine months after the fire</u>

The crops are coming up ruined. Worms! Anders says if birds and insects had returned, they would have eaten the worms. I cried quietly out on the land where Anders and Matthew could not see me. Anders talks of going back to sailing at Green Bay.

. . . <u>October 1872, one year after the fire</u>

Matthew and Chepi got married. The wedding day went nicely. I felt the presence of God, joining Matthew and Chepi together. I was pleased to cook for the festivity. There were jokes about feeling old. Anders spoke again of sailing in Green Bay. I could not live through that again.

<u>. . . Spring, 1873, a year and a half after the fire</u>

Anders and the men are planting the whole homestead acreage. In three months' time, we have some meager crop yields. Half goes to the tribe for their help. Beans, squash, corn and more. Everything has changed and the future looks positive. Chepi is expecting.

<u>*. . . 1874, two years after the fire*</u>

Chepi had a healthy boy, Robert. We now have a very busy, crowded and loud household. Chepi and I are so happy that Robby has Menominee heritage. I hope he will know both worlds.

In March, Father Pernin came for the baptism. It was the first celebration of surviving and rebuilding after the fire. Even Beulah came with her new husband, Monroe. He'd been a child slave like her, escaped to Canada, trained as a cook and came back to Green Bay for work.

Father stayed overnight. After cleaning up from the day, I came into the main sitting room where he sat before the fire with his bible. With two years of tough times behind us, I asked if he'd join me in a bit of brandy in a cup of tea."

He closed his book. "I will."

I told him I felt I had such good fortune to have a family, a home, good work cut out for me. I told him that dark time after the fire still troubled me. "Even after you said the pillar of fire didn't mean anything bad, it still haunts me." I started to choke up. "So much death and destruction. And through what was like the pillar of light for the Chosen People!" I wondered aloud if the fire was what the Virgin Mary warned about, people not converting and punishment. Everything came blubbering out of me.

Father listened patiently, nodded and sipped his brandy tea as I carried on. The fire happened exactly twelve years after the apparition. What sin did Peshtigo commit? Why did the miracles happen?

The fire crackled and Father Pernin said, "I'm not sure," he said. "I've been thinking about it all, too. I plan to write about it someday." He exhaled slowly. "It was an extraordinary terror." He sighed with a brief smile. "Time helps, a little."

He said I really suffered from grief. He agreed it looked like a pillar of fire but that was only the night sign. During the day, the Exodus fire changed to a column of smoke for the Israelites. "Nobody saw that in Peshtigo." He didn't think it was a chastisement – because of the Tower of Siloam in Luke's gospel.

"Some Jews went to pray at the temple and the gospel says 'Pontius Pilate mingled the men's blood with their sacrifices.' We don't know why that happened but later, some men asked Jesus about this event which horrified the Jews. A little like you, they were wringing their hands, wondering what had been the men's sin that led to Pilate's men to murder them.

"Jesus said those men did not suffer because they were greater sinners than anyone else. He said it just happened – like the Tower of Siloam. That was a known tower that had collapsed and killed eighteen."

We both stayed quiet for a long stretch.

Father said the fire was probably natural. "The biblical story is to warn people to remain spiritually ready. A collapsing tower, or a fire that kills isn't necessarily a punishing thunderbolt from God." He paused again and smiled. "Illyanne, I can see now that the Peshtigo pillar of fire has been your Tower of Siloam."

At that moment, the memory of what the driver said on the way to the chapel about President Lincoln jumped into my mind. 'The Almighty has his own purposes.' That's what he came to understand about the terrible war dragging on for so long. Maybe there was something like that about the fire.

Father Pernin tipped back the last of his tea. "We all knew of Peshtigo's wicked side, the near worship of prosperity, the little reverence for man or nature." A flash of anger came over him. "Did you know, on average one man everyday got killed on the job? At the sawmill, the woodenware factory or logging? Often, they couldn't find a body for Last Rites or a funeral, when a man was crushed in the logs floated down river."

He said the "feverish taking of so many trees was like a gold rush of the Northwoods. A madness.

"I can tell you, I do believe in the miracles. Of course, they're only signs that faith is true.

Almost without thinking I said, "Maybe God doesn't want us to fully understand all these things."

Father Pernin tilted his head and looked at me.

"He might want us to be searching, to ask Him for answers. That's probably why sometimes the Bible says things nobody can figure out."

Father Pernin slapped his hands on his thighs. "Why Mrs. Illyanne Eriksson, you'd make a very fine theologian." He smiled and got up from his chair. "I must turn in now. I have an early morning of it. Goodnight."

That old sea shanty entered my dreams many times. "As we set forth upon the Great Lakes, show us the fruit of your womb, for without your Son we are lost, aimlessly casting about, Adrift at sea." Eventually, a larger picture emerged out of the dread of the fire, the bone chilling terror of shipwreck, near drowning, the long, aching, tiring search for my family, and the backbreaking struggle to rebuild.

A spiritual easing came over me. I could see it now, like a ship becoming visible through a lifting fog. She had been helping me through my own gloom. It was Mary, Star of the Sea, mother, messenger, navigator, who lit my way back from being lost in my dark and stormy seas. I had been almost hopelessly adrift in a sea of shock and burned landscapes. I have arrived at that haven of peace, to a mending heart, to love, family, friendship and a faith being renewed.

39

EPILOGUE

This is the final entry in the diary of Illyanne NeeNAH Eriksson, written before she left with Anders for Green Bay to work in the Spring of 1881. They did not return for winter as expected. In November of that year, word came. The ship Anders and Illyanne had sailed upon failed to arrive back in Green Bay. A telegraph message reported to the Lumber Room, that the ship never arrived at its destination. The vessel, her crew and cargo were all presumed lost at sea during a bad storm.

1881, TEN YEARS AFTER the fire

By 1875, things looked good for Matthew and Chepi and Robert and little Sarah, too. The crops improved; the yield increased. Anders longed to return to sailing. After the fire and the troubles that followed, I never wanted to sail again. But We left Sugar Bush together and went to Green Bay.

After the fire, Anders had become a man with a larger heart. It was in his encounters with me, Matthew, Chepi, sailors and townspeople that gave me a new outlook. I asked what changed him. He said it was from the night of the fire at the chapel with the fire approaching. He said, "I knew the gospel stories and prayers, but there was a point where the words disappeared. An understanding took over. Something more under my skin than words, a higher feeling – of being, really. It's stayed with me. It just blended into everyday life."

I could have cooked alongside Beulah and Monroe at the Lumber room and lived very satisfied. Slowly, the understanding of my world converted to seeing the benefits of sailing again. To my own amazement my fear faded away. Eventually, I saw that I really took the cook job aboard the Henry B. Jones because I wanted to go and experience the delight of sailing.

Now, Anders and I sail as a team. I cook and he works as a crewman. I often bake bread and make the men Booyah the evening before we leave port when it can simmer for a long time.

The sights, sounds and smells of the Sugar Bush woodlands remain ingrained in me. We still spend winters there. I have expanded my appreciation for nature. I relish the thousand shades of blue and green and white water and sky with the changing light throughout the days and seasons. I enjoy the motion of the waves, their commands and freedoms. Now, I savor the aroma of the lake breeze, like fresh air mingling with the scents of decaying leaves. Often there is a trace of the mineral scent of dissolving stone and fish but the mixture of it all is the smell of wild beauty. The timeless night stars dazzle and inspire.

The meaning of my child's fever dream vision has at last unfolded itself to me. I was not a bird flying high. My spirit was riding on the back of a bird. The landscape without trees was not the black burned landscape that I had suspected. It was not land at all but the night sea's dark blue water. And, the bird wasn't carrying a light on its head. It only appeared so. I was flying toward a light, a great star that watched over mariners on the seas.

There is a great calm in arriving at my foretold path. My soul is set on a true course, that channel of peace and wonderment that is sailing the Great Lakes with Anders at my side. I am content to continue to ride the dips and swells of the vast inland seas until the day I reach my ultimate safe harbor.

AUTHOR'S COMMENTS & NOTES

This is a book of fiction. However, much of it was based upon true history.

<u>Real life characters, places, events</u>

Father Peter (Pierre) Pernin and 'Sister' Adele Brise are the only real historical persons used in the story. The event of the 1871 Peshtigo Fire was a real historical event and it happened the same day as the better known, Great Chicago Fire. The true number of people who lost their lives in the fire is unknown but estimates run from eight hundred to as many as two thousand, four hundred. It is also estimated that the fire destroyed 1.2 million acres of land.

In 1874, Father Pierre Pernin, a French immigrant Catholic priest, wrote an article of his experience of living through the Peshtigo fire. Originally written in French and translated to English, this writing became a major original source about the fire for historians. In 1971, this memoir was reprinted. (*The Great Peshtigo Fire: An Eye Witness Account;* see https://digicoll.library.wisc.edu/WIReader/WER2002-0.html).

'Sister' Adele Brise, a Belgian immigrant is reported to have actually experienced the 1859 Marian apparitions. Although the book refers to one on October 8th, there were actually two more appearances on October 9, 1871. After the apparitions, Adele dedicated herself to teaching children in the area. She formed a group of Third Order Franciscans to help her mission. She died in 1896 and is buried on the shrine grounds.

The shipwreck of the sailing schooner, Henry B. Jones, is based upon a true event. A lumber schooner named, the *George L. Newman*, ran aground on the shoals of Green Island on the night of the Peshtigo fire and it was abandoned as a wreck. The location was an official island lighthouse which was deactivated in 1956. Today, Green Island is a private island.

The two reported miracles of the saved tabernacle, and the spared chapel and grounds in the midst of the Peshtigo fire are actual reported events. Father Pernin wrote that after the fire, the tabernacle, found two days after the fire, was wholly preserved. After the fire, Father Pernin noted that the Marian chapel grounds shone like an emerald island amid a sea of ashes. Local Catholics generally regarded those as miracles. The Wisconsin rural site today is known as the National Shrine of Our Lady of Champion. In the year 2010, the Catholic bishop of Green Bay, Wisconsin declared the 1859 apparition to be 'worthy of belief.' It is the only officially recognized Marian apparition in the United States. The shrine is open daily and receives up to one hundred and fifty thousand visitors per year. In May, the traditional month of Mary, there is an annual pilgrimage *Walk to Mary* event. In 2024, approximately 6,000 people participated.

Peshtigo, Wisconsin maintains a Peshtigo Fire Museum and a Peshtigo Fire Memorial. The tabernacle recovered from the river is on display there. Peshtigo identifies itself as a "city rebuilt from ashes." Its population in the 2020 census was less than four thousand.

<u>Fictional people, places and events</u>

The Belgian characters are fictional but the general history of Belgian immigrants to Wisconsin's Door peninsula are derived from real history. Door County, Wisconsin was one of the largest Belgian immigrant populations to the U.S. In the town of Brussels on the Wisconsin Door County peninsula, an annual summer Belgian Days festival still takes place. Booyah and Belgian pies are among the delicacies which are available.

Sailing schooners like the ones Illyanne and Anders Eriksson rode upon in the Great Lakes dominated cargo transportation the late Nineteenth Century. Some two thousand schooners operated on the inland seas during that era. Perhaps the hustle and bustle of the industrialization age caused a sentimental longing for the beauty, grace and quiet of the old days of sailing. In the year 2000, professional shipwrights and hundreds of volunteers completed a composite design of a Nineteenth Century three-masted Great Lakes schooner in Wisconsin.

That ship, the sailing vessel, *S/V Denis Sullivan*, was homeported in Milwaukee until 2022, when it was sold to the World Ocean School in Boston. In Milwaukee, the *Sullivan* operated as an educational, sailing trainer and tourist vessel. There are other historical educational sailing ships in the Great Lakes and coastal areas as referenced in the *Tall Ships America* organization. During construction of the *Sullivan*, the Menominee Nation in northeastern Wisconsin donated six, seventy-five, foot white pine trees harvested from its forest for her masts. The ship flew the flag of the Menominee Nation in addition to the U.S. flag.

The *S/V Denis Sullivan* honored the romantic, Golden Age of Sail on the Great Lakes, the maritime history of Wisconsin and the sailing livelihoods of thousands of Americans and immigrants. Aboard the *Sullivan*, there was a near magical ability to go back in time and sail for a few hours, or overnight, like sailors did in a foregone era. I sailed aboard the ship for one of its two-hour educational tourist events. The experience on the open water offered passengers a purity, a love of nature and a means for them to search their own souls while their feet are not pressed upon the security of land.

The Lumber Room in Green Bay is a fictional invention for dramatic purposes only.

In regard to Menominee cultural information, I have consulted with an enrolled member of the Menominee tribe on an early draft of this novel for sensitivity and accuracy feedback. The Menominee Indian Tribe of Wisconsin and their lands, over 200,000 acres, are authentic. As of 2019, there were approximately 8,700 Menominee members living on their lands, mostly in or near the village of Keshena, Wisconsin. The Menominee are one of eleven recognized tribes living in Wisconsin.

The Menominee tribal forest is very diverse, including about 30 species of trees. The tribe's forest management continues to be recognized as a model of logging and ecological sustainability. In 1995, the United Nations recognized the Menominee and other tribes for excellence in harmonizing land use with sustainable forest practices.

The Menominee forestation model is attributed to Chief Oshkosh ("*Start with the rising sun, and work toward the setting sun, but take only the mature trees, the sick trees, and the trees that have fallen. When you reach the end of the reservation, turn and cut from the setting sun to the rising sun and the trees will last forever.*") Satellite images from space clearly show a dense green rectangle where the tribal forest is located. Today, Menominee Tribal Enterprises (MTE) employs approximately 300 people. It harvests 15-20 million board feet of lumber every year. It operates a lumber mill and manufactures wood products marketed globally. It is noteworthy that the Menominee have provided maple wood floors for the Milwaukee Bucks' basketball court. MTE has 35+ years of providing wood floors for NCAA Final Four tournaments and more recently, for the 2021 Tokyo Olympic basketball courts.

<u>Fire cause: Theology, Marian messaging and Star of the Sea</u>

In the many years after the Peshtigo fire and Great Chicago fire, people have tried to understand what caused such devastation. In large part, weather has been blamed. An extremely long, dry period of time preceded the fire. Railroad construction workers left cut-down trees alongside the tracks after they laid them. Farmers cut down trees constantly and burned tree stumps and roots. Saw dust piled up all around Peshtigo as a byproduct of the sawmill and the woodenware factory and it was spread on the streets to soak up mud. Some have argued that the fires could be attributed to a meteorite shower or from fragments of *Biela's* comet. Others say that there are no records of meteorites ever having been found to cause of fires. During World War II, the British and American militaries studied the Peshtigo Fire and tried to recreate its conditions as a weapon of warfare. Based upon that research, they 'firebombed' several Axis Power cities, (Dresden, Hamburg, Tokyo).

The theological idea that the Peshtigo fire may have been, in part, a chastisement, is one from my own embellishment for dramatic literary purposes. Other articles and blogs have discussed it. I derived the notion primarily from the Virgin Mary's own words, that if sinners did not convert, (i.e., repent and convert their hearts), her Son would be obliged to punish them.

Her message in 1859 is akin to other Marian apparition messages. In particular, Our Lady's message can be viewed as a precursor of her message to three children at Fatima, Portugal in 1917. The Champion message was more generalized, seeking religious education, prayers and sacrifices for conversion and reparation for sins. Fifty-eight years later, in Fatima, the message was more specific (i.e., need for specific religious practices; advice for how to obtain peace; warning about the spread of worldly errors and wars if requests were not done to atone for wrongdoings). Illustrative of the link between these two apparitions, the grounds of the Wisconsin shrine, Our Lady of Champion, includes an outdoor statuary garden memorial of the Fatima apparition and the three shepherd children seers.

I found no evidence that the Catholic Church either supports or denies the idea that the Peshtigo fire was a form of chastisement. All Marian apparitions are considered private revelations which Catholics are encouraged to believe but not obliged to. Mary has urged people toward prayer and penance for sinners, who have much offended her Son. A common theme in Marian apparition messages has been that prayer should be offered in reparation for the outrages and ingratitude of humanity and to seek conversions, (e.g., 1858-Lourdes, France; 1917-Fatima, Portugal; 1973-Akita, Japan; 1981- Kibeho, Rwanda; 1983-1990-San Nicholas (Buenos Aires), Argentina, et. al). Thus far, there are 26 approved Marian apparitions in the world.

https://media.ascensionpress.com/2020/05/30/the-ultimate-guide-to-marian-apparitions/#bishop

The *Star of the Sea* shanty is derived from ancient prayers to *Stella Maris* (Latin for Star of the Sea). In this book, I used a modified version of the prayer by St. John Paul II for the story's sea shanty. The devotion to 'Mary, Star of the Sea' dates back at least as far as the fifth century. Ancient sailors relied upon the stars for navigation. Early Christians apparently merged that guidance concept with Mary's religious role as a spiritual navigator. Like the constant North Star, the Star of the Sea metaphorically guides people toward her Son, toward the safety of land, through the storms and vastness of the perilous seas (and lands) of earthly life.

The epigraph in the beginning of this book from J.R.R. Tolkien relates to the Virgin Mary. Tolkien, a lifelong Catholic, described his *Lord of the Rings* trilogy as a "fundamentally religious and Catholic work; unconsciously so at first, but consciously in the revision." His character, Galadriel in *The Fellowship of the Ring* was inspired by the Virgin Mary (aka, Star of the Sea). In Tolkien's posthumously published *The Silmarillion*, Galadriel, was described as "the mightiest and fairest of all the Elves that remained in Middle-earth." In the story she possessed a vial which held the light of a star, emblematic of one of her many monikers, Star of the Sea.

Star of the Sea is a title which has been widely used to name churches, schools, colleges, health care and housing facilities, songs, and many paintings and prints. There is a *Stella Maris Catholic Church* in Egg Harbor, on Wisconsin's Door peninsula. A worldwide church mission, Stella Maris began over 100 years ago in Scotland. Its network offers hospitality and pastoral care for seafarers, fishers, port personnel, their families and all who work or travel on the high seas.

About the Author

Alicia Connolly-Lohr, author of *Fire and Apparition*, is a retired attorney and military officer. After working in the South, Japan and Washington D.C., she returned to Wisconsin. She traded in her legal brief writing skills for researching and writing fiction. For over 15 years, she has been a serious hobbyist writer. She has self-published three prior novels, *Lawyer Lincoln in Transit to Freedom*; *President Lincoln's Other War*, and *Coastie Kid: A Hurricane Katrina Mystery*. Intriguing real people and actual past events have served as inspiration for her historical fiction.